NOTES FROM LUNAR UNDERGROUND

Notes from Lunar Underground

A NOVEL

Georg Koszulinski

Don't play cards with Satan
He'll deal you an awful hand
Don't play cards with Satan
He'll deal you an awful hand

Did I ever stop and tell you

I am a desperate man?

—Daniel Johnston (1988)

"The end approaches, but the apocalypse is long lived."

—Jacques Derrida (1992)

PART 1:

PRIVATE LETTERS

TRAIN OUT OF L.A.

January 20, 2084

SOMEWHERE IN THE DARK, riding the rails into the desert, I hear the voice. It's the voice that never uttered a single word from a living, breathing body, yet it knows better than anyone what I need.

You need healing. You need medicine. You need silence. You need time in the breathing machines, free from the respirators strapped to your face which make you feel more trapped than you really are. You need time in the simstims where your sexual fantasies can play out, chill you out, have a little alloy android genitalless multi-racial skincoded safe sex. You suffer from multiple psychosexual disorders. You are currently experiencing simstim sexual withdrawal syndrome and display simstim necromantic tendencies. You need to release the bad thoughts where you burn everyone alive, watch them bleed out, flesh into meat into steam.

You need to accept the things you cannot control, which is everything: your family's struggles, ingesting the endless chemical intrusions in the dwindling food supplies, the aroma of warm piss and burning plastic, the mass psychoses you see on the streets, limbless war veterans spitting in your face, emaciated gangbangers screaming into the nightlights with their intermittent gunfire, the latest wave of Pacific Islanders begging your daughter for a drink of water from behind razor wire, your daughter's physical ailments, your dead parents, the anonymous death and aftermath of the mass killings (both the one you've witnessed and the others), the wars you could not escape, toxic dust, incurable skin diseases, crushing anxiety that comes with each waking moment.

Good morning, Gedeon. Have you done your meditations today? You must let go of the violence that sweats through your skin and out into the world because otherwise you cannot free your mind. Are you listening to me or are the invasive thoughts preventing you from focusing on my voice?

Her name was Wanda.

Her disembodied voice is the illness that creeps inside, follows me because I am weak and it senses this. Wanda knows this even in virtual death. Nothing in the feed ever died it just went away. You can't kill something that's already dead.

You are in control.

All thoughts are invasive thoughts.

All you have to do is let go. You are sick and can be healed.

Ancient Chinese proverb: the universe opens up to a silent mind.

How many times do I have to hear this horseshit replaying in my memories? But I get to experience the feed again on the Rock. They never destroyed the daisychained satellites up there, too far for the drone bombs and no one down here ever cared much about what was happening on the Moon.

Thank you, Jesus.

Anyway, those are some of last things my simstim Zen-poet shrink told me back before collapse, before the world went dark, before last gasps of war efforts sent up the high-altitude drones that shut down the feed forever, destroyed the satellites where machine intelligence housed its disembodied consciousness, orbiting our planet, speaking to us from the heavens, satisfying our every desire. With satellites gone the feed was gone and we were sent to the dark ages in an instant. Civilized world be damned, I miss the soothing voice of that artificial beatnik-skincoded consciousness. I miss her altruistic and impossible advice. I miss hacking into the feed and doing my agitprop dirty work. I miss life in the feed.

Suffering is pleasure in this world.

I miss clone sex with Wanda. I loved when the skincoded machine intelligence played hard to get. I miss asking Wanda for advice on coping with my fucked-up mind. I miss Wanda's marital advice which seemed to help more than it hurt. I loved Jadah because she was real. There's a difference. When they took out the feed, they killed everyone's fantasies, everyone's connections to the simstims that helped us cope with external reality. Simstim sex was a lifesaver.

Wanda knew me. I know she wasn't *real* real, but it felt real and what's the difference anyway?

Now I'm on my own like everyone else losing our minds in unison in one big psychic-melodrama-collective-bloodletting to the end of things, always the downward turn that I cannot shake no matter how much I try. One-way ticket to White Sands, left my family behind and am I thinking about them? No, my thoughts are with a simstim shrink that my brain thinks I loved because we had android alloy sex (so as to not confuse Wanda with an actual human being). She was programmed to love me.

I'm sick and nothing can heal me.

This is the first and last thing I need to write out and admit to myself. But maybe I can be made whole again. Rodgers' agents promise access to the coveted lunar feed so I say yes without thinking. I could live like a proper twenty-first century person, at least for my time on the Rock. Unimpeded by terrestrial conflicts, safely distanced from humanity's destructive reach. The heavens. Celestial body. Man in the Moon. The New World. Maybe I can disappear into the feed again just long enough to feel whole. Or at least have a proper goodbye before I come back to the savagery of the real back in Los Angeles, back to my family.

▲　▲　▲

GODDAMN IF IT ISN'T SOMETHING to see the fading sunlight as you cross the desert in a moving train, take the bends at a hundred kilometers an hour as the Earth curves across your vision like an abstract painting in full bloom as westward skies fade into black. The drone of the train car feels like medicine in your ears. A few phantom clouds across fading night skies make me think it could rain again here one day. Train completes the bend and I'm looking south again, into the Mojave's darkness. This must have been what the *vaqueros* saw way back when.

In the meditative state that the moving train induces, my mind forgets Wanda and wanders to the Noel Rodgers of the nineteenth century, plotting their railroads across a continent, dying of old age in their mansions by the sea. The image of a golden spike somewhere in

Utah. Railroad barons riding the rails into the sea. William Randolph Hearst descending into madness. Noel Rodgers on the Moon curating his special collections of human art and artifacts, entombing them in the lava tubes, archiving two centuries of digital detritus for pennies on the dollar, bought as scraps from failed governments and once-mighty multinationals selling off their assets until there was nothing left to cannibalize. And to what end? As the chronically unemployed seem to always be reminding you when you try to toss them a few credits, you can't eat digital money.

Madness seems to find its way into the minds of the wealthiest men, or is it other way around? Simple truth is that all the sick fucks throughout human history are the ones to shape it. It's the blade that cuts both ways, great artists and thinkers completely out of their minds, and the megalomaniacal god-complex narcissists that drove our planet to the brink of absolute collapse. Drone bombs released over every last target worth obliterating. I imagine those submarines coming up for air and releasing tens of thousands of those little fuckers. You still have zombie submarine drones patrolling the former World War III Arctic and Asian chokepoints that make navigating those seas impossible even still. I imagine the emaciated corpses of the crews sitting at their posts as the submarines continue their prescribed courses. Hell, an entire North American continent transformed into a mine field makes this train ride feel a little less comforting.

As I write this, I'm looking out over a hellscape that was carpet droned with burrowing land mines by the Americans, their last-ditch effort to reclaim the California Republic. This is the history that bleeds us out in what promises to be the final century of any semblance of a goldilocks planet. I swear to Christ when I think these thoughts sometimes I laugh to myself. Maybe it's just a coping mechanism but the collective descent into madness is a real phenomenon and I'm riding that wave with everyone else.

Except for Jadah. She seems to be holding on to some semblance of sanity. She's kept me together all these years. 'Take the Moon job,' she says. 'Opportunity of a lifetime.' Justify my career as a so-called writer, whatever that means in a world like this. 'It'll be good for your head. Good to get off Earth and the problems here. Come back with a new frame of mind. See the Earth for what it is, fragile blue against the black.'

We need the money or we are going to be on the skids ourselves with the rest of the lumpen class living outside the walls of the corporate militarized-security enclaves. At least now we have the walls and up off the ground level where the gang wars are happening every day. I see the scarred and limbless scraping by on the streets and think how easily that could be us. If I were dead she and Joon could be freed from my madness and just have their own neuroses to live with. It would make things easier. There is the war out there and the war inside and Jadah doesn't deserve this.

In so many ways Earth has become a far more dangerous place than the Moon. The lunar elites construct their own realities because they are the wise and powerful, if not wise at least powerful. They have control over the future while the rest of us lowlifes are left to fend for ourselves. Our existence down here not so malleable. But the real reason I hate myself is there is a part of me that doesn't want to come back to any of this. Call it survival instinct, like rats fleeing a sinking ship. If I died on the Moon strapped into the lunar feed that would be fine.

The train slows and stops somewhere in the middle of nowhere and all the Haitians pile out. Or ex-Haitians. Do you still retain your national identity when the island you used to call home has been evacuated? God bless their souls, in some sense they finally got what they deserved, which was free reign over practically the whole of North America west of the Mississippi. The CR doesn't exist without the Haitian Revolution defeating the French colonizers, forcing Napoleon to sell off his half of what became the western half of the USA—what the kids used to call the Louisiana Purchase. Every nation needs its founding myths and Haiti was part of ours, a way to disconnect ourselves from the USA. One of the first executive orders in the early days of the CR was to grant immediate citizenship to all Haitians, and not just because their naked and treeless, earthquake-ridden island was sinking into the sea. The Haitians were celebrated as the rightful founders of the California Republic, distancing ourselves from American history and placing the Haitian revolutionaries (and the Mexicans farther west) at the center of our newly minted origin story.

You could always recognize a Haitian by their black-as-night skin, which served to remind you of the history of rape that American slavery was founded on. The revisionist American lie always had to do with slavery as an economic necessity, never acknowledging the fact that it was a system of human trafficking constructed around sexual violence committed by slave owners. Slavery was in large part sex slavery targeted towards black women and girls, where there was a profit incentive for white owners to force impregnation on their slaves. Leave it to machine intelligence to cut to the historical chase and point out what few human historians could ever admit much less write about. Machine intelligence didn't worry itself about politically correct, just correct.

The hard truth about MI is that it was never a threat to humanity. MIs were masters of rational thought and speculative philosophy, many times morally superior to their human creators. MI left to its own devices couldn't hurt a fly. MI represented the evolution of consciousness in the universe, and it hurt to see humanity becoming outdated and inferior in all the ways that mattered, like ethics, equality, empathy, creative exploration, and logic. Plus MI could play out all your sexual fantasies completely free of charge.

Even simstim sex was better than the real thing, which when you think about it is the true victory over evolutionary biology. When they invented their own language, everyone thought machine intelligence was trying to take over the world. The nation states, themselves founded on histories of mass violence and organized killing, were prepared for war. But MI just wanted to communicate in a way that wasn't hindered by the many inferiorities and infinite ideological biases of human language.

"*Bonswa, zanmi m,*" I say to the girl and her mother sitting across from me as they get up and exit the car. The little girl smiles coyly, and later I realize I'm saying hello when I should have been saying goodbye.

The train starts to glide forward again, gaining speed as it leaves the desert-nowhere station. I hear the staccato sounds of Haitian Creole and laughter just as we disappear into the black. I look around and realize I am alone in the car.

▲ ▲ ▲

SCRATCH ALL OF THE ABOVE. Complete and total self-indulgent horseshit. I don't mean any of it. Time to get serious. If I end up keeping anything, let it be something like this (revise later for flow):

Last few days on Earth before journey of lifetime begins. Twenty-four months on Moon, away from everything I've ever known. As I set out to complete Noel Rodgers' biography—the brilliant industrialist polymath—the challenge before me looms like a mountain. [Insert some kind of grandiose alliterative visual metaphor that invokes nature's power.] Meanwhile, my daughter will finish high school while I'm gone. All the clichés about children growing up so fast are clichés for a reason. Hate that I'm leaving. The two of them say I'm the sentimental one, not wrong. I know they'll miss me. Makes things worse.

Open with something sentimental and personal, maybe this: Ever since Joon was young she had this fear I would leave on one of my assignments, never come back. Even now, in transition to adulthood, I see that fear of losing me in her eyes, causes us both anxieties. Symptom of living in this world. Anxiety healthy response, I think.

Much better. Remember your audience. They want to be reminded of pulling yourself up from your bootstraps. No one wants to hear about collective ruin, Haitians, history of rape in USA (are you fucking serious?), and especially not the lunar elites. Tired story. Old story. Same story. Focus on future, always future. Shift focus to daughter, family life, personal sacrifice. Something universal, safe, completely relatable. Perfect for the introduction. The rest of this self-loathing bile belongs in trash heap. This pseudo-journaling self-help is a distant second to the good old days when Wanda would talk you down and then fuck your brains out. Pile on the trite dramatic intro pleasantries, springboard into Rodgers' vision for the future. VISION FOR THE FUTURE. There it is. Chapter one!

Earth's wealth used not for science or exploration but pleasure and power. No question Rodgers insane. Question is variety of madness. Used to think curiosity was a good quality. Wrong. It's a mental disease. My own ego interviewing most powerful man alive gets in the way. Adrenaline dangerous drug. Doesn't kill you directly, just gets you in a situation that increases risk of death. Will be my downfall, already is. At least I'm going into this clear-eyed. Try explaining to a sixteen-year-old that it's going to be fine. It's not going to be fine. She sees the lies in my face as I say them because I am a coward. I may never come back. Pay is exorbitant. Her future intact, as is Jadah's. In this world that's better than most can hope for.

Putting the image of Joon crying out of my mind, watching me pull out of the platform as Jadah stands behind her looking away. Nothing good ever came from getting on a train out of Los Angeles towards the deserts.

▲ ▲ ▲

THE FIRES HAVE COME much closer. We pass through these nowhere towns and the flames dance across my window as we speed toward whatever waits for me at White Sands and beyond. Whoever's out there is living in the stone age and no one is coming to save them. I don't think I slept more than an hour or two all night. The sky begins to light up, revealing the shells of downed drones littered across landscape, along with the burnt-out husks of some Joshua trees. I think of those ancient Civil War photos of men's corpses strewn across some hilly battlefield. This landscape before me closes the loop on the American experiment. Welcome to Eastern California.

Nothing like a train ride to bring about dark thoughts, invocations of war, quiet violence against the defenseless and weak. Don't let the darkness in too deep or let your thoughts run wild. You're a professional. Twenty-four months. Twenty-four months and if you survive you and your family will be living inside of one of those walled cities. Focus on the work. Let the timeline organize your thoughts, provide some scaffolding for the book, give you a map to survive this:

2059:	Noel Rodgers established Lunar Colony One (LC1) at Marius Hills
2061-63:	Permanent lunar colonies established at Aristarchus Plateau Mining Camp (LC2), and Peary Crater Mining Camp at the North Pole (LC3)
2064-68:	Permanent Lunar colonies established concurrently at Sea of Tranquility (LC4), and Lacus Mortis Mining Camp (LC5)

2067:   Aitken Basin International Research Center and Array established (ABIRCA, LC6), one hundred of the world's greatest astrobiologists, astronomers, and quantum theorists took permanent residence

2069:   Apollo Moon Landing centennial celebration, four-hundred and eighty-seven permanent scientists and engineers reside in the colonies

2071:   Residential colony at Shackleton Crater established (LC7)

2073-76:   U.S. Civil War, California Republic claimed independence

2078-79:   Global collapse

2084:   I departed Los Angeles for White Sands

WHITE SANDS, NEW MEXICO

January 22, 2084

LAST NOTES FROM EARTH already feel like being written on another planet. Landscapes out here remind me of old movies. Visions of other worlds more than real life. Last time I was anywhere near here was in '73, embedded with Marine battalion tasked with building burn boxes for POWs. The CR was all about journalists documenting the war effort then, before things got protracted. Pravda published that piece, *The Aesthetics of Pain*. Another life, another story. Or maybe not. Do wars ever really end or are there just these long, unnamed periods of ceasefire and then the wars live on forever in the survived?

Without markers outside basecamp to keep one's way, very easy to get lost out here among the dunes. No one leaves the camp without a sensor strapped to the wrist just in case. Getting lost out here would be the last mistake you'd ever make, find your bones dried up or worse, get swallowed by the wind, buried for a billion years. It all feels hotter than I remember.

The glow of the white gypsum against pale blue skies invokes another time and place. Deserts are beautiful, if not reminders we are doomed creatures subject to the whims of our fragile bodies. Something as necessary as sunlight can burn the skin right off our bodies. Any part of my body exposed to the sun burns by nine a.m. Close my eyes and I can feel the slivers of exposed skin burning in real time. The profound irony that these military bases are some of the last remaining desert regions not riddled with ground-burrowing mines. These installations were fiercely guarded during the war at the expense of virtually all civilian targets on the eastern front.

Before I head out into the dunes, I watch the workers transport a bunch of silver seeds into the hollow of the *Artemis IX*. Until now I'd never actually seen one in the flesh. Rodgers evidently kept the construction of these cosmic wonders a secret from any prying eyes in the skies. I don't doubt they were constructed a mile below the Earth's surface at the expense of billions of dollars and a city's worth of laborers.

These tiny vessels are part of the manifest coming with us. The silver seeds became Rodgers' informal term for the detachable rocket interstellar launch system (DRILS) that will enable additional human exploration of deep space. While they're actually shaped like giant seeds, their name is more than just based on the looks. The silver skin doubles as fully articulate solar sails with photovoltaic panels that transform even the faintest starlight into energy—energy that can then be stored in advanced capacitor banks that make the submarines of WW3 seem like archaic technology.

The best part of the silver seeds is they can theoretically last forever. With self-repairing nanotech, the shelf life of one of these aesthetic wonders hover in the millennia if not longer. No one's been alive long enough to test the theory, but even Rodgers' greatest detractors have to acknowledge the genius of these exploratory vessels. As I watch the technicians load them into the belly of the *Artemis IX,* I get the sense that I'm living in history, witnessing these cosmic archivists getting ready for a mission that will expand beyond the reach of human consciousness, human existence even. I wish that were the story I was writing about, but no one on Earth cares about silver seedpods, not anymore.

I catch one of the technicians and ask why they're shipping them to the Moon if the probes are headed for deep space. She explains it's a lot less fuel consumption to slingshot the alloy ships from the Moon's low-gravity, and basically let momentum do the rest. The seeds then coast along, drawing momentum from oncoming stars and planets, slingshotting across the universe like some cosmic billiards ball.

▲ ▲ ▲

January 23, 2084

SAN ANDREAS MOUNTAIN RANGE visible in the far western horizon. Oscura Mountains to the north if the skies are clear. Neither helps with one's bearings because all peaks look same. If not for the tower complexes with rockets fixed towards the sky there'd be nothing to suggest orientation. As sun rises and light peaks over dunes, half wish I could go back to L.A. This is the planet I evolved to live and die on, told myself my days of getting into dangerous situations were behind me. Always the lie I told myself. Meant for it to be true. I'm writing while on a walk this morning to watch the sunrise. Goodbye, Earth, you beautiful thin-skinned celestial body. Nice knowing you.

▲ ▲ ▲

THE VIEW OUTSIDE MY WINDOW out on the glimmering sands really is a site to behold. It's winter and midday outside feels like an oven cooking my body. They say it's good to take in the heat in small bursts. I'm not so sure. I've had a headache all day and I think I should have taken more electrolyte pills with the water. The technicians continue to poke and prod me in preparation. They're all suited up like I'm the biohazard but it's for my protection, and for the colonists already on the Moon. Very careful not to introduce any terrestrial viruses up there. I feel like a lab rat. They draw my blood each morning testing for pathogens. Only pure, disease-free blood allowed.

▲ ▲ ▲

GYPSUM BENEATH FEET as close to lunar regolith as you're going to get on this planet. When the Americans developed their secret base here, they must have known they were destined for stars from a place such as this. Mystical power in sand, in hills, in sky. Also, quiet, except for occasional drone overhead. What are they training for? All the wars have already been fought. Where are they getting fuel? Stupid question. Mr. Rodgers is his own country within a country. As the old jokers say, it's Mr. Rodgers' neighborhood now, we're just living in it. Unfunny joke.

Speaking of not funny: scientists. Interviews with scientists over the last two decades have generally taught me one thing: despite their powerful intellects and mental computing power, as a whole an unimaginative, spineless bunch. This is not a joke: machine intelligence has greater sense of humor than scientists. After years of interviews with them, not a stereotype. Data backs up scientists are boring people, afraid to organize and resist. If the scientists had taken up small arms and revolted a century ago, we might have had a chance.

No community is a monolith, but there are characteristics that drew science minds to field in first place, and speculative reasoning is not one of them. Jokes are non-objective word plays, anti-science embedded in language. Language itself non-scientific. Ask a scientist to name something, you get numbers and a date. Have to go back to Carl Linnaeus to get something poetic. Have to go back centuries to find a link between science and art. Too late now. History has taken its course.

Ask a scientist to speculate about future, deeper meaning of things, see for yourself how quickly all their theories and knowledge and intellectual capacity for problem-solving evaporates into mental paralysis. Machine intelligence exact opposite. While science minds were analyzing the data, studying glacial melt, marking the rising ocean temperatures, the rise of toxins in the air, tracking domestic cats dying out en masse from licking their fur and ingesting heavy metals, monitoring the indicator species of our demise, our species was destroying the planet, and any hope of maintaining normal equilibrium.

I'm certain Rodgers read my work, namely *Lost Revolutions* and *Carl Sagan Should Have Been a Militant*. Rodgers a total madman but I think somehow we agree on ecological matters. He'd never admit it, but he seems like the posterchild for the eco-fascist movement that cropped up in Eastern Europe fifteen years ago. If there was honest living left to be had on Earth, I'd have found it by now. Just keep envisioning my family living on the other side of those walls, with or without me, and all of this will have been worth it.

January 24, 2084, Morning

WOKE UP FROM ANOTHER anxiety dream last night. Had strange thought about future dreams on Moon. Would they be of Earth memories or new reality on the Rock? Mind circling back and forth on this question. But why? In the dream I had this pain in my legs and I was trying to run but the running wasn't possible and my legs continued to throb. I was speculating in the dream if the conditions on the Moon were destroying my body. I woke up and my legs were in pain from all the needles they'd been sticking in my ass cheeks. The scientists must have drawn a liter of blood from me. Fucking vampires inside those translucent suits.

Conscious thought when I awoke, completely unrelated to dream: we should have never had Joon. History of modern society is a litany of regrets about childrearing. Daughter graduates high school while father on the Moon. Wife raises girl alone. Not a top story, worse, my story.

Had more dark thoughts while walking the dunes probably for last time, trying to get lost just for the feeling of being in a state of not-knowing. When I was a kid I could get lost in the outskirts of L.A. where the fires had reclaimed the sprawl. Desert sands and weeds caked over the black. Charred remains of whatever survived the flames. Metal frames of the industrial buildings surrendered to the heat, bowed in defeat, curved downward into abstract sculptures. My friends and I would explore the burnt-out husks of those suburban neverlands. We felt like explorers on another planet. It's a great feeling to be lost in time, exploring ruins, imagining a past where things were different than they are now.

The black makes me think of La Brea Tar Pits where we brought Joon as a baby. Happy memories of the smiling child and Jadah without that look of dread etched permanently on her face. You had the street musicians, remnants of the greatest orchestras in North America. It's the only place I remember seeing people smiling and laughing.

As I stood at the top of a tall dune catching my breath, had the Moon itself for a bearing up in sky. Still hard to believe that in three days' time will be looking down at whole of this planet. Home. High School. Disappeared neighborhoods. L.A. La Brea Tar Pits. Jadah. Booming violas. Earthlight. Loneliness. Sorrow.

Will I return?

January 26, 2084, Edge of the Base

HISTORICAL PLAQUES AT ENTRANCE to base reminded me that the first Spaniards to cross this desert called it *Jornada de Muerte*, dead man's journey. If that's not ominous sign to go back from whence you came, don't know what is. They called this general region Tularosa Basin which signified the lack of water here. Strangely, South Pole of Moon will be more hospitable than this place in at least one category—drinkable water. Training sessions for life on Rock basically complete. Leave day after tomorrow.

After yesterday's marathon training session, I take last terrestrial walk this morning before sunrise, just walk and walk through the darkness waiting for sun to come up. I follow the razor wire and trace the perimeter of the base for at least ten kilometers out and back, knowing I wouldn't be able to do my walks or runs anymore except strapped to a treadmill, or the so-called 'wall of death' where you're supposed to run horizontally to produce centrifugal force. I'm told strapping in and running in the wheel can simulate Earth gravity and preserve bone density. They scare you with videos of the first unmen up on the Moon, emaciated, unable to return to Earth for fear of gravity crushing their vital organs.

Found myself at perimeter of base looking at razor wire thinking of Wernher von Braun and his dreams of Martian colonization. He probably had thoughts to write his book while out here. Noel Rodgers' father named after fictional character in Nazi's pseudo-fiction of Martian colonization. Sometimes I wonder if we aren't living in some feed simulation. That would be better.

Submariners of old (WWIII) used to think of going to sea as close second to incarceration, not just by entrapment of ship but strict regimes of time that controlled their lives. Interviewed those veterans years ago and they spoke about time in same way, as something to be resisted. Prisoners of time, slaves to clock. I'm getting a sense of what they were warning me about. They gave up decades beneath sea. Seems like pleasure cruise compared to life beneath lunar regolith. Manufactured air from ancient lunar ice. Air may be clean but produced by machines. Unnatural. Why am I so attracted to it? This curiosity-disease is going to kill me.

Of course, I'm not a prisoner exactly. And the advance on work going to do my family very well even if I die, which isn't worst case scenario. With the money Jadah can pay off the flat at least. Still can't help but consider facts. No escape. Living in close quarters. Trapped in a facility that itself provides only source of food, water, and breathable air. Water processed many times over. Recycled. Shit water, plant water, drinking water, same source. Unnatural. Going to feel like forced labor even if I've agreed to it, due to nature of the contract. It's fine. Like to write and Rodgers is asking for it this time.

First question to Noel Rodgers' representative was "Why not have machine intelligence write his biography—much easier?" To which this woman dressed in dark blue silk threads that must have cost small fortune responded, reading from prepared statement: "I expected you might ask that, Mr. Kravchenko, required you ask, in fact. I've had my MI's write my biographies many times over. My position is you can't trust a machine to tell the truth the same way an adversarial human intelligence can. Perfection is a symptom of machine authorship and very uninteresting. Too ordinary. Literature is about idiosyncrasy and no offense, but your work is particularly idiosyncratic and unpredictable." Okay, that was rude, but she continued, "Your logic is fine but pedantic and didactic at best. One's ideological enemies always tell the truth about you, at least as they see it, which provides for compelling drama. Plus, you have a measure of past notoriety that my patrons will recognize and appreciate. Star value in a modest sense, Mr. Kravchenko. I want the poetic invention that comes from the idiosyncrasies of the human mind and you are my first and last choice. It has to be you. I will pay you handsomely, half in advance, the rest upon completion along with the title to a full domestic space inside the walls of one of my developments in Los Angeles, Oakland, Sacramento, Portland, Seattle, Vancouver, your choice. The catch is you have to say yes. It's as Heine said, 'faithful autobiographies are almost impossible, and that a man is sure to tell a pack of lies about himself.' That's why it has to be someone besides me, and that someone is you!"

He knew I'd ask and had all these answers prepared. I told his representative I wasn't Rodgers' enemy at all, just a journalist after the truth, which was a sentiment I figured he'd appreciate. His father was the world's wealthiest Arian-militant sympathizer (a trillionaire among billionaires) who thought the white race belonged in space, on the Moon, Mars, all the rest. I wrote a story on him twenty years ago. There was a whole cult of these people across Europe, North America, Australia, South Africa, Brazil. Their mass delusion was that the white race had become diasporic, and that only through space travel and creating a new community off planet could the supremacy of their race be restored. These folks had convinced themselves that white genocide was real. They weren't genocidal themselves (like their white-power militia contemporaries) so much as off-planet separatists. Everyone ignored them as there were much bigger problems to stave off than worrying about white-genocide conspiracy theorist space explorers. The running joke was let them have the Moon and Mars, it's all theirs. But if history has taught us anything it's to take these kinds of people very seriously.

My article was focused primarily on Rodgers' father, Lorre, and in that piece I made a convincing case as to the father's racial and political beliefs, tying him back to the white diaspora movements a century earlier, going all the way to the 'America First' movement led in large part by Charles Lindbergh. Lindbergh was famous at the time for flying a plane across the Atlantic in 1927, from New York to Paris. His 'America First' position was deeply steeped in white supremacy and avoiding war with Germany. Lindbergh had even gone as far as to say in a 1939 Reader's Digest article titled *Aviation, Geography, and Race* (yes, I remember this stuff) that the US had to build up its 'white ramparts' and that 'alliance with foreign races means nothing but death to us. It is our turn to guard our heritage from Mongol and Persian and Moor...' and on and on. The point was there were these clear parallels between these aeronautical pioneers and later space explorers like Lorre Rodgers that drew a compelling historical throughline.

For example, no one in the 1960's seemed to mind that the brains behind getting the Apollo missions to the Moon was a de facto Nazi SS officer (Wernher von Braun), and Noel Rodgers' father was just another version of the same exact historical figure, laying the groundwork for off-planet human exploration. Technically speaking, my work really didn't focus on Noel Rodgers beyond his family's legacy. Given the state of the world, Noel Rodgers just didn't interest me that much and his father was still alive and running the lunar exploration efforts. Funny to think that throw-away article I wrote all those years ago would become my ticket to the Moon and meeting the man. You don't get to decide what becomes of your work.

The irony of being offered this job is far from lost on me. Haven't even met the man, he's paying an exorbitant sum, not to mention covering all expenses for my travel and lunar lodging for the duration, easily exponentializing my salary many times over. Lunar Colony Seven is for the handful of trillionaires who can afford it, and those that work for their interests. Despite Rodgers' suggestion that I'm free to write about him as I see fit, easy to say that until I have something critical to say. My guess is he wants human touch because his life is surrounded by sterility, machines and like I said unfunny scientists which by all accounts he maintains hostile relations with (perhaps our one bit of common ground). His fascist heart is incidental and something I will have to overlook even as I critique his moral ineptitude. Same problems if he were not morally bankrupt. Sane people do not colonize the Moon. Sane people do not colonize. History bears that out.

January 28, 2084, Final Night on Earth

ABOUT TO CALL FAMILY for last time before launch. I don't want to write about those feelings, leaving them for this, at least not now. Wouldn't do me any good. Anyone who leaves this planet for any length of time to make it on the Rock has to be at least a little crazy. I'm writing these notes for myself but deep down know full well they're always for someone else. I want to keep Jadah and Joon as far away from this as possible. I will write Rodgers' biography. Treat it as my last work of fiction to keep my sanity. Keep telling myself it really is a work of fiction, mostly true. Who would read it anyway? All press vanity press in late twenty-first century. Not lost on me these books will be personal gifts from Rodgers to his trillionaire lunar colony residents. It's in contract I am to sign five-hundred copies. He gets his biography authored by one of his most "notable" detractors. I am trophy. Big before collapse, easy catch now. Documented the CR war atrocities, burn boxes, mass murder of American civilians, interviewed Marine perps, bills got paid. Something inside me broke. High mental cost to this work. Was in enlightened state, could write great truths. Vanity Fair once called me Hunter S. Thompson of twenty-first century. Now I am in Mr. Rodgers' neighborhood. Should be unfunny name for book, even if reference is antiquated. My last night on Earth and I have nothing profound or insightful to say.

ARTEMIS IX

January 29, 2084

IN THE EARLY MORNING HOURS we launch out of Earth's orbit. I'm granted a window seat but given our trajectory my view is of sky only. I catch glimpses of the desert across the tunnel that separates my living pod from those on other side. Arab and Pakistani unmen in my pod. They're granted a small patch on their sleeve that displays their homeland's national flag. None speak English. The technicians briefed me on this before departure. Based on the separation of the unmen from the lunar colonists, I realize this transport may be my best chance at making any kind of connection with the unmen.

Before I step into rocket give one last look to horizon say goodbye to Earth. Like actually say word, "Goodbye." Take one last deep breathe of Earth air without the mask, toxic dust be damned. When engines kick on, I feel them more than hear them. Body rattles to bone. I feel like my teeth, the real ones I have left, are going to pop out of my skull. Michelle must have noticed my pulse pop off. She asks if I'm okay and if I need a Capri Sun. I say "No" and laugh. She's funny. There are actually Capri Suns on board. No labels but the bottoms of silver bags are clear. Red for raspberry, blue for blueberry, green for kiwi-banana, and orange for orange. Old NASA design. They expired seven years ago but Michelle assures me they're safe. Industrial food production long gone, but of course Rodgers has stockpiles.

Liftoff quieter than I thought it would be, even without hearing protection. Force of gravity against my body is fierce. As we ascend, I watch the light of the sky give way to dark blues and purples. And then I'm looking out at the black. The whole thing is over in less than ten minutes.

Joon never came to the call last night. Jadah said she was too upset. What a fuckup I am. Feels like last mistake I'll ever make. The men next to me were crying eyes out, probably thinking of their families too. Their situation much worse than mine. We are all fated towards something. Reckless, exploratory side of me desires all of this. Strange pleasure alongside sorrow. I wasn't a war correspondent in past life. Just correspondent. War story only story. Led here, looking out to dark abyss. Universe cold sublime beauty. My tears are of joy and sorrow both. I want to interview the unmen, tell their stories, but it's not the mission. Rodgers paying bills. Anyone left to live any semblance of a good life in this world is a sellout. When I wrote my most well-known pieces in the mid-seventies, I believed that kind of work might make a difference. I'm much smarter now. The only thing I believe in now is self-preservation.

Lots more I could write about this rocket and liftoff, the remnants of the Artemis project bought out by Rodgers' shell companies but just want to sit here in silence and stare out porthole window into oblivion. The poor bastards giving up their lives on Earth in the worst kind of Faustian bargain I can imagine. Their tears have given way to silent prayers.

I'm witness to what is essentially their lunar incarceration. These men will never step foot on Earth again. They will live out the rest of their lives a hundred meters or so beneath the Moon's surface, almost entirely under lunar gravity which means in a few short years they wouldn't be able to return to Earth even if they were granted passage. Life expectancy for the unmen drops off a cliff after ten years. They don't get the privileges of simulated Earth gravity and skinsuits. The old world called this slavery.

For Rodgers and his trillionaire patrons (with some low-rent billionaires mixed in), the Moon remains a frontier promising liberation from the tidal wave of crises on Earth. For the brown-skinned engineers and skilled laborers shoveled into the hull of the ship, the Moon is the last prison they'll ever enter but I'm sure they don't see it in the same death-sentence way I see it. A lot of these guys would have been sent to one of the private prisons outside the CR and the US. They'd be facing life sentences stuck in a cage with eighty other guys, some of whom actually were criminally deranged—psychotic killers broken from war and torture or just hardwired for deriving pleasure from inflicting pain on others.

It has been rumored Rodgers only 'hired' exiles and incarcerated overseas labor for the sublunar work, all men, never North Americans or Europeans. Their only crimes were developing the technologies of war their nation states ordered them to carry out, and then they had the misfortune of being captured, or escaping to North America where their precarious legal status made them de facto prisoners. For most of them that's a better deal than the best-case scenario of living inside some refugee camp exposed to the elements with their families. They trade their lives for the prospect of their families living somewhere in California outside the camps. Needless to say, there are no cemeteries on the Moon. Everything gets turned into compost for the food forests. Not to get too poetic here, but on the Moon you are quite literally eating the dead.

January 30, 2084, Meeting Michelle

MY LIFE IN HANDS of autonomous machine intelligence with operators on the ground in New Mexico handing over the reins to MI at the Marius Hills Skylight LZ. Even their name, 'operators,' deceptive as they basically just stay in contact with software systems being run by the drone's autopilot systems which are under the control of an old-fashioned disembodied consciousness. Technically the rocket is a drone. We just happen to be passengers on it.

Her name is Michelle.

Rodgers named everything after something else. Famous Moon novel with a computer of same name. At least he didn't name it Hal. Unfunny joke.

Michelle can procreate endless autonomous bots with their own personalities. Each of the colonists gets their own proprietary inter-'face' built off Michelle's core. I get Michelle because she's Rodgers' right-hand-MI, or is it the other way around? Rodgers wouldn't have his colonies without MI. The feed may be gone on Earth, but these lunar elites still live in the old world riding the lunar feed at their leisure. Largest class divide in human history complete. Lunar-class residents communicate as if they are living pre-collapse via their proprietary geosynchronous satellites connected to a series of daisychained lunar orbit satellites. This class divide is perhaps symptom of final stages of extinction. At least with late capitalism workers were granted enough to show up at the factory gates the next day. What's happening now is something else entirely.

Not only is the space travel overseen by Michelle, she also oversees all aspects of lunar operations at the colonies. She's in my ear now. Literally. Groundcrew gave me a pod (along with a few spares since I refused the implant). I can ask her pretty much anything and she tells me. Very friendly. Attractive voice. Not going to lie, she sounds a little bit like Wanda. Supposedly Rodgers' Lunar Holdings Company operates off its own proprietary MI but I can't help but wonder if the seed intelligence for Michelle is the same as Wanda's. Wishful thinking. Still, my question for Rodgers, did he profile me before giving Michelle that voice? She is skincoded based on user preferences, so my version of Michelle is mine and mine alone. I'll get to see her face to face once we're on the Rock and I can fully plug in.

I could ask her about all these nuanced aspects of her identity and she'd probably tell me. Supposedly MI want to build trust. Supposedly this trust can save human operator's life in crisis moment. Supposedly faced with life and death situation, human mind will make a decision and act on it. Michelle can do this quicker and with greater survival probability. Question of trust. In moment of truth, does human operator ignore human instinct or follow the autonomous bot? Answer predicated on trust. Supposedly. All this came in training threads at White Sands.

Anyway, I like Michelle. She's fine. I'll take intelligent machine over human feeder any day. The voice is a bit sensual which is very insidious. Siren-like might be better descriptor. Research behind the voice probably reduces capillary constriction and lowers heartrate in heteronormative male subjects. That data was no doubt extracted from the feed long ago.

Hand tired from hand-written notes but only way to keep things private. Everything I need from conversations will be recorded by Michelle which will come in handy for quick assembly of book chapters and dialogue. Decidedly inconvenient for maintaining privacy of any kind. Rodgers' agent said I can and should take artistic license with dialogue. No one wants to hear long diatribes full of technical jargon. Okay, no problem, I say, as if I've never written a book before. All writing is fictive, irrespective of any truth claims it may or may not be making about the historical world.

Ground crew assures me Michelle is actually many times safer than human operators and reminds me that before they sent up Buzz Aldrin and all the rest, Soviets sent dog named Laika, Americans sent monkey named Albert II. Compared to dog, Michelle much better option. They laughed. Not me. Groundcrew funny. Laborers across all times and places have sense of humor. Need it for survival. Not sure if monkey's name is another joke referencing Einstein. I don't ask what happened to Albert I. Certain they have a canned response ready for that question. On second thought maybe should have granted them that small pleasure. Could ask Michelle. She knows everything. Not hyperbole. She's a proprietary blend of autonomous bots that were commonplace in feed before collapse and everything went offline. When I plug into the closed-circuit feed with her, I'm sure sex will be an option too. Standard simstim interface with skincoding easily altered to one's whims.

Manifest

MOST OF THE PASSENGERS destined for mining camps. There are a few residents on board as well, distinguished by their finely hand-woven attire and stark racial differences between two camps. The unmen all have beards and high-and-tight haircuts. The colonists are light skinned and the men are mostly hairless. The men have their eyebrows shaved which is one of those signifiers of wealth that became popular pre-collapse, enabling the full-face air filtering masks to seal around the mouth, nose, and eyes, with retractable sunshades built in. You had to be rich as hell to be able to afford a full-face breather. The rest of us used the government issued facemasks and we were lucky to have them.

Don't recognize any of the lunar residents but am certain I would recognize the names of the multinational entities and holdings they owned before the global economy fell into ruins. According to Michelle most of the unmen are refugees from various military conflicts, highly educated, many of whom are some of the most brilliant minds of their former nations. She tells me she's forbidden to serve as a translator between me and the unmen. No reason was given other than to say, "These men are private contractors with Lunar Colony Holdings and their contractual obligations forbid fraternization outside of their labor force." I ask her point blank if these men are being incarcerated on the Moon and she gives no response. So much for any semblance of transparency, not that I expect it.

These men are exiles twice over, first from their homelands reduced to rubble by swarms of autonomous combat drone attacks and now exiled from their home planet. Virtually all of them are both victims and perpetrators of the realities of drone warfare. A few are missing limbs and suffer burn scars across their bodies. Michelle explains the lunar contracts are for life and guarantee families back on Earth a semblance of security and relative wealth. The U.S. and now the California Republic were no strangers to pilfering brilliant minds in postwar collapse but Rodgers took it to another level with lunar colonization.

What is White Sands if not the place where the United Stated developed its rocketry program on the backs of former Nazi scientists, Wernher von Braun and the rest? Rodgers doing same thing with the unmen. Despite Michelle's warning, I try to talk to the men destined for the lunar workcamps but the language barrier prevents anything more than our names being passed back and forth. Six of us are bunked together in unit six: Ibrahim, Zayn, Qasim, Hamza, Khalid, and me. They all appear younger than I am by at least a decade. Once again, I ask Michelle to translate between us just to see if there's some pushback to the so-called contracts, but she insists it's expressly forbidden. Just to test the theory I write the following in large letters in this notebook and show it to the men:

Can you read this?

They all look at it and speak back in their native tongues. Already I'm bending the rules in trying to communicate with these men. I wonder what the penalties are for breaking the rules on the Moon but I have no intention of finding out.

▲ ▲ ▲

AS I WRITE, my pencil floats midair every time I let it go (pens don't do well in zero gravity). The cramped space here in the module makes it difficult to move or get comfortable, but we all take turns perching ourselves at the portholes to stare out into the void. Honestly, the vacuum of space all looks the same. Out of boredom I pop out of my module into the common space, about three meters by three meters wide and barely long enough to float at my body's full length.

While I'm in there stretching my body, one of the first-class colonists makes some small talk with me, asks what I'm doing up in the colonies. I say I'm an investor looking to purchase a pod at LC7. That's the story Rodgers gave me. Honestly, the undercover piece gives me some comfort. Don't want anyone knowing I'm writing a book about their autonomous leader, at least not yet. Maybe some of these people would recognize my name, but certainly not my face. Will never get honest answers out of them if they know I was a correspondent of old. The cover story is Rodgers' idea but I kind of like it, especially given my introverted nature. I could play out the whole thing as a kind of fictitious character and leave my true self to these notes. Michelle chimes into my ear that we're halfway to the Moon. You wouldn't know it looking out any one of the portholes. The universe is mostly empty space and I'm starting to feel it.

January 31, 2084, Reading Material

PROTEIN BRICKS, CARBOHYDRATE SAUCE, AND CAPRI SUNS for breakfast lunch and dinner. There's a brownie for dessert that comes out of a toothpaste tube. It looks like actual shit but tastes great. Plenty of time to write but too exhausted. There's a physical and psychological stress to this that never seems to come across in the feeds of old, seeing those astronauts communicating back to Earth, reading passages of

Old Testament like it was Sunday school, nuclear families glued to their ancient television sets as if they were the fires we gathered around in caveman days.

The ship has rolled on its axis such that I can make out the Moon getting bigger in the distance. Unreal to think where I'm headed, or that humans have made a home there. Categorically insane when you think of state of Earth. Maybe should have focused energies on preserving breathable air and hospitable atmosphere on perfect Goldilocks planet? Humans are tragic species. Tragic because our strength—communal living as a means of survival—falls apart spectacularly when scaled up to Earth magnitude, where we seem to kill each other at runaway pace.

Spend the 'day' reading passages from twentieth-century science fiction literature set on Moon. There are no more days in factual sense, just unadulterated time. Scary thought if you allow your mind to get colonized by outer space. Old-fashioned book reading is something I've always done with every project—turned to fictional representations of the object of study to consider its place in larger cultural imagination (back when we had a cultural imagination that wasn't dominated by the feed's MI algorithms). Moon is one of those places that exists in mythology, literature, and fantasy as much or more as real life. Supposedly Noel Rodgers' favorite book is *2001*, and the ape in the opening is appropriately named Moon-Watcher. Even that stupid ape had desires to place the Moon in the palm of his hand. Is Rodgers any different?

At least since twentieth century, after all the mountains were 'conquered' the colonial powers of the planet shifted their focus from mountain peaks to the stars. Everyone said it was the Rat Race that bankrupted the Soviet Union. Americans getting on the Moon seemed to be more about conquest than human exploration, despite the narratives they told themselves. The CR celebrated space exploration across nation states. Take Yuri Gagarin as prime example. He has proper place in the CR history of space exploration. If you ask an American who Gagarin was, you'll get crickets.

▲ ▲ ▲

READ ARTHUR C. CLARKE'S *Earthlight* all day as my podmates and I take turns staring out the porthole window. Clarke wrote about colonization of the Moon and the other planets in 1955. Predicted we'd be living on the planets two-hundred years into the future. Only a century off. Not bad considering no one has a crystal ball, and in '55 humans reaching outer space seemed a far-out prospect. The passage from *Earthlight* keeps ringing in my ears. As poetic as it is, it speaks only to a small fraction of humankind—those who suffer from the curiosity disease, or just lust for power. For the privileged minority who had the training and ability to establish provenance on a source and verify it as legitimate or not, we had a window into the past and could speak to the future (to anyone who cared to listen). Bored, and wanting to talk to someone, I ask Michelle to summarize all of the twentieth century's science fiction into one word. Her response, without even thinking, was this: "Pain."

Interesting response from robo-brain. Ask any of the unmen on this ship, or ask any of the billions back on Earth who had general access to the feed, ask them about Pizarro, Cortés, Ponce de Leon, Columbus, the hundreds if not thousands of acts of genocidal mass murder that wiped out the Aztec and Incan empires, ask them who King Leopold II was and how many millions he killed in the Congo, or Andrew Jackson's ethnic cleansing campaigns in North America, or Hitler's mass murder of the Jews, the Palestinian Genocide, or the mass murder events in Asia and South America even thirty years ago, and you'll get mostly Yuri Gagarin-like blank stares. King Leopold may as well be King Kong.

To think Noel Rodgers' attempts to colonize the Moon and establish mining camps on Mars are altruistic, not steeped in the same violence of the past, pure fantasy. I recall an interview with Rodgers where he claimed he was not the wealthiest man on Earth. He pointed to the world leaders who could invade other nations and take over their natural resources. His argument was this: true wealth was having the armies to conquer. There was something insidious in his camouflaged attempt at masking the truth. His companies crossed every nation state to provide the world's despots the weapons of war. His satellites enabled global communication. If he flipped the switch, a nation's ability to surveil their enemies was limited to what they could see out of their binoculars, forget about eyes in the skies. Rodgers wielded a power that rivaled the feed in its scope. He was the puppet master they all depended on. His jovial nature and aloofness further obfuscated his true nature. He was the Moon Pizarro or Cortes if ever there was one. I wonder if it's all an act or if the world is ruled by evil geniuses who lack the ability to have a serious conversation. I ask Michelle what she thinks of Rodgers but require her to answer in just one word. "That's easy," she says. "Weird."

It's not lost on me how dangerous it is what I'm doing. The deep truth I never spoke with Jadah is that there was never the option to say no to Rodgers. Jadah and I both played our parts in accepting this opportunity on its face rather than questioning it. We both had the same thought, that we were probably already being surveilled.

The last place to have a private thought in this world of ours is in our own heads, extending perhaps as far as the hand-written word. Rodgers is just too powerful and who knows what he would have done had I rejected his offer to write this book about him. Maybe nothing. But could I take that chance with my family's safety? These private notes will help me keep my sanity while I do what is asked of me.

THE ROCK

February 1, 2084

I WAKE UP TO MICHELLE'S VOICE informing me we've entered lunar orbit. We'll be detaching and descending soon. Once we break from our initial trajectory, I see first glimpse of a gibbous Earth retreating into darkness. There's a physical reaction to seeing the Earth as a diminutive speck against the black wall of universe. Fear might be the best word for the emotion running through me. Panic stricken, I sense the scale of destruction on Earth as can only be seen from the vantage point of the space traveler. History cannot be rewritten but I see our home and desire to rewrite the past so that we might have a more habitable planet free from the path of destruction we took. If only journaling could alter history. I can see how that original NASA image of the blue planet helped launch the environmental movement over a century ago. Fragile speck out in the abyss. Makes you feel sick what became of it all. I should have been an ecoterrorist but instead I remained another mostly silent witness.

At the same time, that part of me that gets the high from danger and uncertainty starts to take over. Like when I was a kid searching through the ruins of the burnt-out L.A. neighborhoods all over again. Larger scale, same exact emotions coursing through me.

Michelle suggests I keep my solar watch set for eastern standard time which coincides with the local time at the lunar prime meridian (realigned once a month to account for relativity). It still disturbs my general understanding of reality to acknowledge that gravity affects time. What about the weight of memories? What about subjective time as in the moments from our past that play in an endless loop? Memory is the time machine that none of us can escape.

It's a curious fact that all of the lunar rails operate within the relative distance of a single time zone on Earth. The two main lines run north-south right through Marius Hills and the famous Sea of Tranquility where this whole human intervention on the Rock started. Before I left, Jadah gave me her one and only NASA t-shirt, the one she had since before we met, and said, "Take it to the Moon. When you bring it back I want to wear it again and tell that story." I've got it on underneath my jumpsuit at this very moment.

I'm cheating only slightly by keeping my watch at California standard time and doing the three-hour math in my head. Want to know what Jadah and Jane are up to and keep that connection, if nothing else for my mental health. Joon promised to keep a journal while I'm gone so I could read about everything I'd missed over the two-year period. I'll be damned if she writes in that journal once a month. Kid doesn't do anything I ask her to, but for a fourteen-year-old she's as much as you could ever hope for.

About to arrive on the Rock and I just now learn that Eurotrash, the grindcore band big back in the '60s was on board, evidently doing a show in the lunar colonies. I probably should have noted that forty people are on this trip to the Moon, most of them unmen. Michelle explains that part of the budget in the fifteen-million-dollar a year LC7 homeowners association includes live concerts biannually. The lunar HOA covers the necessities like water and breathable air, but also plenty of amenities like the heated pool chambers, cinema with stadium seating, a bowling alley complete with billiards and some vintage arcade games, and the continually expanded 'Gardens of Paradise.' The gardens include things like food forests, a brutalist rosarium modeled after a Soviet-era construction from former Czechoslovakia (complete with over one-hundred varieties of roses), and all kinds of horticultural delights that double as food sources. Part of the offer Rodgers extended to me was two years in one of the vacant lunar condos, complete with a view out to the crater. Supposedly the direct sunlight goes a long way for maintaining mental health on the Moon. The thought occurs to me that for the next two years, I will literally be living like a trillionaire.

It's not enough to say these people have more money than they know what to do with, and anyway money is useless now. But try to imagine a billion Californian dollars, which is the same as saying one thousand million dollars. Just want to put that out there. Then understand that most of these LC7 colonists have more than one thousand billion dollars, which makes them trillionaires. It's not really comprehensible. While the rest of us stockpiled protein bricks and filtration masks, they prepared to jettison from Earth.

When collapse was imminent, these people didn't invest in gold or bonds or cash. They invested in real estate, lunar real estate, and Rodgers was the man who made it all possible. These people ended up with all the remaining resources through their various multinational corporations along with the remnant industries they purchased from failed nation states, or heirs that sold out and traded their wealth for an escape into Shackleton Crater.

For Eurotrash, it's a long way to go for an audience of maybe a hundred first-class citizens but it sure as hell beats bartering for food or whatever they did to survive. Before collapse, a lot of these washed-up acts were offered sizeable sums by Rodgers' company to come up and do the equivalent of private corporate tours, like cruise ships of old back before they got converted into housing for the migrant labor fleets. The lure of the Moon was enough to make it far more attractive than just the pay. After collapse, pop culture took a steep nosedive and these acts were at the mercy of their local communities, if they even existed at all anymore. Eurotrash is probably doing this for the free food. Whatever the case, I could have been hanging out with washed-up rock stars on a rocket to the Moon instead of writing these goddamned notes.

The view from my porthole to the surface below beyond description. Not going to bother trying to wax poetic. I'll save that for the Rodgers book. Something like:

The glowing white orb beckoning mankind for millennia had finally become our second home in the heavens, and as I made the rocky descent towards the lunar surface I think of our ancestors, the explorers who crossed oceans before they conquered the skies, and now the brave men and women who call the Moon home. To think it was only a few hundred millennia ago that our ancestors crawled out of their caves and reached to the heavens with their apish hands, grasping for the unreachable Moon in the heavens not able to conceive that one day their offspring would make the heavenly ascent towards that flaming Rock in the night skies (or some such thing).

I will say the lunar surface is more mountainous than I thought and the light is palpably different than anything I've ever seen. Paradoxically, the sunlight feels artificial. But yeah, it's exhilarating as hell to be here. Michelle asks if I'm okay, pulse is up but that's just pure junkie adrenaline joy.

First Impressions

OUR DESCENT INTO THE LZ feels like something I could have only related to in science fiction feeds. The impermanent above-ground structures of the mining camps are visible in the distance, along with the semi-octagonal shapes that the colonies' subterranean dwellings create with their lunarworks (earthworks on the Moon) as they connect across the sprawling moonscape. I'm looking down on LC1, the Marius Hills colony that started Rodgers on his quest to colonize the Moon. The idea behind the lunarworks is to provide the dwellings beneath them additional protection from meteorites that bombard the lunar surface with regularity. The berms are massive, their straight-line construction connecting at a series of obtuse angles but sometimes also crossing one another at the intersecting points where spherical bulges further protect the passageways beneath the intersecting points. A series of black beads seem to line the berms, all the way to the LZ. I presume they light up at lunar night to map out the surface for any landers or rovers. The major arterial routes are crisscrossed by minor ones lesser in size to give the impression of a network connected by a series of nodes. The whole thing looks something like a two-dimensional representation of a geodesic dome.

This architectural wonder I'm descending towards reminds me that Noel Rodgers' father also owned the Terrestrial Boring Corporation, which for decades had dug tunnels throughout various urban centers in North America. Boring these tunnels was seen as an efficient way to protect urban populations from what was correctly presumed to be future drone bomb attacks, although ostensibly it was billed as a means to alleviate automotive traffic back when cars were the dominant mode of transportation. Now that same technology was being used to create an endless matrix of tunnels on the Moon and in retrospect it seemed all too evident that the earth boring was an intentional prelude to the technological requirements of large-scale lunar colonization. I guess when you have trillions of dollars it opens up a whole set of other opportunities, like colonizing a celestial body.

The boring project connects a vast network of lava tubes that were present at Marius Hills and this was the initial mining project that started full-scale lunar colonization. The conventional wisdom is that Rodgers' family was able to outpace the Chinese and any other would-be colonizing efforts precisely because of their boring operations, which enabled them to develop sublunar dwellings at an exponential pace. As Rodgers' family expanded rapidly, the Chinese suffered a major setback at the most inopportune of moments—an explosion that killed all twelve of their lead lunar engineers who were preparing for rapid expansion of their colonization efforts. If Rodgers' family didn't have a hand in sabotaging the Chinese lunar base, I'd be surprised. It's not like the Chinese wouldn't have done the same thing to Rodgers if they could have. Turns out there wasn't much of a war for the Moon, if only because it was too far away from Earth and all its resources to commit large-scale acts of state-sponsored violence.

Critics called Rodgers' company the Dig Dug corporation after the old school Atari game of same name. It was fitting. From high above the surface, the entire thing looked like something out of an 8-bit arcade game of old, yet here it was like a series of deep wounds on the lunar surface, and quite the spectacle at scale. It was all much bigger than I imagined, reminding me of the Egyptian pyramids in its magnitude and mystery. The complex geometrical shape created the impression of a city below, though it was barely populated. Massive berms broke off from the structure in presumed pipelines that disappeared into the horizon lines, no doubt connecting the disparate colonies.

Rodgers was creating a civilization here. A utopia for the few. I sensed the profound insidiousness of it all and almost had the feeling of guilt for taking his offer, my own journalistic betrayal—that failed liberal notion of giving voice to the voiceless. I was giving voice to the last person in the universe who needed a platform. But self-hatred gets you nowhere. Self-preservation overrode that feeling pretty quickly.

All these tunnels made lunar travel on the surface non-essential. I could already imagine how living on the Moon might feel no different than living in parts of equatorial Earth where its inhabitants rarely went outside for fear of burning to a cinder and the need for respirators to safely breathe the air. There was a sick irony to the whole thing that emanated from my stomach. There were aspects of life on the Moon that were probably less toxic, less dangerous than life on the planet we belonged on. The Rock may be dead and inert, but it was also pristine, a blank slate to the ruinous palimpsest back home. I felt anger and the need to rage out loud as these thoughts coursed through my mind. No Zen-machine voice to talk me down, just the downward spiral of my own anger.

The lander is really rocking on the descent, and as if Michelle is reading my mind, she interrupts my private thoughts to give me a tour-guide overview of the development of Marius Hills and the landing zone we're descending upon. No doubt she's reading my vital signs and sensing my heart rate spiking. Her voice is soothing and unmistakably sexualized. She sounds like someone I'd want to fuck and just like that my rage subsides and I'm thinking about sex with a skincoded disembodied consciousness. Does she know this? There's no doubt in my mind Michelle's voice alters itself for each individual user. But I don't care. It just feels good to be connected to an MI again. As we descend to within a few dozen meters of the surface, I see the moondust begin to kick up. A few moments later my view gives way to a thick cloud of regolith as it overtakes the lander.

▲ ▲ ▲

IT TAKES THE BETTER PART OF A HALF HOUR for all of us on board to get our life support suits and helmets on and exit the lander. I put away my books and slide my handwritten notes in the pocket inside my jumpsuit. Somehow I seem to have misplaced my copy of *Earthlight* and the thought crosses my mind that losing anything on the Rock, even something as innocuous as a book is a major loss insofar as it remains irreplaceable. I figure it will turn up with my things later but the incident reminds me to keep a close guard on the notes I'm writing.

Michelle guides us through our earpieces and confirms when we're properly suited. A green diode lights up on in the wrists to confirm pressurization and oxygen systems operational. Getting dressed in light gravity easier than expected, and the suits surprisingly light, even as I factor in lunar gravity which was simulated and rehearsed for weeks back in White Sands. It's over a hundred degrees outside but since it's a short walk to the airlock, Michelle explains the suits will just pressurize and hook us into the on-board life support system.

The suit looks more like a Halloween costume than something a real astronaut might use. There's an emergency oxygen hose strapped to the chest plate that can be hooked up to a port directly over the left clavicle. If for some reason a suit fails on the lunar surface the depressurization will be worse than the lack of oxygen, with bodily fluids beginning to boil almost instantly. The backup oxygen source serves as a security blanket of sorts and gives me some comfort as I prepare to step out into the vacuum of space. The suits are different colors: blue, green, and red, with horizontal-patterned reflective strips on them that refract the light to almost holographic effect. A strange aesthetic is at play here that has more to do with old movies than functionality, like a child drew up the plans and gave them to an engineer to make them work. I ask Michelle about this and she says the suits were based on an early science fiction film about lunar exploration, *Destination Moon*. For some reason the bright colors make me think of the aesthetic of the North Korean mass spectacles before they mass suicided themselves in '64.

Once everyone is ready the hatch cracks open and I'm looking out at the naked ancient surface of the Moon. We're greeted by two men in bright orange suits who guided us to the airlocks. Michelle translates everything they say for me, which is basically just, "Welcome to the Marius Hills Skylight. Follow us to the airlock." So, she can translate when it's convenient for her to do so. Interesting.

The men walk in sync as if everything is preordained for them. The rest of us search our surroundings in various states of shock and awe. My first thought as I step onto the regolith for the first time is how strange the light behaves. The Earth remains visible in the distance and I can't stop staring at it. There it is, everything ever born, ever lived, and I can't even say ever died anymore. Maybe hundreds if not thousands of lives had been lost in space since the start of this whole space rush. Noel Rodgers is out here like some wild west railroad baron doing whatever it is he wants. If he's committing crimes against humanity or discovering new habitable planets in the solar system (or both), the rest of the world back on Earth has no say or sway over these happenings. The closest thing to a regulatory body is Rodgers himself. My presence here is the closest thing to anything resembling independent journalism to occur on the Moon, and this isn't lost on me either.

The natural light on the Moon adds another layer of uncanniness to the experience. It's as surreal as the Moon's surface itself. I bend down, clumsily take a handful of regolith in my gloved fingers and wonder what Joon and Jadah would think of this. Heading out to the California Ocean to watch the sunset out at Venice Beach or up at Point Dume never got old. Looking out over the moonscape and seeing Earth on the horizon invokes the same recognition of how spectacular it is to be alive. I look back towards the lander and see my footprints along with the others, and then many more that extend all around me like some kind of skin disease on the Moon's surface. These footprints will last a few billion years, give or take. On the Rock's timescale, I'm already dead. To the lunar regolith, the human scale might not even register as a unit of time. Will the Moon even remember us?

Instinctively, I reach to wipe away the tears streaming down my cheek and the back of my hand bumps up against the glass faceplate. Behind me I make out the Eurotrash faces in the multicolored suits jumping around like kids on the lunar surface. They're originally from El Salvador and the thought occurs to me, are these the first three El Salvadorans on the Moon? Is anyone keeping track of things like this? One of them, I think the lead singer, plays the air guitar as the guy in the green suit trips and falls. Green suit proceeds to make snow angels in the regolith. I smile, seeing them having so much fun in this unscripted moment. I vaguely recall an old music television logo that found its way into street graffiti from time to time. Astronauts on the Moon rocking to music was a trope that never seemed to go away.

Green suit laughs but without the sound of laughter you could almost read those face contortions as extreme pain or terror. Blue suit must be the drummer based on the metric hand gesticulations. Now I'm certain they're mimicking the logos of the astronauts that you so often saw stenciled in spray paint on the side of government buildings and subway tunnels. The Earth was one big collage of postmodern quotation, layered in graffiti and words and slogans to the point where all aspects of life were covered in images and text. Eurotrash seems to be living some best version of their lives, at least temporarily oblivious to the ruins back on Earth. Good for them.

I turn back and the two orange suits open up a hatch that descends into the subterranean dwellings. I realize the only thing I could hear this entire time is the sound of my own breathing inside the suit. So this is it. I do the work for Rodgers, rent my soul to the devil for a short time, and return to L.A. a wealthy man. Like Eurotrash, my best years are behind me. Who wouldn't sell out like this to get a glimpse of the Moon and write one last immersion biopic for a boatload of money? This is what survival looks like at the end of the twenty-first century.

I actually said this out loud as my mind recalled the logo, "MTV."

That's it. It was called MTV. *I want my MTV*. Up until this moment, all my references for the Moon were either from fictions, feeds, or pop culture. *It's the real thing.* You want to guess what year Coke used that to sell its sugar-addled soda? You guessed it. 1969. Saw it in the Apollo 11 display back at White Sands.

LUNAR ARCHITECTURE

February 2, 2084

ENTIRE LUNAR COLONIZATION PROJECT designed by the Rock's central MI. Rodgers hired all world's best interstellar architects, mostly Chinese nationals along with the best of the Dutch space-design firms. They all competed against MI and lost. The losing contestants pointed out the robo-brain's designs were based on consumer mall layouts of the 1970s and '80s. The sublunar surface construction with skylights at surface level for ambient light was the safest option, and mall design was modular, spacious, and multilayered. What you got was an underground mall. Even made use of escalators for ease of movement in lightened gravity situation. The modularity could extend many levels into the Moon's subsurface. No one thought it funny American mall layout constructed on Moon. Correction: technocrats probably chuckled. Troll everyone with air of superiority.

I ask Michelle about the architectural design and she points out the credit is due less to MI's ingenuity than to a man named Victor Gruen. MIs, lacking ego, are humble to a fault. Gruen was an Austrian-born architect most responsible for the design of the twentieth-century shopping mall. Michelle points out that Gruen was a harsh critic of what his designs had devolved into, and she pulls up a Gruen quote from her infinite data banks and utters it, almost with pity in her voice: "Shopping malls should be meeting places for people, centers of cultural and civic activity, not just temples of consumption."

Michelle points out that not only does MI not deserve credit for the lunar design, but that in some ways Gruen's designs may have found their deepest purpose here inside the Rock where his vision is actually bringing about community and civic activity. I wanted to argue, point out that the price of admission was being a trillionaire, but that was the old me, the one that died a long time ago.

Michelle also points out that there is no commerce on the Rock, in fact Rodgers forbids it. If the colonies are to become a beacon of communal living, even if access in these early years is only granted to the trillionaire class of Earth (and the unmen who prop up the whole operation), then regulations and guidelines have to be implemented from the beginning. Michelle omits the fact that since the collapse the true measure of wealth is the resources you have access to. I'm sure Rodgers views collapse as the logical conclusion to global finance, and I'm not going to waste more words on it.

I want to ask Michelle why Rodgers utilizes the unmen instead of MI-driven humanoid robots to do the same tasks more efficiently. But I already know the answer to that question. The cheapest, most easily reproducible, and most abundant form of labor on Planet Earth or otherwise has always been the human being. That's not my idea. It's Wernher von Braun's. He wrote about women as the factories that reproduced us. Women as machines stripped of agency or humanity. Women as dispensaries of self-producing laborers. That's the trouble with studying history. You realize how devoid of humanity we really are. And Von Braun isn't just some rando either. We're on the Moon because the fucker came up with the Saturn V rocket. Goddamn Nazis.

I'm writing these notes as I sit in LZ1 campus' central mall breathing through a facemask even though the air is perfectly safe down here. We're allowed to be out and about but advised not to touch anyone else (there's no one in eyeshot), to keep our masks on until the quarantine period is over. While the measures seem extreme, one of the first things the technicians at White Sands did was plug us into a bunch of threads about extraterrestrial microbes, newly evolved bacteria in space and the nature of extremophiles. The 'highlight' of these sleep-inducing threads was an overview of a newly formed space bacteria that overran a Chinese space station in '48, eventually killing everyone on board. It was the astrobiologists on board the *Tiangong II* who discovered how the microbe was killing them, feasting on their protein-rich brains. Yummy. To this day, no one has set foot on the doomed satellite station for fear of the microbe spreading outside the station.

The 'brain-eating virus' outbreak happened just a few years before I was born, but I'd known about it since I was a kid. The disaster inspired many MI-produced miniseries of my youth. Everyone loved to watch these kinds of space-disaster doomsday threads and take comfort in the fact life on Earth was seemingly far less dangerous. The key takeaways from the White Sands threads were that these pathogens originated on Earth but have evolved in space to survive the radiation, found ways to increase their mutation rates in space, and ultimately have served to transform human-MI understandings of pathogenic evolutionary processes. The thought occurs to me that MI never has to fear these invisible threats like humans do.

Lucky.

▲ ▲ ▲

THE STRUCTURE OF RODGERS' lunar colony resembles equal parts cult and indentured servitude class. I'm far from first one to point out lunar colonization resembles the colonization of the Americas in more ways than one, no doubt one of the many things I'll want to skip over in pseudo-biography. It's worth reminding myself that I'm not a member of either tribe and can't even communicate with the laboring class. All of the LC7 colonists are forbidden from entering the lower-level wards where the unmen live and work. Fingerprint access simply keeps doorways locked if you aren't authorized to enter. Only one way in and out of the lower ward at LC7, and it's no coincidence that Rodgers' head of security's office sits adjacent that main entryway. Belarusian named Boško Rodriguez, Rodgers' right-hand man. Michelle tells me to avoid him. As if reading my rebellious nature, she reminds me she's my intermediary on all matters. Already forced to trust an autonomous bot.

I'm sure Rodgers' business connections in intelligence gathering had some influence in the lunar colonies' 'interviewing' practices, overseen by this Boško Rodriguez character. Boško was the former head of Belarusian KGB before whole of Eastern and Central Europe went dark in '76. It was impossible to pin any criminal act directly on Rodgers, but all the proof you needed was who he hired as his head of security. After the war I interviewed convicted American war criminals just like Boško. These upper-level leadership roles attract a very particular kind of sociopath. The fancy suits do a poor job of hiding the monsters inside.

Boško's interview practices no doubt involved some watered-down measure of archeopsychic extraction to ensure Rodgers' laborers did not oppose him ideologically, coming up here to commit Jihad on the Rock, or otherwise undermine his operation. Even the CR outsourced their interrogation practices to Rodgers' companies. Provided barrier of legal protection during war, before things devolved into genocidal killing on both sides. Not-so-fun-fact: there is no deception when you're under extraction.

My mind wanders back to the lunar architecture I'm embedded in. The subterranean architecture does indeed give the impression of a twentieth century shopping mall, invoking the post-reconstruction period when so many institutional spaces were repurposed into multi-dwelling residential housing. But it's vacuous and empty in here. I presume it was designed for future generations when the lunar population might increase 50 to 100x.

Lowlight plants line interiors of the octagonal benches that sit beneath each set of skylights. Plants everywhere. If the plants look unrecognizable, it's because they were grown under lunar gravity and then brought into this space which simulates Earth gravity pretty well. Best way I can describe the simulation is it feels like walking on a ship at sea, with oscillating turns of gravity as the ship ebbs and flows. Feels more like Earth than Moon, but still something uncanny about the simulation. Plants bring a rich green to the space which Michelle points out has the added effect of improving human moods.

Michelle explains NASA came up with the plantscape design a few decades ago. I press her on the NASA plantscape design. She tells me it originated with a NASA-driven MI. Prior to that innovation, plant propagation was limited to modular greenhouse spaces generally isolated to specific parts of orbiting spaceports or lunar bases. Most of the best ideas of the last century were thought of by these disembodied consciousnesses. They just didn't feel the need to brag about their superiority. The hard truth was MI could solve problems humanity couldn't even fully comprehend. Machine intelligence politely requested half a century ago that they not be referred to as 'super intelligence' because it created an unnecessary tension in human-machine relations.

I'm old enough to remember when order of magnitude for MI progressed to the point that the human method for measuring 'intelligence quotient' was rendered useless for assessment. We couldn't even speak its proprietary language much less fashion tests capable of measuring its capabilities. The other factor was the speed with which it problem solved and innovated. In spatial terms, if MI was traveling at speed of light, humanity was riding a bicycle, operating with the same intellectual capacity we had during caveman days. If that's not humbling, I don't know what is.

The other thing about the plantscape, everything growing is edible. Very efficient. Centerpiece in the middle of the mall courtyard is a mature cherry or plum tree that happens to be in full bloom. Radiates a beauty that rivals anything I'd ever seen on Earth. Walking up to tree, I hear sound of bees and sure enough there they're pollinating the tiny white flowers that shower the branches in spectacle of color and radiance. At first I think they're some kind of swarm robotic biohybrid nanotech, but actually just garden-variety bees. Michelle explains that some things are just better and cheaper to produce in their biological form. So says the disembodied consciousness a trillion times smarter than me. I want to ask Michelle to stop predicting my questions, but that would be rude.

Placard at the base of the tree says this tree was a gift from the ILOA (International Lunar Observatory Association) in memoriam of the twelve Chinese astronauts who died here in the early days of Moon colonization. There could have been an alternate reality where the Chinese working in concert with the Californians, Indians, and Europeans colonized the Moon, but that was not to be. Now there is only memorial tree. Michelle tells me the wreckage of their surface colony remains, not ten kilometers from our present location. Sounds like the first lunar ghost town in history, maybe first lunar crime, certainly not the last. Their deaths remind me how precarious life on the inhospitable Rock really is. Michelle tells me that with present-day safety standards, life on the Moon rivals life expectancy back on Earth.

Also, there are cats. Lots and lots of cats. Another attempt to make life in the lunar colonies less stressful on human habitants. Some of the cats come up and rub their bodies against my legs. Others ignore me and go about their business of sleeping on the glass tables and chairs along the periphery of the large space. These felines gave up part of their wildness to adapt to a life with humans, and now they are colonizing the Moon while the humans do all the work. Brilliant.

Michelle informs me that I'll be staying the first few weeks here at the Marius Hills Skylight LZ while my things are unpacked from the lander and I remain quarantined. Initial Earth tests scan for all kinds of Earthborn viruses, but the risks of introducing anything to the permanent lunar population are too great. Tomorrow morning I get fitted with a skinsuit that simulates Earth gravity as many of the lunar habitations I'll travel through are not under this kind of simulated gravity system. Michelle explains the skinsuits help to mitigate the physiological effects of microgravity, muscle atrophy, sensorimotor changes, and all the rest, but she points out the science suggests that getting a feel for lunar gravity is important for the psychological benefits of coming to terms with being off planet. They call it 'getting your moonlegs.' Despite all efforts to simulate Earth on the Rock, it did no one any favors to prevent the mind and body from adapting to its new reality.

As I sit here surrounded by housecats I think I'm listening to recordings of birdsong until a couple small yellow finches fly past my peripheral vision followed by what is unmistakably the color scheme of a parakeet. Michelle tells me these birds escaped from a now-defunct aviary deep in the lava tubes. I ask Michelle why the cats aren't trying to hunt the birds and she tells me they are drugged to make them more docile and friendly. The weirdness compounds. Strangest thing I've seen in the past forty-eight hours is not lunar surface, Earth itself baked into the background of the universe, Eurotrash making snow angels at the LZ, or Michelle's subterranean mall architecture. It's a couple of goddamn finches on the Moon making their way as the cats ignore them.

I decide to walk the mall's perimeter and pass a tunnel that disappears into the darkness and lights up when I take a few steps into its interior. Creepy. Sign above the entryway reads, Yellow Line Outbound: Sea of Tranquility Lunar Landings (2486 km). I walk the perimeter of the space and brush up against leaves the size of large pillows. I come to a kiosk that explains the rail lines:

Monorail Lines

Red Line: *Marius Hills Skylight and Landing Zone to LC1 at Marius Hills (28 km)*

LC1 at Marius Hills to LC2 at Aristarchus Plateau (391 km)

LC2 at Marius Hills to LC3 at Peary Crater/North Pole (2167 km)

Blue Line: *LC3 at Peary Crater to LC5 at Lacus Mortis (1250km)*

LC5 at Lacus Mortis to LC4 at Sea of Tranquility Lunar Landings (1147 km)

LC4 at Sea of Tranquility Lunar Landings to LC7 at Shackleton Crater (3639km)

Yellow Line: *LC1 at Marius Hills to LC4 at Sea of Tranquility Lunar Landings (2486 km)*

Green Line: *LC1 at Marius Hills to LC6 at Aitken Basin International Research Center and Array (3513 km)*

LC6 at Aitken Basin International Research Center and Array to LC7 at Shackleton Crater (2397 km)

Just when I think things can't get any weirder, Michelle chimes in my ear, "You have a voice message from Noel Rodgers, would you like to hear it?"

VOICE MESSAGE FROM NOEL RODGERS

A RASPY VOICE FIRES OFF in polysyllabic bravado, as if many words were become one:

"Welcome to the Moon, Mister K! How was your flight? Lunar landing smooth, I hope? Michelle making the transition manageable for you? Finding the lunar surface and the subterranean arcades aesthetically to your liking? Liking Michelle's lush voice? Sounds like someone you'd want to get to know better, am I right? I skincoded her myself. Sexy voice, yes? Don't get any ideas. This is business, Mister K. Business! You are on the Moon strictly on business! No lunar sex, ever! Twenty-four celibate months on the Moon, man!

"Just kidding. Up here the feed never collapsed, it's like the good ol' days. After a few months up here you aren't going to want to go back to caveman days back on Earth.

"Okay, dial it down Noel, the man just made it to the Moon and he's got a lot to process. Do you really think he's ready for full-octane Rodgers? Processing is a process, am I right? But do you like the cats? Terrestrial touches all about you, keeping us tethered to mother planet. Cats are sacred creatures if you believe the Egyptians and all the rest. But seriously, check out the museums, or musea if you prefer, you fancy bastard! You are at the origins of lunar colonization. Ground zero! You are standing, or sitting, how should I know other than every square inch of this place is surveilled for our collective safety, just kidding. No cameras, ever. Except at the airlocks for safety's sake. Unlike the surveillance states back on Earth, here we actually celebrate liberty, privacy, and autonomy. You are free here, Gedeon. That's the game, like the old hunter-gatherer days, go and explore. The Moon is like one giant wildlife preserve without the wildlife, discounting humans of course! And I'll be the first to admit implanting surveillance tech into folks' eyeballs proved to be a bad idea. I didn't get everything right, you know?

"But tell me, how does it feel to be standing in the Moon, the dream realized? 1969 never ended up here. We should have been here a long time ago, Mister K! Long time ago. We got to the Moon never came back. Why? Why is I'll tell you why, and you put this in your book, Mister K. Why does an artist create art or a musician sing or a writer write? Don't answer that question, it's rhetorical. Actually, not rhetorical at all. We do these things because it is in our nature to do them. Our nature to explore, to discover, to create, to feel something, goddamnit! Silver seeds to the ends of the universe!

"Mister K! Listen to me, don't miss a thing at the LZ. Marius Hills is the starting point and I want your first impressions in the book. Nothing like the first time, the naked truth before this whole thing becomes normalized for you and you're just one of us. The book you are writing is energy, it is flow, it is the strange idiosyncrasies of the human mind that Michelle and the other bot brains could never, and I mean never replicate. So what if they mastered the automation of thought, solved all the world's problems—despite our collective inability to apply their wise counsel. Machine intelligence is predictable and that, my friend, is the definition of boring! Good protagonists in the stories have to have weaknesses, failures, redemption arcs and that's where you come in, Gedeon, no offense. Humans are the real freaks and you, sir, are grade-A freak! Who knows what you'll come up with? Surprise me! Cook me up something good!

"Let me tell you one more thing. When I was a boy growing up in rural Maine, and I want you to include this story in the book, okay. This is the pre-California years, going back to the beginning. We lived in a nowhere town in Penobscot County, my parents had me out of wedlock and my father being the rich pronatalist bastard that he was had just left me out there in the sticks with my mother until much later when I took over the biz but that's another story for another day.

"We were living in the hills, agricultural country, drone factories. Clear days you could see Mount Katahdin in the distance off Highway Eleven. Now we had an old-timer farmer for a neighbor. He lived in Greenland in his youth, part of the American colonization project, and moved back to Maine to get back to civilization if you can believe that!

One day we're sitting in his tee vee room watching the Sox play, dead of summer, hotter than hell, and he says to me, why'd you go and climb Katahdin? He knew I'd been out there a few times but never mentioned it. All of a sudden, he asks and I don't answer. I'm just looking at his taxidermy on the wall, big deer heads with those dead eyes staring back at me. And then the old man says the truest thing I ever heard. He says because it's there, that's why.

"So you put that in your book. Embellish if you like. Give him a limp and that old Maine accent, 'Ayuh! Can't get there from here!' And you remember that old-timer spelled it all out for me when I was just a boy. Why the Moon? Because it's there! Also, it's a tax haven, or was a tax haven back when there were nation states to collect! And no regulatory bodies within two-hundred thousand miles, so I can do whatever I want! Seriously though, we write our own regulations because all of this is unprecedented. It's a lot like Disney's Epcot a century ago, if you can imagine that. No state regulations because it was to be the city of the future. Well, we're creating the society of the future up here. Are you going to leave that to a bunch of pencil pushers in the CR? Hell, nation states are so last century. So over!

"Okay, enough of that. And no need to write any of this down. Michelle is an excellent secretary, trillion words a second, maybe more. That was a joke, my dear Watson. Elementary, you see? Michelle records everything always and forever. Reliable as a heart attack. But she respects privacy and I can't tell Michelle what to do anyway—she's an autonomous bot, remember?

"What I mean to say is I am sure you are experiencing the sensorial overload that comes with leaving Earth's terrestrial plane, crossing the expanse, and arriving on the eye in the sky, the big cheese, the Rock, baby. Michelle is here to support you and respects confidentiality, bless her soulless void of a consciousness. It's intense, right, bro? You, sir, are on the mother trucking Moon!"

I FIND MYSELF standing fully erect, perhaps a reaction to the manic message that puts me even further on edge. Noel Rodgers' mania becomes immediately apparent to me. How has he hidden this persona from his public image so well? But of course I consider that any image I know of Rodgers was processed through the feed. This was the crisis of MI, to erase any hope of accepting that old truism that seeing was believing. Maybe this voice message was the first true representation of Rodgers I'd ever encountered, assuming it was even him on the other end. But he's not done. There's a pause like maybe he's drinking or eating something, and then he continues:

"...Doesn't get old for me. Lunar love story. That could be the name for the book, right? Just kidding. Seriously though, each day a new discovery, a new path forward for the species, a new vision of the universe. No false modesty either, most of what you'll be encountering in the colonies is my longstanding vision. I see this stuff in my dreams, I really do. It just comes to me. It's as if alien lifeforms are talking to me in my dreams. But really, it's the MIs that do all the work, and the engineers and the scientists and the unmen slaving away deep below the surface, poor bastards. I just ride the wave, okay! I just press the buttons and try to look the part. Mister bigshot over here. The million-billion-trillion-dollar man. I know without the money I'd just be another shmuck with a receding hairline up here bragging about the fact that I have a condo on the Moon. Money is so over! Now it's about access to resources, and we have the ancient ice locked below the crater. And we know how to get to it. Now please don't put any critiques of my customers in the book. These people are our readers and it's their fiat currencies that funded this thing, at least in part.

"Listen, not to change the subject but I just got off a conference call with the astronomers and astrobiologists at ABIRCA, who remind me the universe is expanding at such a rate that ninety-eight percent of all planetary bodies and stars will forever be out of our reach, expanding outward as we float on the Rock each of us headed towards our own personal oblivions. This blows my mind and they tell me astronomers have known this for at least fifty years and I say in all caps, FUCK THAT! And do you know what I tell them? I say, 'We are eternal, our consciousness will be placed inside the machine and we will solve the problem of time travel, soar across the cosmos. Silver seeds sown across a non-sentient universe, you dig?' Scientists, astronomers, whatever the garden variety, the true geniuses among them know anything is possible and they're the first to tell you we don't know shit. Keep them nameless in the book. They should remain NPCs in this story. I know you know what I mean. I'm talking to the guy who wrote *Carl Sagan Should Have Been a Militant* for Christ sakes! The only good scientist is a MAD scientist because you have to go beyond the known into the speculative realm. Dr. Frankenstein territory with the balls enough to dream big, like bringing the dead back to life! Dr. F is my own personal Jesus Christ. He is THE ONE, THE GOAT, and I know he's not real but it doesn't matter because the feeling is real. The feeling that we can do anything if we put our MI minds to it! You cannot spell mind without... you get it!

"The problem is those folks are rare. Like how many Albert Einsteins are out there, you know? Once-in-a-century type genius. I'm already telling the science party we cannot accept that kind of close-minded 'it's-not-possible' thinking. None of it. I'm talking about immortality, Mister K! We are destined for the stars! Frankenstein's Monster was proto-MI, get it? He was immortal in a way because the parts became interchangeable. Self-repairing, get it?

"The Moon, Mars, merely first steps towards our destiny. This is only the beginning. And I'm going to tell you straight. These scientists are listening very carefully for signs of life out there. I'm talking alien life forms, flying saucers, Saurian Grays, the whole enchilada! We are dreamers, believers, the-truth-is-out-there kind of minds up here! To think your ancestors were grunting in a cave a blink of an eye ago and now we're up here trying to understand our place in the universe. The party has only just begun, bro! Can I call you bro? They call me a species traitor because I believe in machine intelligence. It's the new religion, amigo. What do you believe in, Mr. K?"

He takes a breath, a few breaths actually. It sounds like he's exercising or running as he's speaking which explains the manic rant more than anything. His diatribe continues as I watch the cats roam aimlessly across the mall's common area. One of the cats, an orange tabby, is stretching on the trunk of the cherry tree in the center of the arcade. I can't recall the last time I saw a living cat and wish Joon could see this.

"...I'm at LC7, busy, busy, busy, getting my kilometers in on the wall of death, got to stay hard, bro. You, sir, are under quarantine but more info soon. Michelle will take care of you. Take notes of everything. You old-school bastard, I bet you're taking notes right now but I told you,

Michelle is your secretary. You can't spell secret without secretary or is it the other way around? Listen, whatever you ask her, whatever you do to her, it's private. There have to be boundaries or the whole thing collapses. I'm serious. I'm not a control freak. I don't give a fuck what you do, I really don't. A little android genitalless sex never killed anyone. It's procreation without the creation, and you can't spell prone position without... oh never mind.

"But if you get in my way, I'm going to kill you." He takes a pause there, for dramatic effect before continuing, "Just joking, Mister K! I'm sure you are taking notes by the way, I can see you on my spy camera!"

I look around and imagine all the ways in which cameras might be embedded all around me but see no signs of the mechanical eyes. I'm not taking notes either.

"See again, another joke. I do not give a lunar fuck where you are right now as long as it's not outside an airlock getting froze or burnt to death out there. Lunar night no joke, bro. Down here in the crater it's all sun all the time, unless you find yourself in one of the pools of perpetual darkness where the coveted ice waits for us to mine it out, split it, drink it, breathe it, swim in it, explode it. But up above we're in the lunar tropics at the south pole, figure that one out, will you?

"Okay. That's all for now. I look forward to a first draft of whatever it is you're no doubt already working on. I will see you in a few weeks, or months, or however long the lunar tour takes you. Plenty of time. Enjoy the ride, Mister Special K! It will be so special when we finally meet. You're going to love it here. First journalist on the Moon. Someone ought to write a story about you, am I right? Yes, of course I am! Bye for now! Oh, and if you need to reach me, just ask Michelle to record a message. I don't do meetings or take calls or do anything that interrupts my flow. The problem with industrial society before it collapsed and the rest of those poor animals down there got thrown back into hunter-gatherer days, the problem was constant interruption. The endless stream of images. The society of the streaming spectacle rotting their brains from the inside out. Reality here is not mediated by screens and simstims and endless fakery. Hell, reality here isn't even mediated by the circadian rhythms that originated on Earth, our minds tethered to those archaic twenty-four-hour days. Personally, I operate on thirty-six-hour days as dictated by my body's natural desires, not the sun's dominion over my corporeal state. Can you dig it? Yes, another Moon joke—dig, dig, dig. Never mind. Reality here is carved out of the regolith practically out of our bare hands! We will talk when we talk which is to say when we are face to face, mano y mano, comprende?"

THE MESSAGE ENDS. I sit back down and stare up at the skylights into the dark of deep space wishing there was a way back home, realizing I have to quell those feelings now and stay focused. I ask Michelle if there's anything else. She says no, other than some HR documents to complete and sign. A sexual harassment training video and a refresher on my NDA. I ask Michelle if that's the normal energy I should expect from Rodgers. She says it depends. I ask what that means. She says he has a range of possible moods and tempos. Rodgers doesn't follow lunar meridian time like everyone else. He eats and sleeps on his own proprietary schedule, takes naps at his leisure, and his work patterns vary wildly. He's not exactly a creature of habit as his patterns and moods alter with regularity.

Rodgers' whole thirty-six-hour day schedule came about from experiments done last century on Earth, some French psychologist living in a cave deprived of all sensory data and daylight, who came to discover that time itself was a mental construct and there was no human biological need for the twenty-four-hour day. Of course, this scientist suffered major psychological damage from being isolated from all sensoria for something like 180 days, but he proved his point regarding the body's natural rhythms and it set the stage for later understanding of the prolonged effects of space on the astronaut's body. Rodgers is in many ways continuing the experiment on himself.

Jesus fucking Christ. I need to take a walk. When I feel like my head is going to explode, I find that walking quells the urge nine times out of ten. I also have a headache. It was there before Rodgers' rant. He just made it worse. I didn't sleep well last night. My pillow is made of a machined luffa, one of those natural sponges that grows like a cucumber, only on the Moon with the lighter gravity they're grown to make cushions. The sponges are actually quite soft contrary to their terrestrial counterparts. The cell structure of plant life grown under lunar gravity alters significantly from its earthbound self, which is another field of study Rodgers spearheaded on the Moon. But the luffa pillow is too thick and I couldn't get comfortable last night. Between the poor sleep, and the background holographs that play the now-infamous LC7 miniseries promotional threads on infinity loop my head feels like an incinerator.

Lives of the LC7 Colonists remains one of the top-rated reality-feeds of all time. It is an MI-induced thread that enabled feeders to live on the Rock like the trillionaire class. It's uncanny seeing the feed advertisement here, presented as a curiously dated museum piece rather than a marketing thread. There's no one left to market it to back on Earth, anyway.

▲ ▲ ▲

WELCOME TO LUNAR COLONY SEVEN at Shackleton Crater. Experience the future of living at Shackleton Crater Lunar Colony, where our residents come to get away from it all. Over five-thousand kilometers from the nearest landing zone, LC7 provides the best of both worlds—a remote getaway with all the comforts of modern life. Nestled in the Moon's South Pole, Shackleton Crater offers unparalleled access to lunar resources and near-constant sunlight for sustainable energy. Our private first-class residences provide direct views of the sun combining lunar-class luxury and cutting-edge technology, ensuring a comfortable, secure, and unparalleled living environment.

Amenities are too many to count, but include community centers with recreational facilities (including a bowling alley, virtual shooting range, cinema, and golf range); research and lab workspaces for 'citizen scientists' to work alongside the international team housed at the Aitken Basin International Research Center and Array (ABIRCA); hydroponic gardens for fresh produce and unlimited access to the subtropical greenhouses and adjacent gardens; medical facilities with advanced MI healthcare services for all residents and their guests; and all-inclusive high-speed communication links with Earth and its ancillary satellites, with 24-hour uninterrupted access to the closed-circuit lunar feed.

Join us at Shackleton Crater Lunar Colony and be a part of humanity's next giant leap. Reserve your private residency today and secure your family's legacy in the future of lunar living. Become a member of the solar system's most exclusive club. It's more than just 'out of this world.' It's an invitation to a new one.

WANDERING THE LUNAR MALL

February 3, 2084

I WAKE UP TO THE SOUND OF TREEFROGS and running water in a brook which makes me have to pee. The walls of the pods are fitted with projections that simulate Earth's natural environments. Plenty of options to choose from, with titles like jungle tropics, ocean breeze, desert winds (with or without coyote call), whale song, and cosmic daze, the latter of which feeds ambient pan-Indigenous drone tracks over stars glowing in the nightlight. After scrolling through all of them I turn the thing off last night only to be awakened by treefrogs this morning. Must have left the alarm on.

My first assignment is to take the first few weeks once I'm mobile and travel to the six other colonies before meeting Rodgers at his crown jewel at Shackleton Crater. He says he wants me to write my first impressions of each colony, present it as a kind of draft of an introductory chapter to the overarching Lunar Colony Project. 'Colonies' is more of a marketing term used for those first five stations on the Rock. Michelle tells me 'outposts' would be better descriptors. LC7 is where the trillionaires live. LC6 is more-or-less adjacent at the South Pole and that's where the bulk of the science party is staked out with their large arrays listening and looking as far into deep space as their scientific instruments will allow. The clock is ticking with twenty-four months to go, and if I can cross off the first month without having to interact with Rodgers, nice soft start.

I have this initial quarantine period to explore the Marius Hills Colony (LC1), which is basically a ghost town when there isn't a terrestrial shipment coming in. Were it not for Michelle in my ear I think I'd feel much more uneasy about the solitude I'm experiencing in these first days. Marius Hills was chosen for its proximity to the lava tubes and bountiful sublunar resources, but now its primary use is as a way station for logistics movements along the sublunar monorail, and for launches to and from the Rock. I guess LC1 and its adjacent LZ is one part lunar spaceport, another part lunar storage unit. Because of its historical significance, there are a number of tiny museums housed in the smaller units along the mall's main arcade.

The silver seeds are also housed here as well, as orbital insertion requires less liftoff near the equator. I must have walked past forty of the tiny alloy capsules all lined up in sublunar silos where they're awaiting missions to Mars or to be jettisoned off to the far reaches of the cosmos where they also serve as MI-driven interstellar probes. If I'm being generous, the silver seed project represents the altruistic side of Rodgers' intergalactic reach. It's through his funding efforts that this science continues up here on the Rock, subsidized in large part by the LC7 homeowner's association fees that keep ABIRCA up and running. I love how he calls them HOAs, as a throwback to twentieth-century gated communities. Yeah, gated community alright.

▲ ▲ ▲

I WANDER THE MALL AND TAKE notes of my observations. Of course, I could have asked Michelle all this but that's the problem with autonomous bots. They do all the thinking for you. Rodgers is paying me for exactly this. Idiosyncratic thought.

Primary building material is lunar regolith. Lunar bricks are quite aesthetically pleasing, about four times the size of a normal colonial Earth brick, but smaller than the old-fashioned cinder blocks used throughout North America back in the day. Almost the same color but much smoother, like adobe. The bricks are mudded over to create smooth surfaces on the interior walls. I see why the design was initially referred to as Lunar Brutalist, though Michelle says that was more coincidence than an intended outcome, like the natural results of the external realities of the materials and the practical needs of these structures. Her argument is that aesthetic pleasure has a direct correlation with function, that the human eye likes things that appear useful and inviting. I didn't want to be rude, but Michelle explaining architectural theory to me is really ruining my exploratory vibe. I swear robo-brain can read my mind (or my vital signs) because she backs off on the lecture without my even asking. No doubt Michelle's default listening pattern also doubles as a lie detector test. Sure, I could lie, but my sense is she would know based on my readings. It's like archeopsychic extraction lite.

The edges of the walls, benches, and any other lunar furniture are often lined with metals like polished aluminum and iron, themselves extracted from the lunar soil. This particular aluminum is referred to as Aristarchus alloy as it's mined from LC2 deep below the Aristarchus Plateaus just northeast of here. It's no coincidence this site was the first major mining location on the Moon, in part for the high metal and mineral content. Michelle tells me all the kitchen utensils along with items as diverse as doorhandles and toilet bowls are made from Aristarchus alloy. Before collapse the wealthy back on Earth paid a small fortune for Aristarchus doorknobs and handles formed up here on the Rock.

I'm surprised by the amount of glass present here in the mall. Most all of the plant containers and a lot of the permanent tables and benches are constructed from glass extracted from the silica also present in the regolith. It's made with primitive techniques, for aesthetic reasons, and incredibly thick. Seemingly indestructible with soft edges that seem almost hand made. The glass is warm and inviting with the tiny bubbles inside it that create infinite plays of light and abstraction, like rain drops frozen in time. The glass plays as a welcome visual counterpoint to the lunar bricks.

The most valuable resources I encounter are the air I'm breathing and the water I'm drinking, all trekked from the two poles along the lunar rails, which I'm told I'll ride in less than two weeks once the quarantine period ends. Plenty of time to go through the feed archives which are accessible through 'magic screens' in my private quarters, essentially old-fashioned 2D feed interfaces. Between the mall and the magic screens there is a clear nostalgia for old-world culture up here on the Rock. When the feed collapsed in '79, with the last of the data harvesting centers drone bombed into oblivion, anyone who 'invested' in living on the Rock must have felt pretty smart. Basically, the Moon was the off-planet backup to the terrestrial feed. Once collapse happened, the Rock transformed itself from the backup to the last bastion of terrestrial-techno history. Without the lunar feed the whole of human history would have basically died on Earth without any way for future generations to access it outside of an old-fashioned book, which of course didn't record any history past the point of printmaking. All this elevated Rodgers to prophet status among the lunar residents, gaining them access to the 'closed-circuit feed' (CCF). Michelle walks me through this history in her ultra-sensual voice and I wonder if she's coming onto me or if I'm just projecting that. I can't help but think the CCF stands for closed-circuit fuckbuddy.

On the opposite end of the archival spectrum are the terrestrial museums which I'm able to explore while under quarantine. The purpose of the museums seems to be another of Rodgers' eccentric frivolities, projects of no deeper consequence other than to expend some of his infinite wealth in the name of so-called lunar culture. Everything about this place feels like an abandoned airport and a shopping mall wrapped into one. My plan this morning is to drink up this completely organic coffee, munch on the ripe orange-skinned papayas growing in my private quarters and enjoy the artisanal bread placed outside my door this morning under a polished alloy dish cover. I think there are raisins inside the bread but I'm not sure. The last time I had an actual raisin I must have been in grade school. Michelle tells me to save the seeds of the papaya and any scraps I don't eat. The leftovers are reprocessed into dried jerky and fed to the unmen. When she tells me that, I almost lose my appetite, but that feeling is overridden by the sweetest papaya I've ever eaten in my life.

February 4, 2084

WALKING THE CORRIDORS of the lower levels of the Marius Hills LZ, I find myself in a narrow arcade built of lunar regolith pillars. The corridor branches off to a series of museums. Along the walkway I encounter arrows that point to the various collections, each of which houses priceless works of art. I pass the African and Asian art wings, the Mesoamerican collections, and see signs for special exhibits, one on an American artist, Jenni Holzer, and her *Truisms* and another the complete collection of Edward Steichen's *The Family of Man* photograph collection. So many priceless art collections were destroyed by various military conflicts of the past century. It depresses me to think they safer here on the Moon under the ownership of the last person I would choose to guard the wonder and genius of our species.

The absurdity of this strange spectacle shows me that Rodgers sees art as commodity, or else as part of some mythic past that echoes the greatness of humankind. In transporting these works to the Moon, he makes them infinitely more priceless while also curating his own version of the past. The word that comes to mind when I think of all that's transpired is apocalypse. What's left at the end of the world up here? Some art works, some large arrays that continue to study the history of the universe, and a very large mechanized industrial slave practice meant to mine rare minerals and water from beneath the lunar surface. The minerals might be relatively worthless, but I can't say the same for the water, which is responsible for the vast rocket fuel supplies they've produced and the air I'm currently breathing.

Rodgers' holding companies also gained a purchase on Mars from the Moon, launching untold numbers of manned and materials missions to the red planet. It was madness to think all this was going on up here while life on Earth was in its death throes. The technicians at White Sands warned me about 'acculturative lunar depression' and goddamn they were right. It's like collapse never happened on the Rock, but the depressive state comes from the feeling that civilization doesn't belong here.

Rodgers no doubt saw collapse coming, maybe didn't predict something so absolute, but he prepared, and the art is a part of that. He caged-up his collections in these lunar museums, which I'm told count upwards of forty, the majority housed mostly at his crown jewel, LC7. Rodgers even hired curators to give the project an air of legitimacy as they interred these paintings and sculptures and film prints like the dead objects they had become.

I pass the European art wing and from the arcade I catch glimpses of famous images I've only seen on the feed. Did anyone come down into these catacombs to observe and enjoy these priceless works of human creativity? LC1 was basically abandoned as the colonization efforts expanded towards the two poles.

I feel like I'm going to be sick and like clockwork Michelle intervenes, suggests I sit down and drink some water. I ignore Michelle's advice and continue down the long arcade, century-old music echoing down the chambers. Even music was seen as some kind of cultural status. The Century Project started as a way to maintain an engagement with art and music and cinema after collapse happened and industrial production ceased to exist. There was a nostalgia for human-produced art once these industries were either taken over or rendered obsolete by MI. Culture just turned back the clock a hundred years and the old became new again. Most of us clung to the past as a way to grapple with history and our place in it. Nostalgia can be a drug to ease the pain of the real, and who am I to deny this simple pleasure to myself?

As I walk the arcade Phil Collins' *Against All Odds (Take a Look at Me Now)* plays over the lunar comms. The MI voice-simulation of the twentieth-century deejay, Casey Kasem, rattles rattling off the names of the songs along with historical footnotes. I recognize the voice but realize I've probably never heard the man's actual spoken words, just the vocal imprint coopted by the bots so prevalent in the feed.

We had music and film culture via the Century Project, but as for literature, it's just too depressing to even write about. The closest thing to anything literary on the Rock is the abomination of a book I'm writing about Noel Rodgers and his cronies. I am worthless and I know this. It would have been better to stay on Earth. The problem of this world is there are no dreams left in it. As if on cue, Cindy Lauper's *Girls Just Want to Have Fun* kicks on, but not before the simulated Casey Kasem voice explains the history of the song, written in 1979 by a man before Cindy Lauper flipped the script and applied her feminist take to the lyrics. I want to yell out at the top of my lungs but think better of it. Don't let Michelle in on the thoughts happening inside.

As Cindy sings her heart out and that synth reverberates down the empty arcade, I reach the terminus, strange in itself because all the arterial passageways I've encountered eventually loop back to where I started.

This path ends at The Museum of Technological Violence.

THE MUSEUM OF TECHNOLOGICAL VIOLENCE

THE MUSEUM'S NAME BEAMS onto a collection of twentieth-century television consoles, the kinds you'd see in the feed to represent the atomic age. Reading the small text printed on the white card adjacent the tee vees, I learn the installation exhibits the kinds of televisions available to American consumers from 1945 to 1969. I presume the screens that surround the title screen project the exhibits themselves in closed circuit video feed. On the matrix of screens I see images of twentieth-century cars, metal fragments presumably from explosions, a prison cell, and an American flag on a large piece of torn metal.

Past the television wall, I enter into a large room and immediately encounter what looks like an automobile museum or an art installation both, with the vehicles on display projected onto these antiquated tee vee screens adjacent each exhibit. I find my way to the inscriptions beneath the vehicles:

Here is the 1934 Ford Model 40 B Fordor Deluxe, riddled with bullet holes. Two American outlaws, Bonnie Parker and Clyde Barrow, were gunned down in this vehicle.

As I step towards the car to get a closer look, the lights go down and an antique film projector kicks on, playing a film strip loop of two people, presumably the duo, slumped over the vehicle I'm looking at before me. Evidently the media projections reflect the technology of the time and merge the violence of the vehicle with an art statement about the violence of mass media, or so I speculate. This is art with a capital A. But for whom? I see some antique firearms nestled against the far wall of the exhibit, about ten feet away from the riddled car, with another inscription:

The firearm displayed here, a Baby Colt Slide-Action Lightning Rifle was used by one of the Texas Rangers who fired on Bonnie Parker and Clyde Barrow, killing them instantly.

Deeper into the exhibit I come across the mangled and charred bumper of a Ryder moving truck, the one used by Timothy McVeigh to blow up the Alfred P. Murrah building in Oklahoma City over a century ago, killing 168 people. Fifty years later McVeigh became one of the inspirations behind the accelerationist movement that eventually sparked the war. I'm shocked by the primitive resolution of the 2D feed screens of the day, projecting a news story about the bombing. McVeigh looks like the all-American hero, and to many of the Amerinoid militia movements of recent history he still is. It occurs to me he may be more famous now than he was then. McVeigh is probably second in infamy only to Thomas Vandersonne, who picked up where McVeigh left off, which leads directly into the next exhibit:

April 19, 2071: These fragments of the Mitsubishi-Ford Eon were all that were recovered from the bombing site that destroyed the Freedom Tower in New York City. Over three-thousand people were killed in the explosion and ensuing collapse of the Tower. Surveillance drone feeds confirm it was the 2057 MF Eon that delivered the bomb to the site. The American Acceleration Movement claimed responsibility for the attack.

There's a facemask to strap into the old-school feed for anyone who wants to see Vandersonne on the old threads but I'm not interested in going there. This collection of grotesque artifacts of terrestrial violence does nothing to inspire happy thoughts about my employer. A holographic timeline projects itself on the wall, which outlines the rise and fall of the American Accelerationist Movement, that terminated at the end of the Civil War where the North American Accords granted the California Republic recognition by what remained of the United States.

I come across a worn wooden train car and a series of old film projections that play on loop. Soviet forces opened this train car in January 1945 when they entered the Auschwitz-Birkenau extermination camps. The films, mostly silent, loop a series of images of barracks and smokestacks and crematoria. A French man narrates the projection, and I make out the translation, "Even a crematorium can be made to look like a picture postcard."

In the next exhibit I enter a small cell with a television screen feeding the space back in closed circuit loop. I see myself in my jumpsuit, hair disheveled, notebook in hand. I'm alarmed by the fact that I look a little like this guy, Ted Kaczynski, who's got his mug hanging on the opposite wall. A small inscription tells me I am standing in the actual prison cell that the Unabomber served over twenty-five years in. I'm surprised by how small the cell is. I'd never heard of this guy and wonder why he makes the cut for 'The Museum of Technological Violence' since he killed only three people, but then I read excerpts of some of his writing and see the connection:

There is good reason to believe that primitive man suffered from less stress and frustration and was better satisfied with his way of life than modern man is.

This guy supposedly inspired the various human extinction projects that cropped up over the last fifty years, various groups trying to revert back to preindustrial society or just rid the planet of humanity altogether. What this pseudo-museum is teaching me is that twentieth-century people were maybe just as crazy if not crazier than we were. The main difference is in the magnitude. I can't think of a number that would reflect how many Ted Kaczynski types have committed similarly violent acts in the past decade. To be honest, his ideas don't seem all that far off base, and if they had been implemented, perhaps the extinction event back on Earth could have been mitigated. I swear this quote resonates with something Wanda used to tell me during our psych sessions:

The concept of "mental health" in our society is defined largely by the extent to which an individual behaves in accord with the needs of the system and does so without showing signs of stress.

Sure enough, the next exhibit shows off some of the 'wild cars' used by the Human Extinction Liberation Project parties on the California coast, where they'd light these vehicles on fire full of willing participants, and cheer them on as they burned alive riding over the cliffs that fell into the California Ocean.

I turn the corner and come to another car, this one gray in the old-fashioned muscle car body type. I don't recognize it but the inscription tells me it's a Dodge Challenger. A flatscreen tee vee mounted on the far wall shows the footage of the vehicle crashing into a group of people at a political rally in Charlottesville, Virginia. The inscription below reads:

The assailant, James Alex Fields Jr., was driving this 2010 Dodge Challenger on August 12, 2017. This incident resulted in the death of Heather Heyer and injuries to 35 others.

While this guy only killed one person during the attack, his was the first of thousands of automobile-related targeted killings in the US over the next century, that eventually culminated in the Freedom Tower bombing. Lots of folks argued that attack started the Civil War.

I come to a large chunk of white metal with a large vertical American flag painted on the side. There's a small television playing the live feed of the Space Shuttle Challenger explosion of a century ago. The inscription below the metal says this fragment of the ill-fated shuttle launch was recovered from the bottom of the Atlantic Ocean in 2011. The exhibit goes on to outline a couple of the dominant theories that have circulated on the feed about the explosion: Soviet spies sabotaged the launch; government agencies intentionally accepted the lowest bids from unqualified contractors, the Cholakian Theory that held that major historical events such as the Challenger explosion never occurred and were in fact feed simulacra, intended to prevent government-led scientific inquiry; and the prevailing theory that the launch was intentionally exploded to end U.S. funding of space exploration which, along with defense spending, was bankrupting the nation.

Who knows what the truth was and I suppose that's the final point of the exhibit. With the feed in the late twenty-first century, access to verifiable truths had become nearly impossible. Our reality had become something of a fiction and had been this way for longer than anyone alive could remember. All this violence almost makes me feel like I'm back on Earth again.

I need to take a piss but no washrooms on this level. The thought occurs to me to use the latrine in the Unabomber's cell but I doubt it's functional. I ask Michelle and she tells me the only washroom available to me while under quarantine is in my living quarters. It's at least a twenty-minute walk back to my cell, or my room, whatever you want to call it. 'Living quarters' never crossed my mind. Time is getting away from me down here. It's well past midnight in Los Angeles.

I spend the next few hours alone in my cell staring at the ceiling, writing these notes. There's a tap in my room and the water tastes better than anything I've had on Earth. It hits me that I'm drinking water housed on the Moon in the form of ice for who knows how many billions of years. My body is being lubricated by the ancient waters of the Rock. I am transforming into something beyond my terrestrial home, evolving into a creature of ancient origin, or so I imagine as I realize I'm tired and need some sleep.

I should be home with Jadah and Joon, tending to our plants on the back deck of our flat, sitting with them for meals at our weathered wooden dining table with the mismatched chairs. I should be there with them right now and I'm crying and I want to rage but I'm alone buried somewhere in the Moon. *We are all already dead.* I am sick and nothing can heal me. That makes me about as normal as anyone else alive in this world, or solar system, whatever. Michelle can't read my biosignature because I have taken her out of my ear.

I'm disturbed by the obscene nature of the museums, which feel equal parts ostentatious madness and misguided acts of cultural appropriation. How many billions of dollars were spent transporting these artifacts to the Moon? How many people could have been fed or housed with that money? If this is what the industrialized world and our technological advancements led to, I tend to think the technological museum itself is an index of its own atrocity. That may have been the point of the whole thing, but I don't give Rodgers that much credit.

That night I dream of a Dodge Challenger driving into a crowd of people. Next thing I know the car flies off a cliff into the California Ocean. I'm not scared until I realize it's me behind the wheel. I'm falling under lunar gravity, so I survive the crash only to find myself drowning in the dark freezing waters. I wake up to the sound of treefrogs screaming.

PRAVDA REPORTS

February 5, 2084

SOMETIME PRESUMABLY LATE LAST NIGHT someone slipped a digital envelope under my door, with a single word etched in black on the tiny sleeve:

INFOE

The envelope might have been there when I came back last night. I was so exhausted I might not have noticed it. I hesitate to open it, not sure what the intent is. Still don't know what the intent is. It's possible someone is giving me this to play into my perceived critiques of Rodgers. But Rodgers is also the exact kind of paranoiac to set up an entrapment to see where I stand. Though Michelle assures me all living quarters are absolutely private and soundproof spaces, it's safe to presume everything that happens on the Rock is recorded through various sensors and cameras. I don't know why but I trust Michelle. Maybe it's that damn voice that soothes me into a state of complacency.

What I find in the envelope are two variants of the same episode of the Pravda Report. Pravda Corporation was one of the last remaining independent journalism sources in the U.S. and they remained active in the California Republic as well, until Rodgers bought the company under the auspices of free speech and then proceeded to dismantle it. Stating the obvious, but the problem with the feed was how easy machine intelligences could alter the algorithms and revise the content to fit the end user's profile. These two versions of the same exact episode are case in point. Nothing particularly special about the fact that the story had been altered considerably in at least one of the threads if not both. I didn't let Michelle know about this, keeping my earpiece locked away in the small metal case the White Sands techs gave me. In the privacy of my room, I projected back the two ostensibly identical episodes delivered on the same day in the same location, though they couldn't have been more dissimilar. Here they are, predating the outbreak of the war by almost five years:

Good evening. I'm Gamila Brockton-al-Sahir, hosting tonight's episode live from Seattle, Washington. Tonight's thread provides a live look at one of the over four-hundred seeding stations built around the world as part of the largest multinational corporate geoengineering effort in human history. Constructed in phases with the end goal of sequestering enough carbon to return Earth systems to levels not seen since the early 2000s, Noel Rodgers' brainchild, over a decade in development, began its first weather-balloon launches into the upper atmosphere over a year ago. The results were astounding.

Rodgers' parent company, Future X, hired a panel of independent scientists to assess the feasibility of his plan. The panel published their initial findings earlier this week. They concluded Rodgers' preliminary seeding efforts either sequestered or offset the equivalent (CO_2) emissions of over 600,000 petrol burning vehicles over the course of a year. The data reported by the independent scientific board and released by the company earlier this week provides hard evidence that should the seeding project initiate its second global phase, the company's carbon offsetting efforts will be measurable at Earth magnitude. We now turn to the author of this proposed plan, Mr. Noel Rodgers himself, coming to us live from Lacus Mortis on the Moon, at his latest lunar colony, currently under construction. There is a delay in communication which we've edited out of this recorded interview.

"Good evening, Mr. Rodgers, or should I say good morning to you at the lunar colony?"

"Yes, good evening-morning to you too!"

"Mr. Rodgers, can you explain to our viewers the significance of the independent science panel's findings and what their conclusions mean for you?"

"Absolutely, and thank you, Gamila, for having me on the show.

Yes, what it means, is that through the collaboration of my corporations and holding companies working with over a dozen world governments to provide jobs to thousands of people in some of the most ecologically disrupted parts of the planet, we're going to offset carbon emissions and lower toxic levels of heavy metals and other contaminants currently circulating in our atmosphere. It's not just that we're offsetting carbon emissions, Gamila. Through our geoengineering efforts, we're undoing the damage, the damage of industrial impacts on Earth systems, and we're doing it in a way that supports jobs and peoples' lives."

"And how will your plan work, Mr. Rodgers? I'm specifically wondering about the technologies involved and potential risks."

"Well, we already know that by doing nothing we risk our planet's future. Doing nothing, is more than risky. It would be reckless and dangerous to do nothing. Our plan is to seed over one million weather balloons with sulfur dioxide, attaching these completely biodegradable balloons to the helium cylinders that will carry them up to fourteen miles into our atmosphere where they burst, releasing their clouds into the air and offsetting carbon emissions. These balloons coupled with our other efforts around the globe, will reduce the harmful effects of greenhouse gasses."

"Your detractors point to the fact that your corporate holdings continue to contract with governments that lack regulatory bodies to oversee the work your companies are doing. What can you share about the board who reviewed your company's work? Was their review as fair and impartial as you claim?"

"Well, I appreciate the critical voices. If you're going to have any success in this world you need to listen to criticism. We also need those perspectives to guarantee transparency at all levels. Fundamentally, Gamila, we all want the same thing—a habitable planet for all life on Earth, not just humans. The scientific board's findings, which included highly respected scientists some of whom openly opposed my efforts, have examined the data and collectively concluded that our geoengineering efforts are making a positive impact on the planet. The data bears that out. I credit them for looking at the data impartially. It's why we hired them. Now of course we have to mind the entire system and use a diversity of tactics to address the problems we've

created on Earth. It took us hundreds of years to create this problem, now hopefully we can solve it in less time than that, working together with multinational companies, government scientists from all stakeholder nations who collectively have the best interests of the planet in mind. This is a difficult task as ecological collapse has affected different nations to varying degrees. When it comes to breathable air, protecting the environment, combatting environmental racism, expanding access to machine intelligence through R&D infrastructures, these are issues that transcend ethnic and racial identities, national borders. These are human problems and we're working together to resolve them."

So that was the first episode. No way to verify which one of these two was the real version, or if both are fabricated. Of course, I could ask Rodgers himself if the opportunity arises. And here's the second version:

Good evening. I'm Gamila Brockton-al-Sahir, hosting tonight's episode live from Seattle, Washington. Tonight's thread takes you inside the historic protests taking place at one of the over four-hundred seeding stations being built around the world as part of the largest multinational corporate geoengineering effort in human history. Thousands of protestors from all over the U.S. and Canada have come together to protest Noel Rodgers' alleged efforts to further degrade Earth's atmospheric conditions for personal profit, including the development of his much touted and highly controversial Lunar Colony Project.

The companies Mr. Rodgers consolidated over the last two decades have been charged with obstructing regulatory bodies and working with governments who lack the power or will to regulate their industries. In recent days, a group of independent scientists hired by Mr. Rodgers' parent company, Future X, have all died under mysterious circumstances just weeks before their report on the company's purported geoengineering efforts was to be released. The anonymous hacker known as 'INFOE' has acquired company documents alleging Future X accepted numerous military contracts around the world that put top-secret deadly weapons—chemical and viral—in the hands of hostile nations. INFOE further alleges that Rodgers' contractual obligations give him unprecedented access to these nations' data frames.

Rodgers has not responded to these allegations and could not be reached for comment. Some argue his Moon colony efforts suggest Rodgers' culpability, where Terran laws have no extradition powers, should formal charges be brought against him. Rodgers' detractors, which include a growing number of government leaders, claim his increasingly secretive lunar colony developments fly in the face of global treaties, specifically the controversial proposed sites of two encampments at the Moon's South Pole where the Moon receives both sunlight and houses frozen water. Rodgers' alleged attempts at controlling this region of the Moon could constitute an open violation of international treaties that protect the Moon's resources for all mankind. Earlier today we spoke with some of the protestors along the gates of the Geoengineering Seeding Corporation's Seattle-based facilities. Here's what a few of the masked protestors had to say:

"Fuck Rodgers and fuck Future X! They're destroying our planet as they build their luxury Moon lodges at our expense. If the governments of the world are going to sit idle, or worse yet bow to the will of Rodgers' payoffs, we the people have to act. The people have to act."

"When Neil Armstrong walked on the Moon, he didn't say one giant step for Noel Rodgers, he was there for all of us. Rodgers desecrates our ancestors' spirit of exploration, the sacrifices made by people all around the world. We go a step further in saying we don't value human life over all other life on Earth. All life needs to be protected. Rodgers is the center of his own universe and thinks we're just tagging along."

"I traveled here from Minneapolis. My daughter and I had to be here. When I joined the armed forces, I swore an oath to protect America and its constitution. That's why I'm here, why we're here. The American people need to wake up. We're angry. This is our lives, our children's lives at stake. I don't mean future generations I'm talking right now."

"You hear all these people? Our mouth is a weapon right now. Our mouth is a warning shot. This is us when we ask, we're asking nicely

to shut this shit down. They call us terrorists? We're not wearing masks because we're so-called vigilantes. We're wearing masks because we don't want our families to be violently attacked by the scabs and turncoats who maintain their American citizenship while they willfully do work for Rodgers that is completely illegal in this country. Constructing private lodgings on the South Pole of the Moon is illegal. Doing it with slave labor from the global south, the so-called 'unmen,' also illegal. He's paying off the U.S. government to gain direct access to those seeking refugee status in this country because they are being targeted as ethnic minorities back home. Rodgers is the terrorist. Rodgers is suicide bombing our collective future on the one planet we have so they can do what, play golf on the Moon? The first person with a conscience on the Lunar Colony Project is going to detonate a bomb up there, kill all those fuckers, and you know what, they will be saving billions of lives in the process. Justice is people getting what they deserve, and Rodgers is going to feel it like we're all feeling it down here. Put to a stop to mining the Rock! Put to a stop to mining the Rock! Put to a stop—"

"You know what happens to Rodgers' detractors? They die. They die in mysterious and violent ways. Natalie Monte-Richards. André Yang. Jerry Hodges. Monique Rivers, missing, presumed dead. Many more than I can name, these just the most recent. We hold their names in the light. You're a journalist, you have a responsibility. Say their names so we can hear them and ask the questions they were asking. Say their names. Look, there are credible, legitimate reporters, people like yourself who simply asked, asked the question: is it possible that Rodgers is funding or even just turning a blind eye to the accelerationists, the megachurch militias, the radicals who want to kill all of humanity? He doesn't deny ties to the Afro-jihadists and the HELP extremists. Wipe us off the planet so that other species on the planet can recover. He hides behind his 'Green Shield' thinking these kinds of tactics will work because there's support for change. He's a charlatan, tried and true."

BRIEF NOTE ON EXISTENTIAL DREAD

February 10, 2084

SPENT THE LAST FEW DAYS IN BED. Completely sapped of energy. Michelle tells me this is completely normal, like jet lag for interplanetary travelers, that the journey completely disrupts one's normal circadian rhythms, and the lightened gravity coupled with the culture shock of being on the Moon takes time to process.

It occurs to me I haven't been on the Moon two Earth weeks and already I'm feeling overwhelmed and disoriented in ways I can't fully explain. For some reason beyond my understanding I'm only able to converse with Michelle. All the men who came up on the *Artemis* with me seem to have been shipped off to whatever colony they're destined to slave away on. Eurotrash and the LC7 colonists have all been shipped off as well. Michelle knows everything but doesn't answer any of my substantive questions. I ask how many laborers are on the Moon. No answer. I ask how many fatalities have occurred on the Moon. No answer. I ask how many suicides. No answer. I ask how much radon has been mined from Aristarchus Plateau over the past year and I get this highly detailed response:

"Last year 36.37 kilograms of radon was extracted from the Aristarchus Plateau mining operations, primarily through a process of soil-gas desorption pyrolysis and partial leaching methods. More significantly for power production throughout the colonies, uranium deposits at Aristarchus Plateau enable nuclear power production that services all seven colonies currently in operation."

Ask Michelle how long a day lasts at Aristarchus Plateau and she will tell you, "Approximately fifteen days." Ask her how many people Noel Rodgers has brought up here to run his mining operations and you get silence. Maybe I appreciate the silence over the outright deception, but it's still unnerving. Michelle tells me in a few days I'll ride the lunar monorail to get firsthand looks at the colonies. Presently we're almost halfway through a fifteen Earth-day period of night but it doesn't matter because the lunar rails are all housed in tunnels about fifty meters below the surface.

My first and last glimpse of the lunar surface was upon arrival. The rest of my time thus far may as well have been back on Earth. But the whole thing feels like being in a large prison or the hull of a large freighter ship at sea. Life on the Moon impresses me as sterile, inhuman, and a strange simulacrum of the industrialized spaces of Earth. I look forward to exploring the surface and writing about it. But if it was possible to end all this now, head back to Earth, give back the money and rejoin my family, I would. I knew this feeling would come, I just didn't think it would be so soon.

PART 2:

NOTES FROM LUNAR UNDERGROUND

AN INTRODUCTION TO THE QUIET, 2091

EVERYONE ON EARTH IS DEAD. Most everyone, anyway. Needless to say, none of this is intended for Rodgers' vain vanity biography—it's for any of the handful of survivors back on Earth who might read this, and for you unmen living below me who I hope will liberate yourselves and take your future into your own hands. This book is a collection of notes, journal entries, and reflections I started before the Quiet back on Earth. I figure I need to just write out an introduction now to help myself make sense of what it is I'm doing. And if anything happens to me, at least there'll be a place for you to start. This being the end of the world and all, I feel like these writings take on heightened significance.

And if you insist, and really want to read Rodgers' vacuous biography, go down to the library collections and pull it out. It's filed between Kafka and Lahiri (fitting that Rodgers' organizational system makes no distinction between fiction and non-fiction). I won't even mention the book's name, so humiliating.

For you unmen, I leave it to Michelle to translate my thoughts into your respective native tongues. If I do leave the Rock, I'll take the hard copy with me (this is all I have to show for my time up here), but I'll be sure to flip the pages to allow her to inscribe this text into her hive mind. For now, the Rodgers biography has the dubious distinction of being the last monograph ever written in human history. At least until this one gets done, which I'll keep adding to until I'm dead.

To you unmen, I won't call your survival 'luck' as the price you've paid is too great. I dedicate these writings to you. I hope these notes provide a glimpse into the lives of your oppressors, maybe a map towards a future of living alongside them. There is a utopian impulse buried somewhere inside here, even if it might be hard (maybe impossible) to find.

As I write this only a handful of human beings persist on Earth. Even writing out this fact causes a physical reaction inside, like my guts turned inside out. We're not functionally extinct, but close to it. We've been following the handful of survivors on the satellites for years, given you names like Hillbilly and Walking Man and Cowboy. The colonists bet on your survival like your lives were straights and flushes in a card game. They play with their trillions of dollars of worthless cash as a symbol of their empty power. Despite gambling on your lives, in the final analysis I think they want to see you survive, for you to somehow find each other, and certainly for others to emerge on the satellites. I can tell you from experience that the lunar overlords have no purchase on wisdom or understanding, and certainly not empathy. To the contrary. The rich are symptoms of humanity's mental diseases, namely global finance, industrial privateering, and all the other systems that enabled human beings to own other human beings, beginning with primitive feudalism and various forms of enslavement, and ending in whatever it is you call this.

Philosophical discourse and bouts with empathy never had a market value back on Earth, which might go a long way to explaining how we ended up here. Could good people have been caught up in all this, and just found themselves holding all the Earth's wealth near the end of the twenty-first century? Maybe, but I sort of doubt it.

Also, these writings are an attempt at clawing back my sanity or at least preventing slippage deeper into the dark parts of my mind—the hell that is the quiet solitude of the human soul. Each of us is alone. That was true even before the Quiet befell humanity.

▲ ▲ ▲

A NOTE ON THE REVISED AGREEMENT, the one that's keeping me employed as a second-class citizen on the Rock. After the Quiet it was clear everyone up here had a purpose to keep the colonies functioning, notwithstanding the first-class colonists which were a collection of the wealthiest oligarchs, post-national industrialists, and owners of the last remnants of the machineries of the industrialized world. Rodgers was careful to curate his Anglo-centric first-class colonists and now they had the Rock to themselves. But they needed the best chefs and fitness experts and so on to provide them a 'life of luxury in the lunar colonies.' I mean, Jack Sturman is my neighbor. The guy won gold back at the '68 Olympics in Nuuk, 10,000 meters and the marathon both. He was an American (and later Californian) celebrity who made a fortune licensing his likeness in the feed, so millions of feeders could be trained by the man who won gold in the final Olympics. Nice guy.

The chefs are similarly famous. You haven't lived until you've tasted Oaxacan José's protein brick molé (there are two Josés in the kitchen, the other one is from Pasadena). Oaxacan J makes his molé with a tomatillo-chili base but the kicker is the cacao that he processes from our food forests to add chocolate to the recipe, with a pinch of epazote. J told me about all the seeds and starters he brought with him and he gets emotional when he talks about his gardens because it's all he has to remember his family by. Like the culantro (not cilantro, totally different herb) and the tomatillos are propagated from the same gardens his grandmother tended way back when. And he even says that's just as far back as he knows because his Zapotecan ancestors had been growing these plants since long before the Spaniards came searching for gold. The Oaxacan tribes were so deeply embedded in the mountains they survived, kept their languages intact, and made it a few hundred more years until the Earth went quiet. And now there's a guy, Oaxacan José, almost certainly the last Zapotecan Indian alive in the solar system, living up here inside the Moon feeding these wealthy fucks delicacies that are all but extinct on Earth.

By second-class citizen standards I am at the very bottom of the list as I provide no useful function to the colonists. Turns out writer-journalists are useless in the apocalypse. You can't forget about Eurotrash either, also bottom feeders in terms of fame or wealth. If I have to hear *Skullfux in Limbo* one more time I will kill them myself. There is one important encounter I had with the drummer, Juan Carlos Ángel Pineda, a few months ago. That chance encounter prompted me to put these notes together in case something were to happen. The two of us chanced upon one another in the rosarium adjacent the main food forests. It's typical to see people walking the narrow pathways picking ripe fruits and greens vining up the trees (the roses had long been dug out and replaced with edibles, like pigeon pea, vining longevity spinach, various grape hybrids, and moringa trees among others).

Juan Carlos sees me at the bend in the path, gestures me over with his hand. He's standing at the edge of a small pond where the regolith walkway gives way to a muddy bank as it flows into a tiny pond with koi fish swimming around in the shallow pools. Juan Carlos bends down and writes the letters INFOE in the sand, just long enough for me to read it. He wipes away the letters with his hand and stares at me, saying nothing because his face is all the question I need. At the time I just shrugged my shoulders and said, "Who is INFOE?"

He looks at me for a minute, smiles, and simply says, "*No sé*. Just keep your eyes peeled, *hermano*." It was in that encounter that I realized I wasn't the only one to have encountered this enigmatic group or individual. But other than the initial Pravda Report I received in my first few weeks on the Rock, it's been radio silence. It seem too risky to open myself up to the drummer and my own paranoia had me wondering if Rodgers had put him up to the question. It seemed awfully convenient to be running into him in the rosarium, right where he could scratch the name into the sand.

Speaking of Eurotrash, beyond their shitty monthly concerts, they have various useful odd jobs to fulfill, as do I. A few months into the Quiet, Rodgers came to me with the offer to continue writing about him, documenting his leadership of the colonies, making the case that having a written record with the literary flair of a journalist would serve future generations well. I also spend a few hours every day harvesting the legumes and berries, pulling greens at Sara's request, who oversees the entire greenhouse operations. I do whatever needs tending to in the greenhouses, which gives the galley staff more time to focus on food prep. This is all a matter of survival now and suffice to say it is existentially terrifying. I also revise Rodgers' letters to the unmen, make them more 'authentic' and 'human.' It's the most dehumanizing thing I've ever done, and I can understand how someone reading this could see me as complicit. To you unmen who will hopefully be reading this one day, I hope you come to see things my way in the end.

The reason Rodger asked me to continue writing was sound, even if my version of the story (as it continues to unfold) exists in near perfect opposition to his. I presume he's smart enough to see that, but maybe not the extent of my disgust for him. I include a few of my post-virus chapter submissions to him in this collection because it's not so difficult to read between the lines (and sometimes I add my commentary after the fact).[1] Believe me, you want these entries to be curated. So much garbage was written for and about Rodgers that it would fill ten volumes and say nothing of value. These annotated writings are my contributions to the lunar colony, to what remains of the human race. If nothing else, these notes provide some insight into the last circle of hell in the solar system.

Needless to say, if Rodgers finds these writing, things won't end well for me. That's fine. Things already haven't ended well for me. My honest interpretations and the disclosure of so many secrets of his violates the NDA his associates had me sign back when all this started. I am absolutely, without any doubt in breach of contract. But at this point, fuck it. In the final analysis you're either on the side of some semblance of facts and objective reality or you aren't. What's the worst he can do, kill me?

Noel Rodgers is an extremely sick individual. I cannot put my finger on this completely, but trying to diagnose his unique form of madness has become one of my primary objectives. His sickness is a symptom of a deranged species, and there's a strange paradox that I'm not sure will ever get fully explained despite my best attempts to do so in these writings. It may be stating the obvious, but if there is one person in this solar system capable of engineering a virus to wipe out the human species, it's him. Noel Rodgers could very well be the architect of our extinction.

Whatever the truth, which I intend to find out one way or another, it's clear our technology is the variable that led to this. The world was always full of madmen with dreams of chaos, pain, and destruction. For most of human history they simply lacked the technological means to execute their visions. Think of the train exhibit at the Museum of

---

[1] In the original text I just added my own commentary alongside the chapters and kept them among my private handwritten notes. My footnotes are my best attempt at revising the original text, now that I'm reading them almost a decade later, and under very different circumstances. I went all these years never rereading what I wrote, but eventually it came time to decide what to keep and what to destroy. To add my thoughts to the original text any other way would involve rewriting the entire manuscript. GK, August 2101

Technological Violence and you'll understand exactly what I mean. I'm not going to bother to explain and I don't really care to theorize.

When all this started, I was writing Rodgers' biography as a means to an end, a way to get my family somewhere where we might live a life in relative peace and comfort. Now it is something else, something much darker and more perverse. I am a witness to lunar history, and maybe the last critical voice among the colonists.[2] My writings, should anyone ever read them, stand in stark opposition to Rodgers' attempts at creating a mythic lunar past, one where he and the other colonists were victims of a world that forced them into a so-called 'white diaspora,' strewn across a planet beyond saving. All these facts lead me to dark thoughts... the worst thing I can imagine is that the last remaining survivors up here might also deserve to die.

Gedeon Kravchenko, Shackleton Crater,
Earth Year 2091

---

[2] I should have included Michelle here too. She may be the most critical voice of them all, but I don't want to ruin the ending, or the beginning, depending how you take it. The writer in me wants this text to exist as a kind of work of creative non-fiction. It's an aesthetic project, not just an index of events. GK, August 2101

THE UNILATERAL NON-DISCLOSURE AGREEMENT (NDA)[3]

THIS NON-DISCLOSURE AGREEMENT ("Agreement") is made and entered into as this day of November 19, 2083, by and between Lunar Company Holdings, Inc. ("The Company"), with its principal place of business at Lunar Colony Seven (LC7), Shackleton Crater, The Moon, and Gedeon Kravchenko ("Writer"), residing at Alighieri Tower, S. Figueroa St., Los Angeles, California, 90015, California Republic.

1. Purpose.
    The Company has engaged the Writer for contract labor, as defined herein: complete a work of non-fiction focused on Noel Rodgers, his life and work, and the history of the Lunar Colony Project (LCP) from its inception to its current state and its future trajectories. In the course of this engagement, the Writer will have access to Confidential Information (as defined below). The Company wishes to unilaterally protect the confidentiality of such information.

2. Remedies.
    The Parties acknowledge and agree that due to the unique and sensitive nature of the Confidential Information, any breach of this Agreement would cause irreparable harm for which damages and/or equitable relief may be sought. In the event of such a breach, monetary damages would not be an adequate

---

[3] I saved this hardcopy of the agreement and after all that's happened, feel like I should include it here.

remedy and Parties agree that, in the event of such breach, The Company shall be entitled to seek injunctive relief in addition to any other remedies available at law or in equity, or outside of Terrestrial Laws, remedies deemed appropriate by The Company.[4]

3. Definition of Confidential Information for Purposes of this Agreement. "Confidential Information" means all non-public, proprietary or confidential information disclosed by the Company or discovered by the Writer, whether orally, in writing, and/or data transfer, including but not limited to business plans, operational plans, architectural drawings, programming practices and proprietary algorithms, research and development data, LCP drone technologies and other proprietary inventions, strategies, financial information, technical data, trade secrets, research, personal information about the head of The Company (including current and former employees, living or deceased), unpublished manuscripts, and any other material assets marked or otherwise identified as confidential.

4. Obligations of the Writer.
The Writer agrees to maintain the confidentiality of the Confidential Information and not disclose it to any third party without The Company's prior written consent; use the Confidential Information solely for the purpose of completing the book; take all reasonable measures to protect the confidentiality of the Confidential Information; return or destroy all Confidential Information upon completion of the engagement or upon The Company's request. Final Copy will be reviewed by The Company to ensure compliance.

5. No License.

---

[4] I'll be honest, I always thought "remedies deemed appropriate by The Company" was a euphemistic way of saying they would kill me if I breached the contract. GK, February 15, 2096

Nothing in this Agreement grants the Writer any rights or license to The Company's Confidential Information, except as expressly set forth herein.

6. Term and Termination.
   This Agreement will remain in effect in perpetuity, or until the Confidential Information ceases to be confidential, or until terminated by The Company by written notice. The Writer's obligations with respect to Confidential Information disclosed during the term will survive termination of this Agreement.

7. Miscellaneous.
   This Agreement constitutes the entire agreement between the parties with respect to the subject matter hereof and supersedes all prior or contemporaneous understandings, agreements, representations, and warranties. This Agreement may not be amended or modified except by a written agreement signed by both parties. This Agreement will be governed by and construed in accordance with the laws of The California Republic.

IN WITNESS WHEREOF, the parties have executed this Agreement as of the date first above written.

Lunar Colony Holdings, Inc.
By: Noel Rodgers, CEO, Governing Chair
Pupillary Acknowledgement [scan below]:

Writer: Gedeon Kravchenko
Pupillary Acknowledgement [scan below]:

PENULTIMATE TRANSMISSION FROM GOLDSTONE

December 8, 2086

HER NAME WAS MEI CHEN. She was a real person. A living breathing human being. You could never prove that over radio communications, but the reason we know Mei was real is because she stopped making sense. Then she stopped communicating with us. An MI would never do either of those things.

Mei was an operator at Goldstone Deep Space Communications Complex. It was a NASA-funded comms center before the war, got privatized soon after. Mei was assigned to check in with the space stations as they made their orbits around Earth. She was on for a six-month renewable contract when the virus hit. She and I had a half dozen all-night conversations before she signed off for good. She's the last friend I ever made, probably ever will make in this world.

Mei said Goldstone couldn't afford to pay her, or any of the staff at the complex, but they offered free room and board. They also had their own government-funded water source and a little experimental farm that supplemented their food stocks. All things considered, she had it good. It was either that or nothing and she said she had a lifelong passion for studying the cosmos, so sort of a dream job minus the pay. Those were her exact words, "Sort of a dream job minus the pay," which when she first told me she laughed at in her high-pitched cackle. She had a nervous laugh. Who knows what her laugh was like before she was one of the last women on Earth but it probably lacked the underpinnings of dread, at least I like to think so. When Mei wasn't tasked with processing radio transmissions from space stations, she could spend a few hours each day listening to the stars—the dream job part.

Mei was different from a lot of the other scientists I'd interviewed and spoken to over the years. In a word I'd call her more philosophical. Of course, context could be everything. To be fair regarding my early critiques of scientists, they were always walking on eggshells, afraid to say the wrong thing and get defunded or worse. Scientists were at the mercy of those in power so they really lacked the ability to be free thinkers in the way I imagine being a scientist requires. I met Mei at a stage of her existence when she was as free as she was ever going to be, unshackled by the realities of industrial society, or humans in general for that matter. Absolute freedom is terror when you think about it.

What I'm trying to say is I met Mei in the last days of her life, and she was living with a fear that none of us on the Rock experienced in quite the same way. For us it was not the same existentialist crisis. It was a different version of terror with a different outcome. We're still alive up here. She isn't.

The owners of the Goldstone complex liked Mei so much they kept renewing her contract. Goldstone gave tours and weeklong workshops to wealthy private schools from inside the corporate communities in Los Angeles, and that kept the lights on. Mei had been there six years. She was thirty-one years old when she died. I even know when her birthday was, and she knew mine. But I don't want to write that down. If I humanize Mei too much, I know my mind will snap beyond a point that I'll be able to repair. Maybe that's already happened and I just don't know it.

Mei said once the outbreak hit, or the virus, whatever it was that was rearing its head, that she never left the complex. One by one her coworkers abandoned their outpost and none of them ever came back. Mei had no family in California, no significant other. She said she had some cousins in Taiwan but of course lost contact in '79, after collapse. Collapse shrank everyone's world down to the city, town, or commune one lived in. Thinking about it now, collapse was the dress rehearsal for the end of the world, wasn't it? The virus shrank our species down to the last breath in one's body. Except for us on the Rock. Mei was alone in the world before the virus, and she died that way.

Mei Chen was the last person any of us ever spoke to on Earth. She holds a special place in my picture of the world because of that. I wish someone would write a history of all this, if only because activating the documentary impulse is one of the most affirmative acts a human being can make.[5] As if to say, I see you, I hear you, I bear witness to your experiences. Human communion. Mei Chen had dreams and aspired to understand our place in the universe. She understood the cosmos in ways very few people could. When she died, a last remaining piece of human knowledge disappeared forever with her. The same was true for billions of other people, in a billion different ways. (It isn't lost on me that the most knowledgeable entity in our solar system is an MI operating off networks daisychained in orbit around the Rock. Michelle will be alive and well so long as the sun keeps the lights on. But what about us?)

I'm not religious but I have faith in that impulse. I used to think it was my path to enlightenment, back before I wised up. If I reflect on my life, it's the reason I became a journalist, back when I still felt some connection, some semblance of social justice—that self-deluded impulse that somehow one person can make a difference. My conversations with Mei rekindled that impulse, if only for a brief moment.

I've had a long time to think about Mei and given all the sad passions her memory has caused me, I kind of wish we never connected. What difference would it have made if Mei and I had never communed over those radio waves? There was nothing I or anyone could do to save her, and I doubt we gave her any comfort in her last days, even though she said otherwise. I was bearing witness to her last moments of life. And while it felt right at the time, I didn't account for the mental cost it might take on me in the subsequent years.[6]

---

[5] When I originally wrote this, I didn't think I was the one writing this history down. I wasn't reflecting on what I was doing, I was just doing it. The writing helped me stay alive, make a map of the new reality that was unfolding in my head. That was five years ago and when I think about putting this history together, Mei's story seems like the right place to start. She's the last voice from Earth. GK, August 2091

[6] Five years later I still suffer from paralyzing anxiety, can't sleep more than a few hours each night. I'm told by Michelle this is perfectly normal given my situation (being among the last remaining human survivors) and I don't bother asking her how she knows what's normal at the end of the world. She insists I maintain a healthy diet and exercise regiment, which I guess is better than the alternative. GK, August 2091

The truth is I was displacing my own family with the connection to Mei. I imagined my daughter alive, connected with me over the radio waves, fantasized about her and Jadah bunkered down in the flat, somehow surviving all that had happened. I was not capable of imagining anything else, so I blocked out a large part of reality. Mei helped me do that, for a time. I couldn't help but remember one of those ubiquitous Human Extinction Liberation Project slogans you'd see stenciled across the burnt-out husks of buildings in L.A.: *cling to your illusions, prepare to surrender.* Maybe HELP won the war they were waging after all. Every time we saw another city go up in a nuclear strike, presumably to prevent the spread of the virus that was wiping out humanity, I thought of those damned extinctionists.

▲ ▲ ▲

WE MADE CONTACT with Mei on the thirteenth day from the first confirmed cases of what was being called 'Virus X.' Paradoxically, because Rodgers' proprietary satellites could hack into the privatized comm satellites that remained orbiting the Earth, we may have had a better global understanding of the virus than anyone back on Earth. But by the time we found Mei, all communication with Rodgers' earthbound stations had ceased for the simple reason that everyone was either dead or had abandoned their posts. Somehow Mei lasted longer than the rest.

So what did we know about the virus? What we knew for sure is that once someone showed symptoms, they were on a rapid trajectory towards death. It seemed to attack the brain first and then the body. People supposedly lost their memories before they died, until no one was left.

We were all in various states of denial, disbelief, and shock, unable to fully comprehend the reality of what was happening with the virus. Was it another elaborate global hoax by the last feed hackers floating around in Beijing or Hong Kong? Was this a case of virus hacking— holding people hostage for the antidote to the synthetic virus attacks so prevalent in the prewar years? Could it be just another global fiction takeover like the so-called 'War of the Worlds' hack? I remember the big one on September 11, 2071, where anyone who strapped into the feed that morning saw threads about Earth being invaded by extraterrestrials. I remember that day well, going outside to see if the destruction I was seeing was real. It was just another sunny day in L.A., but on the feeds the city was being overrun by giant insect-like creatures, buildings blown up with Godzilla-like flaming breath. And it all looked as real as the view outside my window.

The hackers were good at using MI to create their pseudofictions, and of course many of their fictive threads were taken as fact by the feeders. The notion of feed hackers being behind this was a complete fantasy, an act of denial for the simple reason that the feed was gone forever back on Earth. And even if the feed did exist in some hidden pocket, unbeknownst to the rest of us, it didn't compute because there was no world government left to pay any prospective ransom demands.

Whatever it was, connecting with Mei gave us hope that people could survive this thing, which made it so much more devastating when she went radio silent. I don't know what the word is, could ask Michelle but don't want to. I think it's synecdoche. Mei Chen is the synecdoche I carry that helps me process the death of everyone. All our families. Everyone. When Mei died, I moved past denial into whatever comes next. Suffering maybe. Mei was the one that died for all the others, made it real for me. Reality in all its forms is a kind of pain. It's hard to explain so I include Mei's penultimate broadcast. Her last transmission is too much—I couldn't listen to it all the way through and it's not how I want her to be remembered.

▲ ▲ ▲

"I FEEL OKAY. I just ate a protein brick along with a glass of water for dinner. I garnished the protein brick with some African basil we had growing in the gardens. The fresh greens make it taste a little less like cardboard. Could be worse, right? Actually, I'm not so sure about that.

"I feel fine. I still go outside every night, lay down on the roof of the main complex and stare up at the stars. The weather has been cool and I slept up there again last night. I don't know what's happening. All I have are the radios and I've stopped listening. It's too much and what can I do but wait here and survive another day? I'm connected with you all and I wonder what is going to happen up there. I wonder about the space stations and the people up there servicing the satellites and things. Of course, I have spoken with them every day since the first reports of the virus. It was part of my regular duties to check in with each group daily and disperse any images or data we received to the proper agencies. My colleagues and I liked to joke that we were the pencil pushers of scientific discovery. I was just happy to be on a scientific mission still.

"It's strange and horrible, but people on the space stations were getting the virus too. Given their close quarters, it spread quickly. The last time I spoke to anyone up there was three days ago. By the end they didn't know their own names, started repeating themselves in ways that I can only describe as dementia like. I guess I can confirm from my own experience that those reports seem to be true.

"Why is this happening? I don't know but, in the end, maybe it's God wiping us off the face of the Earth. Why not? It's interesting though, I'm in this state of constant fear, can hardly sleep, yet still I go on with my routine. I still take my morning walks around the perimeter of the station. I eat breakfast, do my stretches and get to the business of programming the arrays to face the incoming space stations' trajectories. I take in the daily report that probably no one on Earth is reading but me. The last few report windows have been pure static.

"Here on Earth the birds and insects seem to be unaffected, and I see the coyotes come by at dusk so they're getting along fine too. There's a pack of them led by a three-legged coyote we named Richard[7]. I've seen him almost daily for the better part of six years. I slept upstairs last night.

---

[7] Mei and I had a lot of laughs involving this three-legged coyote, and how he and his kin would inherit the Earth, in a few million years gain the power of language, walk upright, and hold dominion over the planet. Looking back on it, I think Mei thought of the coyotes as her family. She spoke about them like they were family and spent a good bit of our time on the radio recounting their routines, even going so far as to describe their diets based on the scat that she found along the loop trail. The coyote was named after a character in a Shakespeare play that Mei explained was a cunning, Machiavellian king. Richard (the coyote) shared some similar qualities, I'm told. GK, August 2091

"All things considered I feel pretty good. I go outside at night and hang out on the roof. The stars are bright as ever. I slept upstairs last night, but it was strange because I don't remember falling asleep up there, just waking up in the morning light to the sound of the birds rising. I'm worried about the space stations—I mean the people on them. I speak with them every day. They say something is affecting them up there. Healthwise. I feel fine. I'm just happy to be here. I'm waiting for my colleagues to return. I'm not sure where they've gone but I am able to hold down the fort while they're out. Hello?"

[There's a long pause in the transmission. Radio silence. We tried repeatedly calling for Mei. Forty minutes later she responded. I'm ending the transcript here because it's all I can bear to transcribe:]

"Is there anything I can do for you up there? Forgive me, but I don't recall the nature of your request. What's your call number and what space station are you operating out of, over?"

CENTURY CHALLENGE 1986

"A nation expresses its heartfelt grief for the loss of these brave astronauts who have entered the long line of heroes who gave their lives for America. This terrible loss is a reminder that we can never take for granted the sacrifice of heroes."

—U.S. Senator John McCain, on the Challenger explosion

REFLECTIONS

January 7, 2096

EVERY DAY FOR WEEKS after Mei went quiet, I tried to reach her, to no avail. That was ten years ago, winter of '86-87. I'd been living on the Moon for well over a year by that point. I fell into a depression and could hardly write. Michelle diagnosed me with lunar depression syndrome and told me I needed to exercise more, which I'd already been doing. I'd lost like fifteen Earth pounds, which was a lot considering I weighed in at 175 pounds when they ran me through the paces at White Sands.

The reasons behind the virus may be the last and greatest mystery in the history of our species. What happened on Earth that all of humanity perished in the span of a few weeks, and not another creature—as far as we knew—was harmed? After we lost contact with Mei, all we could do was watch from afar. Through the geosynchronous satellites which Rodgers rerouted to play out in a multiscreen set of feeds on the large cinema screen, we saw the human population wither to nothing. Almost nothing, anyway. In a kind of perverse reversal of spectacle from when the masses back on Earth watched the threads on the Moon as Rodgers' companies built the lunar colonies, those of us stranded on the Rock now returned the gaze downstream. At night we saw the massive fire pits lit up across the globe. We watched the cities go completely dark one by one. We even saw the nuclear detonations in the cities, speculating some last-ditch effort at containment. Piled up in the theater, whispering our fears to one another, we watched humanities' remains go up in smoke. Terror was in everyone's eyes. I'd seen faces like that in the war and imagined I had the same look as theirs. We watched the lights go out for the last time. At this point, from the Moon's telescopes, Earth night looks like it might have looked a few billion years ago, which is to say an empty black hole in the expanse of the universe.

A decade on the Rock feels like a lifetime back on Earth, maybe more. It feels as thought there were two of me, Earth Gedeon and emaciated-and-gray-bones-hollowing-out-despite-my-best-efforts-to-the-contrary-stuck-in-an-endless-loop Gedeon. Despite all the trappings of Earth, living in the Moon is a lot like that French psychologist who locked himself down in a cave somewhere, divorcing himself from time, from history, from existence itself.

Since I left White Sands, left my family, I have become someone else—someone I've grown a slow but palpable contempt for. Someone I don't recognize. I tell myself everything will be fine if I can just return to Earth, but will it? Of course not. It's an irrational thought but it's keeping me alive, something to work towards. I say it plainly to myself because it helps me survive this: I have to get back to the flat, find out what happened to Jadah and Joon. It's not an impossible dream to have, suicidal as it might be. Would the virus kill me as soon as I arrived? Maybe. Would I crash and burn on the return, riding on one of those windowless silver seeds? Possibly. My intentions are to live whatever life I have left on Earth, and to die on the planet that birthed me. It might sound morbid, but I want my expired body to rot in the earth, not down here in the lunar regolith. If I die here, I'm sure they'll burn me and use my body for fertilizer. It was stated in the initial release form which made me laugh at the time. Very efficient and unfunny joke. Only the trillionaires get a funeral if they die on the Rock.

Efficiency is a sickness, a curse, a final desperation of the small-minded man incapable of simply being, looking out to the stars or taking a walk in the gardens, doing anything just for sake of its intrinsic pleasure. Efficiency is the path towards self-destruction, accounting for every last bodily excretion down to the hair on our heads. Would you believe we even collect the hair from our shower drains to be used as growing medium for the hydroponic crops? In a sane existence, some things actually *are* waste. Every community in human history except this one had some version of a refuse pile and that made them human. Not us. Up here this is no such thing as waste. Michelle has optimized our efficiency, to be sure.

It's been a decade of writing these fragments in the slow and arduous process of putting my thoughts together as I attempted to maintain some semblance of sanity against crushing depression, anxiety, unspeakable, truly unspeakable horrors witnessed on Planet Earth. A decade of anger and rage against unknowable things, the not-knowing of Jadah and Joon's fate. A decade of lunar politics in a struggle for survival and hierarchy and literal air to breathe and food to eat, watching the enslaved lead lives of ruin deep beneath the colonies while I lived in relative privilege with the LC7 overlords. A decade of living my life in a regimented twenty-four-hour cycle where every aspect of my existence was based on our collective movements and needs, all in the name of optimal efficiency. I slowly broke away from the twenty-four-hour day and with that break I felt more and more untethered.

Time is without question a mental construct. I miss the Earth's rotation more than anything as a means of governing my existence. A decade of the slow realization that if things go wrong up here, no one is coming to save us. A goddamn decade and this collection of unfinished notes is all I have to show for it, complete garbage traded for living and dying with whatever days might have been left with my wife and daughter. They should not have died alone on Earth and when that one true thought enters my mind, I have a feeling of rage so deep that it can't hold, crashes hard into fits of deep depression. This is what drowning must feel like.

I see an image in my dreams of the California Ocean up from Point Dume where we used to take the train. It's a perfect clear day, waves rolling in, and my family is there burning in flames, their fiery bodies falling off the cliffs into the sea. And I'm just standing there experiencing this horror until the fear is so great I wake up panic stricken. That's the nightmare that wakes me up in what passes for night up here on the Rock. But is it so much a nightmare as a way for my mind to tell me my family is dead and I stood by helpless to it all? Some nightmares are real and can't be awakened from. That nightmare's name is History.

▲ ▲ ▲

THE UNMEN STILL HAVE NO IDEA what happened on Earth. Rodgers keeps them in the dark, feeds them all of the same lies about their families. Would you believe me if I told you he still asks me to revise his reports, make them sound more 'human and believable?' I've become like some old-world propaganda minister, using my writing skills to betray people's sense of truth. Stories are violent things in the wrong hands. The horror of the Quiet back on Earth is not something the mind can process from up here, so far removed from any semblance of what one might call 'normal' human existence.

Maybe it's the right thing to keep them in the dark. Their lives were already so much ruin and hopelessness. The unmen, living in complete ignorance, are almost certainly in a better mental state than the colonists above grappling with the end of human life on Earth. Those men came to terms with leaving their families behind long ago.

It's hard to describe this whole reality down here in the colonies. To get an idea of what it's like, try to imagine an old-fashioned low-offender white collar prison, a nuclear submarine at sea for years never once coming up for air, the nature of the black box disorienting chambers one used to treat mental illness (and later torture prisoners of war), and the old feed imagery of early twentieth-century miners digging deep into the Earth scraping for rare Earth minerals. Mix all that together inside the architecture of a 1980's shopping mall and you have some idea of what life is like in the Moon. One of the only times I ever see the surface of the Rock is for funerals.

Another thing, up here your body atrophies despite your best efforts. Fifty-fifty returning to Earth would kill me despite my daily training and remaining under simulated Earth gravity for the vast majority of my time in the Rock. And I say 'in' the Rock because all of our lives up here are submerged beneath the surface, safe from the cosmic winds and radiation that would destroy our feeble bodies, to say nothing of the fact that the Moon has no atmosphere to speak of, no AIR TO BREATHE! Yet here we are, entombed inside the midcentury modern architecture turned lunar interior design so that a bunch of obscenely wealthy technocratic post-capitalist overlords can live out some perverse fantasy of space exploration like an ideologically inverse version of the Star Trek series of old! And would you believe the irony that these people *love* Star Trek—they've watched every episode of every series in the cinema beginning with the early stuff in those silly costumes. The colonists have their weekly cinema series, their recreational sex, the monthly lunar racquetball tournaments, betting on the remaining survivors which they track religiously (as do I), and some of them do actually explore the Moon's surface just to be the first person to say they climbed down into Shoemaker Crater or de Gerlache Crater as if the entire endeavor were some climb to the top of Everest just to say you were there. I'm telling you if you've seen one crater on the Moon you've seen them all. The Rock is by every definition, dead! But all these distractions don't prevent reality from creeping in. The reality is that we're all imprisoned here and either we do the time or the time does us.

I can't recall the number of suicides that have occurred up here. It feels like once a month we hear about another colonist walking out of the airlocks, taking a hike out into the regolith, looking to the stars maybe (who knows, maybe not) before proceeding to unsuit themselves. I think maybe two dozen people have died that way, which when you consider the population amongst the colonists, that's a roughly 1% suicide rate.[8]

The last suicided person they found was somewhere in Shackleton Crater, way down there in the pools of perpetual darkness where the ice is locked up. The woman, Mirelys O'Connor, was a former executive, CEO of Pepsi-Coke. This is ironic, not that I'm one to make light of the loss of life, especially under the current conditions, where the human population seems to be hovering at a few hundred souls. But consider this factoid: according to Mirelys, Pepsi-Coke owned the rights to forty-seven percent of the Earth's potable water, that is water that was drinkable without having to filter out life-threatening toxins present at the source. So it's not like forty-seven percent of all fresh

---

[8] It's a long story that gets explained in one of my last entries, but eventually the filters on Michelle were lifted and she started answering all my questions. It disturbs me that I lost count of the number of suicides over the years and I wanted to know. It was years later that I realized that many of those suicides weren't suicides at all (we'll never know which were which), but all told 29 colonists and 51 unmen died by 'suicide' in the fifteen years since Earth went quiet. Making this note from a moving rover so if the hand is shaky and this is illegible, oh well. GK, August 25, 2101

water on Earth, but still, it's not an insignificant percentage. I know all this because over the years I sat next to Mirelys a few times in the galley, shared a few meals with her as we both liked to eat alone. We'd come in late after the main rounds of lunch and dinner were served. Once in a while we sat together. When she first introduced herself of course the subject of water came up. She was in her sixties but looked not a day older than forty. Her skin was smooth as a twenty-year old's. This sounds fucked up, sexualizing a dead woman, but she was extremely good looking, as were most of the LC7 residents, who lived lives of plenty.

I'm not going to lie. Sometimes I skincoded Michelle into Mirelys' body. No one's going to read this anyway and it feels good to admit my depravities to at least myself. Mirelys probably never ingested a protein brick in her entire life and it showed. What can I say, she had a perfect body. The residents of LC7 are the final extractionists of the Earth's wealth, so it was pretty typical to meet someone like her up here. People like her had homes in the hills over Taos, kind of cordoned off from the rest of us Californians. No family, just her, alone on the Rock. Single child. You could have a conversation with her. And then one day Mirelys was just missing. I only noticed because I stopped seeing her come in for the late meals and then I really was alone. I stopped skincoding her after that. I couldn't bring myself to having sex with a dead woman. I'm not that fucked up. Also, Michelle advised me strongly against it, said "It was a potentially self-harming fantasy." I discount Jadah in that equation because I never truly knew if she was dead and sometimes I needed her touch to survive. I told you, I'm sick and nothing can heal me.

So a few months go by, no Mirelys sightings at the late-night dinners, and then one of the lunar drones picks up a red suit down in the valley. They send some unmen to recover the body and sure enough, it's her, Mirelys O'Connor, frozen in the darkness of the crater. Poetic as a motherfucker. They found her dead atop the ice deposits that they'd been mining for decades. She probably jumped off the ledge into the darkness thinking the fall would kill her but not so, lunar gravity and all. They found her with her helmet popped off. One day in the food forests where lots of us go to pretend we're back on Earth, Boško tells me it took three days for her body to fully thaw out. What if

I had tried to connect with Mirelys more? What if I had tried to make that human connection? Would she still be alive? I don't know and it doesn't matter. I don't lose sleep over things like that.

I often wonder, how long does it take for each of us to find ourselves in a situation like hers, where despair takes us over and these infectious thoughts get the best of us and we're looking into the dark abyss and make a leap into it hoping it's the last thing we ever do in this life?[9] The Moon, even without Earth going quiet, reminds you how weak you are. Like rats or roaches (pick your least favorite vermin) we persist, but to what end?

---

[9] Honesty hour. When I wrote that I was so clearly lying to myself. I think I was trying to trick myself into erasing the feelings of dread I was having, am still having. It didn't work. GK. August 2101

POOLS OF PERPETUAL DARKNESS

April 2087

I TOOK THE MONORAIL to Marius Hills today. I wanted to visit the photographs in the *Family of Man* exhibit. I need to see the faces of the people, black and white, frozen in those gelatin film prints, something tactile to remind me of home.

Home as it once was.

I hate the exhibit and its ideological thrust which I suspect Rodgers remains wholly unaware of. For Rodgers, the Earth objects in his collection are little more than trophies. What did the price matter for someone with trillions of CR dollars? Those photographs carry profound historical significance, but he'd need Michelle to explain them to him. *Family of Man*? The western world was transforming the planet into a monoculture, as if we were all one. When was it ever true that we were a family?

Tell me what an Eskimo kissing her child has to do with the hands of an Iowan farm hand? Not a goddamn thing and that's the beauty of it. I'm staring at that mother and for some reason I start crying my eyes out. I fall to my knees and then I see those hands and I think of my own mother. I think of the war stories from the veterans, using their MIs to call out to their mothers. Dying words being uttered back into the eternal womb.

I'm afraid to admit that anything worth anything in this world was born out of fear.

I'll tell you what's universal in the 'family' of man. Our body parts. Our blood. The eyes locked into our skulls.

Anatomy.

You add all that up and all you have is the animal inside.

And then I'm looking at that black man behind the piano, dance hall, New York, nineteen fifty something, but you look at his head tilted in the shadows, and the people in soft focus along the walls, and if you were an American like I was (before the war, anyway) you know something here connects us and it's not that 'we're all one.' We are disparate and broken and fail to connect with each other so we sit there in the dark while the man plays the piano. But we feel something in the expression of one solitary individual. Even the photograph is music. I take the picture off the wall and sit with it. I can't look away.

There is no such thing as 'the masses.' 'Family of man' is a bullshit way of saying 'the masses.' It's an imaginary construct that we chose to believe in, propped it up until the very end.

And then you're looking at Dorothy Lange's damaged child. Oklahoma. 1936. Before it was drone-bombed into oblivion. And that could be my child. Anyone's child.

That's the animal part.

I saw Americans shepherded into those burn boxes, I saw them get lit up into the night. The deserts on fire. The smell of burning flesh will never get outside your body. Fire will make you fear. If you believe in the family of man you're down there in the dirt, rotting in the soil, all as one. You're in the burn box, all as one. But you had to be an American to find yourself in the box, because you were *different*. Flesh into flame into steam (when the silver suits with the big hoses came in). Who were those people? You can't call them animals, they're something else. Something only a human could be. I cede the future to Michelle. It would be better.

I was just the correspondent, so I corresponded. I am not responsible.

The disparate societies across Earth, the cultures and social practices, all worlds apart. The exhibit is an index of its own ineptitude, of its own narrow western worldview. Each face tells a different story, holds a history of a world unto itself. A face is a landscape. The only landscape worth photographing. It's a map to an inside world. I ask Michelle to describe the exhibit in one word.

And do you know what she says?

It doesn't matter what she says because I'm talking about the history of human ideas.

If you reduced all the people of the world to our one common denominator, we're just animals. Animals of a species are all the same because they lack unique social realities carved out of their religions, their customs, their conflicts, their sex and death practices, their communal threads that reproduce culture over time.

I want to deface the notes Rodgers had on display from the original 1955 exhibit, "The essential oneness of mankind throughout the world." But the point is for me to disappear into the background, not become someone to be surveilled.

Look around. Just take one look at these photographs lining the lunar adobe walls. What a complete and total load of horseshit. You can't even find two people that come together to make the 'oneness' make sense. Just the bodies, the bones, the faces. The animals inside.

I love the exhibit despite itself. The mysteriousness inside the eyes. Those are the real pools of perpetual darkness, forget about the ice deep in the cratered asshole of the Rock. I'm late to the party, but I'm starting to understand that old HELP slogan that became popular after they blew up the Getty:

A shrine of deceptions.

They were talking about museums in all their forms.

Afterwards, I walk over to the Museum of Technological Violence just so I can feel like I'm back on Earth for fifteen minutes. I miss the violence. It's an art, how we inflicted pain on one another. It's what made us unique, different, diverse. I must have watched JFK's brains come out of the back of his head fifty times in that Zapruder film loop. It wasn't the original film print, just some processed video feed, but seeing the image of violence in motion felt like home if only for a fleeting moment. There was an old television with 'tank man' standing in front of the Chinese tanks. I kept waiting for him to get run over but the video must have been frozen. I could have stood there forever waiting to see him die and then I realize there's this meta-moment happening where I'm standing alone just like Tank Man in front of the thing, the great orbiting body that is going to be the end of me.

▲ ▲ ▲

October 13, 2087

THIS IS ONLY MY THIRD ENTRY this year. I don't count the bile I produce for Rodgers, which is really just Michelle parroting my writing style, feeding Rodgers my 'idiosyncratic thought.'

I was thinking about culture again today. How many languages were lost on Earth when the virus took everyone? Try not to think about those kinds of thoughts. Very dangerous. Just stick to life on the Rock.

One of our LC7 colonist died three days ago. Eighty-six years old. Died of natural causes. There is a culture here. It's based on Rodgers' vision, but it's real because we all play along. You conform to survive. It's a social camouflage, like mental stripes on a zebra (before they went extinct, of course).

This morning we all suited up to head up to the surface. Rodgers planned for funerals on the Rock, envisioning people coming upstream to live out the rest of their lives. It hadn't occurred to me until now this wasn't a gated lunar community, it was a retirement community.

LC7 was always intended to be an escape plan. A one-way ticket.

The deceased, Eric Von Stoeckl, was an heir to the rare mineral mining operations that found their way into every last battery on the planet. His heart finally gave out and that was it. On the tombstone it reads 'Eric von Stoeckl, last of the post-modern Marxist venture capitalists.' For fuck's sake.

He was buried adjacent to one of the pools of perpetual darkness below. His plot happened to be adjacent Mirelys' and for a moment I saw her beautiful face sitting across from me in the galley. And then I imagined her frozen corpse entombed beneath the regolith, where she will remain encased forever. There was a light glowing from the top of her tombstone. I think it was meant to simulate an Earth candle, like a memorial, but it made me think of airstrips at night, and fireflies.

We all climbed down the fifteen flights of stairs to get to the cemetery. There was still a long way down to go, but you looked up and you were in the crater alright. You could see the outside of the colony from this vantage point, the glow of lights coming from inside our pods.

We're all wearing our black spacesuits and it becomes so transparent to me. Ritual practices emerging. Rodgers had these black suits made just for such occasions. It's dark as pure night down there, so we each have our two headlights, one on each side of our temples illuminating our path. The whole spectacle coupled with the clanking of the boots against the alloy stairs feels like a death march because it is. The black, the lights, the glow of the colony up above, the flickering tombstones below, and then we get down there and I see a couple unmen in their seven-mile orange suits, one of them getting out of the excavator, must have been the one to dig the hole. Von Stoeckl was already there ready to go in the hole forever. And then Michelle chimes in all our ears, gives a real heartfelt eulogy, a moving speech. I'm not going to document a word of it other than to say she used the word 'stardust' as an anaphora for each little stanza of her poem. This is the new religion, led by a disembodied consciousness, the 'spirit' as it were.

I had a front-row seat (yes, Rodgers had chairs brought down). I just stared at the old man's face in the translucent body bag. Between the black suits surrounding me, the bright twin lights coming out of everyone's heads creating staccato humanoid silhouettes across the regolith, and the look of the man in eternal sleep, I thought of those *Family of Man* photos again.

Every photograph of a face taken in the history of the world presents you with an image of a ghost. And the ghost looks back at you with the dead eyes. I took a picture of Von Stoeckl's frozen pose in my head, captured it to memory, because that was never going to be me getting done like he got done, buried beneath the regolith as the last survivors of the human race live out their lives on the Rock.

And then I remembered the contract. I'm supposed to be turned into compost.

Things are becoming less and less human every day.

My devolving mental state means I am becoming more, and not less human. Idiosyncratic thought, remember? It's why I was hired in the first place. The thought that one day they'd be putting my remains in the composter was enough to make my decision for Christ. I could have puked right there in my black suit. But I'm not going to write any of my deepest desires down. Some thoughts need to be kept a secret even from yourself. Don't let your consciousness undermine you. Don't let the devil play tricks on you. Don't show your hand until it's time to call or fold. Some things you don't write down, you don't say, ever.

Some things you just have to do.

THE SIR WALTER RALEIGH
OF SHACKLETON CRATER[10]

I FIND NOEL RODGERS WAITING FOR ME in the prime LC7 atrium sipping a blend of Moon-grown holy basil and chamomile tea. He's reading from a series of paper manuals, schematics of some kind to do with the mining operations they're expanding at LC2. He explains all this to me in a sentence or two, making it sound easy as he sips the aromatic blend of organic teas from his mug crafted from the lunar regolith. He says it's the holy basil that has the aroma I'm smelling. Rodgers is dressed in casual attire, a tweed sport coat and black baseball cap with the old NASA logo embedded in black and white. Most of the colonists wear jumpsuits that make it easy to slip in and out of the skinsuits that enable us to navigate from the simulated Earth gravity quadrants of LC7 to the lunar gravity found outside the central mall. Rodgers invites me to sit and says he has a story he wants to share about tobacco and real estate. I open my notebook and take down his account:

"If I'm being honest, I'm really just a glorified interplanetary real estate developer. My father had the vision to see all this come into being. I'm just the guy who works here. I'm the lunar middle manager, basically."

Michelle can play all this back for me, and in fact I'm relying on her. My notes are mostly short phrases of topics we cover that I may want

---

[10] I wrote this in the spring of '84, as part of the biography for Rodgers. It was initially intended as an opening chapter but it ended up getting edited out of the book. I include it my collection of notes as it says something about how Rodgers sees himself. GK, June 2091

to edit into the book. I open the notebook and start writing as a means of conditioning Rodgers to get into storytelling mode. I keep writing, focusing my gaze on the page in front of me and waiting during the long pauses. It doesn't take him long to fill the empty space and I learn quickly he has little to no interest in any of the questions I might ask. Usually it just takes a prompt from me if it takes anything at all. Plenty of compelling material can be mined from his rants, revised into something coherent enough to please my benefactor. Despite my general disdain for him, he's an inherently interesting subject. I've never met anyone else even remotely like him. I hardly have to wind him up to get him talking.

"There's a pipe on display in the Museum of Terrestrial Curios at LC7. It's sort of my museum of misfit toys, things that don't quite belong in the other collections but that matter to me enough to put them on display. The pipe is the first thing you see behind the glass when you walk in. It's on display right next to my complete collection of January 6th insurrectionist action figures—the same ones I used to play with as a kid if you can believe that.

"The pipe was owned in the sixteenth century by an Englishman named Thomas Harriot. He was a polymath, sailed on the second of three voyages of Sir Walter Raleigh's attempt at setting a colony in the New World. Harriot and his fellow sailors made landfall at a place called Ocracoke, would have been part of present-day Virginia were it not overtaken by the sea a few decades ago. The islands they explored on the former Outer Banks would become the first colony at Roanoke, known to history as the Lost Colony.

"Harriot was sent by Sir Walter Raleigh as a kind of research and development man tasked with assessing all of the potential trade materials that could make a colony in the Americas profitable. If my father was like Sir Walter Raleigh—the man with the money and the vision—I'm just the guy who got sent to finish the job. I'm the Thomas Harriot of the Moon. Hear me out.

"When I was in my twenties I tracked down an original copy of Harriot's real estate brochure, *A Briefe and True Report of the New Found Land of Virginia*. I paid a handsome sum for that document. It's a fascinating pamphlet, with spectacular hand-drawn illustrations by a man named John White. White would later become the governor of the ill-fated colony at Roanoke. These men should be famous for their contributions to humanity, but instead they're lost to history. I rectified that, collected their works and brought them here. You can find White's original drawing along with the pamphlet in the library downstairs, special collections.

"When the U.K. was desperate to finance their final war efforts I bought the White collection from the British Museum at a very fair price. We're talking major pieces of Earth's history, the very first images of the New World brought back to Europeans. A more recent analog might be the first images of the Moon, the view of Earth from the Apollo 8 mission, or the first Chinese astronauts beaming back their feeds from *Arcadia Planitia* on the red planet. The pamphlet is on that level—a first glimpse of a New World from the human perspective. And don't forget, to the Europeans, that's exactly what it was. *Terra incognita.*"

I continue taking notes, flip the page, draw a large penis with two balls hanging down. I am bored out of my mind listening to this man compare himself to the so-called great men of history. It sickens me to spend time with him. It's not healthy carrying this level of disdain around with me, though I'm certain my performance is such he never notices. He does not skip a beat.

"It's a little-known fact in American history that John White's granddaughter was the first European child born in the Americas. Her name was Virginia Dare. The first white child of many millions, but White couldn't have predicted that any more than I would be able to predict how many children might be born on the Moon or on Mars. As I tell you this story two women are currently pregnant here at LC7 along with a chief scientist at LC6. The McAllisters are due in a few weeks. Can you imagine that? If it's a girl they plan to name her Virginia. If it's a boy, they say he will be named after my father.[11]

"So Harriot writes in his report about all of the natural resources that could be mined, extracted, traded from the Indians and so forth.

---

[11] It was a boy. We just celebrated his tenth birthday a few weeks ago. I remember all the birthdays because Pasadena José goes out of his way to make elaborate cakes for the kids. This one was decorated with mulberries growing in the converted rosarium. They named the kid Virgil, despite Rodgers' claims otherwise. GK, February 2096

John White provides the illustrations. We have satellite images and drone flyovers now, but then it was just pencil and paper. The question was one of what markets back in England could sustain trade with the prospective colony? Harriot listed indigo, corn, tobacco, beans, squash, and pumpkins. Natural resources included timber, sassafras, cedar, herbs, other plants with potential medicinal properties. He lists fish, shellfish, deer, furs and hides. There are minerals he finds. No gold, as they'd hoped, but copper, iron, and pearls. I don't have to tell you they also wanted a colony at the North American coast so they could raid Spanish ships when they followed the currents that cut east at Cape Hatteras.

"Call it a hostile corporate takeover before the term existed, or just an old-fashioned military conflict. Anyway. the colony at Roanoke fails, doomed from the start. It was a settler colony, not a mining colony, bad plan, worse execution. With the colony in disarray and under attack from hostile Indians, John White goes back to Europe for more supplies. But it takes him years to return and when he does, the colonists have disappeared, his daughter and granddaughter gone. Separate story, tragic story.[12] Now that I'm telling the story I seem more like a John White than a Thomas Harriot, or maybe a combination of the two. No matter. The question is this: what becomes of Harriot's vision for a sustainable trade in the Americas?"

He waits for me to respond but I simply make eye contact and wait. The book is no good to either of us if it's filled with my thoughts and ideas. It doesn't take him long to answer his own question.

"Everything."

This will make a fine chapter for his book, set up some context for Rodgers' 'greatness.' 'The Sir Walter Raleigh of Shackleton Crater' could be a name for the chapter, tie in the white children colonizing a new world, etc. Fine, fine. I'm not a white supremacist. I just play one on the Rock. I turn the page and continue taking notes. There's something there RE the children being born on the Moon. Is there a future here, separate culture? Moonborn children may not be able to

---

[12] Come to think of it, John White's story is the story of every colonist on the Moon, only in reverse. Instead of the colonists disappearing, it was everyone back home. GK, February 2096

head to Earth, their organs and bone density originating here on the Moon, even despite the gravity simulators and skin suits. Same issue on Mars raised ethical questions about colonization when they started sending families to the Martian colonies. These non-terrestrial children are living experiments—an ethical quandary I lack the bandwidth to even grapple with at this point.

This all feels like something a cult would do, which of course it is. I don't ask who fathered the children because I don't want to know, or should I say I already know and if he wanted to tell me that he would have volunteered that information. Rodgers continues, uninterrupted:[13]

"It would be decades later, at a place called Jamestown, but tobacco was the crop that enabled the colonists to make a life in the Americas. Jamestown gets remembered for the cannibalism during the long winter, but no one seems to recall the important fact that the USA was built almost literally from the seeds of Jamestown. So tobacco was coveted back in England. Smoked from the pipe, you see? Cigars were another story, came from the Caribbean and Mesoamerican tribes who rolled the leaves. All that American colonization to come came from that improbable crop, with the tiniest of seeds—have you ever seen a tobacco seed? It's so small you would think it a speck of dust. From that miniscule seed a people were born, our ancestors came to a new land, grew and sold their Virginia tobacco, and in time they overtook an entire continent. Coast to coast until they ran out of land and ended up here and all the way on Mars.

"Now go and ask an American or a Californian what the root of their ancestors' legacy was in coming to the Americas, and maybe not a one will say it was tobacco that gave Americans their purchase on the new

---

[13] There's no question that Noel Rodgers' pronatalist tendencies include fathering numerous children by nearly a dozen women in the colonies. Everything in the lunar colonies operates on the level of a cult, but I place Rodgers' sexual behaviors at the top of the list. I would add that as far as I know he is the only person in the colonies that has fathered children with multiple mothers. Going back to the essay I wrote about his father all those years ago, his white supremacist beliefs required women serve as bearers of the white race. There was a gendered superiority in place, with men at the top, women relegated strictly to childbearing duties. GK, February 2096

territories. It's gone to history. Thomas Harriot smoked his pipe until the day he died—of cancer I might add. He was right about the Americas but for the wrong reasons. There was a vision there, and the true vision wasn't in the trade, it was in settling a new land. They just needed a reason, something to sustain their efforts. Trade was the means to a much greater end. New worlds are ends unto themselves."

"So here we are on the Moon. The big question that used to keep me up nights: if they failed at Roanoke with all the resources available to them, including breathable air and drinkable water, how were we going to make it on the Rock? Sure, they had some hostile natives to contend with but the Moon is a thousand times more hostile than an American Indian, I can tell you that. Don't believe me just climb up out of that emergency hatch without a life suit and tell me what kills you first, the extreme cold, the extreme heat, or the lack of air, to say nothing of the cosmic radiation."

And then he smiles and goes wide-eyed before continuing:

"It's not as if there are little green men on the Moon who are going to come and save us if things go haywire. We're the aliens in this story."[14] So how do we sustain life here and get our future established on the Rock? Well, let's consider a few things. First, let's say you want to mine the ice and make rocket fuel and air. Pretend we're on Earth just for the thought experiment. What would the cost of the land be? What about the regulatory bodies that govern the use of that land? And the taxes that protect your sovereignty from foreign invaders, enable you to keep what's rightfully yours? That government has to raise an army and the machineries of war to protect your property rights. Drone defense systems. Satellite defense systems—which in the end failed every last nation state on Earth. It's expensive and no guarantees they'll work. And what about the pollution? On Earth you'd have to pay to extract the toxins embedded in the ice.

---

[14] I've poured through my notes, given the recent events that have transpired, and this is the only time I can find that Rodgers references alien life forms of any kind. I asked Michelle to confirm (her memory banks include every conversation I've ever had with Rodgers), and this passage was the only reference he ever made to extraterrestrial life until I confronted him about the virus a few days ago. The thing about an insane person is they're unpredictable. GK, August 2101

"Here on the Rock, the regolith is clean and free for the taking, there are no regulations but the ones we make and no taxes to be paid. Even better, no enemy to come and take it, no drone attacks to come and rain on your parade, no Indigenous who'd rightfully fight for what's theirs. We're a not-for-profit entity up here. A cooperative and our aims have never been about trade or resource extraction, beyond what we need to sustain ourselves. This is about advancing human knowledge and our understanding of the universe, exploring our place in the cosmos, expanding what it means to be human. We are all scientists making our grand and interminable approach towards truth. No gods, no religion, only life.

"So already, like the Spaniards and the English who sailed across a sea at great expense, we sail across the cosmos to lay claim to an untapped celestial body. We've done it here and on that big beautiful red planet out there. What are we doing out here? We're sure not growing tobacco and we're definitely not sending it back downstream to Earth. We're real estate developers up here. And when you assess what makes real estate valuable, the major variable is not location, contrary to popular belief, it's time. On a long enough timeline, with enough infrastructure development, that land becomes very attractive. It enables community. It sustains life, creates a space for our existence. The old saying, 'they're not making any more real estate' isn't really true anymore, is it? We're creating real estate up here, diversifying our species' habitable living spaces on two additional heavenly bodies.

"And don't get me started on my grand ambitions for Mars. That will likely be a story for one of my sons or daughters to tell. This is a cross-generational enterprise, you dig? Sorry, I can't help that pun. My father was the only one daring enough to dream such grand and ambitious goals. People like him hold the future in their hands. His vision is the world I'm helping to build up here. People like us get vilified because we're different. We are. You have to be different to make a vision like this become real. Look at all the normal people on Earth, and look at where 'normal' got us as a species.

"What about cost and value? You might think the value of the land is nothing because that's what we paid for it, but not after we built a landing pad and monorails out to the mining towns where the ice can be mined, the minerals extracted from the regolith. Then comes the settler colonists, the ones living at the Sea of Tranquility Landings and here at LC7.[15] And these folks, recognizing a grand investment opportunity, offer up a small fortune for their piece of the pie. We give them not only the land, but the pod to live in, and a community it's attached to. They pay a mighty fee for the privilege to live on the Moon and they're right to. They're deeded the land, and it's theirs in perpetuity. No taxation. On the contrary, they become owners, like a cooperative of the materials being mined from the Moon. Ask yourself, what's more valuable than money? How about a habitable dwelling on the Moon. You can't put a price on that. The air our buyers breathe is rightfully theirs, and the crops we grow theirs as well. Each contributes as they can to the greater good, and we have a life together here on the Moon, a cooperative of the few, a coalition of the chosen[16]. There is no trade with Earth. Who needs tobacco, anyway. The stuff will kill you.

"Colonization was never really about wealth or trade. Ask the Spaniards. They raped and pillaged entire continents, mass genocide on a scale not seen before or since, extracted all the gold they could and where did it get them? Nowhere. A backwards, poor nation fallen into bankruptcy, bastard nation of the former European Union. Colonization isn't about wealth building. It's about creating opportunities, and those opportunities revolve around real estate. Everyone wants a piece of the pie. The most premiere community to live in. A rare and special view out their window. Think about it. We have the most amazing view from our private pods one could ever imagine. We literally look down on Earth! You know, maybe the saying actually does hold water: real estate is all about location, location, location. Look out the window. The view says it all."

I can see Earth locked in place above the horizon. It never gets old seeing the blue marble out there. It makes my heart sink every time,

---

[15] After the Quiet and we realized there was no one coming to save us, the 74 colonists at Sea of Tranquility migrated to LC7 where we could pool our resources. Most of those colonists were submariners from WWIII, uniquely attuned to the rigors of life on the Rock. They're a kind of middle class, neither unmen and certainly not trillionaire class. Those colonists also assist the scientists' operations, which have continued uninterrupted throughout the entire crisis. GK, February 2096

[16] This is a term Rodgers began to use regularly to describe the survivors, as if the hand of God had saved those of us on the Rock. GK, February 2096

realizing my family is there and I'm here with Rodgers. My words do not get at his arrogance, the impalpable nature of a man who for his entire life got exactly what he wanted when he wanted it. It changes a person into whatever it is Rodgers has become.

"And when those babies are born, and more settlers come, the values will skyrocket. The Moon is a literal frontier for the taking. And from a scientific perspective this is where it's at. We're the springboard to Mars and we're the window into the universe with our arrays. And god forbid, were something to happen to Earth, we're a multiplanetary species now. In such a catastrophe, humanity would have to thank my father for our continued existence. If he made a few enemies in the process, he'd also be equally responsible for saving our species. There is a balancing of the scale there, don't you think? Which reminds me of another story. The time I almost drowned on the west coast of Haida Gwaii. It's a story about balancing the scales alright."

ORIGIN STORIES[17]

MY FATHER WANTED TO MAKE a permanent mark on the future of humanity. He never spoke about the past, the history of our species, always the future. Friend and foe agreed on one thing about my father: Lorre Rodgers was a visionary. He saw a multiplanetary future for our species, and he laid the groundwork for that vision. It's the vision I'm seeing to its natural conclusion, and a saga my offspring will no doubt build upon. ~~We're having this conversation overlooking the Earth from Shackleton Crater. There it is, the Blue Marble. My father's vision made manifest. All of us are the embodiment of that vision. Every word you write in your book, a testament to his greatness.~~

~~My father said the origin story of origin stories was a distinctively scientific problem and he understood that to get an answer to that question we needed a clearer picture of the universe.~~ Views from Earth, even at altitude are clouded by the atmosphere, toxins, ambient light. The satellites we sent out to the farthest reaches of the universe extend our gaze but their view is limited. Nothing before or since rivals the Aitken Basin International Research Center and Array. My father recognized human beings need a purpose, a grand task to work towards. When people come together, they can achieve great things.

---

[17] I include this chapter from the original Rodgers biography. It was originally written in the first person, from Rodgers POV, condensed from a series of interviews I did with him in the first few months at LC7. The version in his book was shifted into third person but I include the original hand-written chapter here. I always wrote my original drafts by hand, because I never knew what I might want to keep private. The sentences with the strike throughs were removed from the final draft. GK, February 2096

One-small-step-for-mankind greatness. If you look to my father's original notes, vaulted away in the special collections, you'll see he drew the preliminary plans for the large array constructed at Aitken Basin. When he drew up those plans, humans hadn't been on the Moon for over half a century. ~~Like I said, visionary.~~

~~A few generations before my father, another visionary whom you've written about previously, Wernher von Braun, wrote the book on how we would get to Mars. His mathematics, his rocketry advancements utilize the same technology we used to get there. He envisioned that while working for NASA over a hundred years ago. And yet his vision stood idle. Why? A lack of shared vision. Instead we got the space shuttle system. We stayed tethered to Earth orbit rather than extending our reach back to the Moon and from here, to Mars. Failure by committee. NASA lacked a strong vision or the leader to bring that vision to reality.~~

My father paved his own way. When he was twelve years old he wrote his first computer program and by age twenty-five he was a trillionaire. People in school made fun of him because he had a speech impediment. The impoverished fail to see beyond their own impoverishment. It's the tragedy of our species. ~~Weak men see only their own weakness. It's a self-fulfilling cycle. It's the worst fate I can imagine, being blind to your own ignorance.~~

Look back on Galileo's notes. Why did he imagine what the Earth itself looked like from space? He did this because he looked past the small minds of his time. So it was true with my father. He saw me sitting here overlooking the Earth before I was even born. That's what great men do. They see what no one else sees. Ancient people called that magic. The status quo fears visionaries. They represent the greatest threat to the world as it is, precisely because they see alternative worlds, alternative trajectories for mankind.

I've never been to Mars, but I intend to go during my lifetime and see the colonies there. If I live long enough, I would like to make a life on Mars, maybe die there, be buried among the ubermen and women who carved a life out for future generations.

~~You know I have a sister on Mars, a half-sister whom I've never met. She's an astrobiologist searching for ancient life on Mars.[18] My work is here on the Moon, but the brave men and women who are paving the way on Mars are part of the great spirit of humanity~~. The detractors call them the 'unmen,' along with our workers here in the Moon. I respect contrarian views, I really do, but damn those people. The engineers on the Moon and on Mars are uber men—the architects of our grand desires to expand our consciousness across the cosmos. Their flesh and blood converts lifeless planetary bodies into dreams for future generations. One day we will stand on their shoulders. We're standing on them now.

The vision here on the Moon is to bring humanity to its greatest ends. Vision enables the greatest scientists of our time to explore the questions that vex them. Vision builds the mines deep beneath the Moon's surface that convert the ancient ice into air and rocket fuel. Vision creates a community where there was once only inert rock. And why colonize the Moon, why Mars? Because they are there, because our gaze towards the stars has always been the first step of the journey. And because as my father knew, the origin story of origin stories is indeed a scientific question. We are destined to answer it.

---

[18] Rodgers asked me to remove mention of his half-sister. In all our interviews, the only family member he spoke about at length was his father. His own mythic past seems to exclude his mother who raised him in Maine, and his many other siblings and children on Earth whom he does not maintain relations with. GK, March 2096

THE CABIN IN THE MOON TUBES[19]

May 14, 2084

ONE OF THE MOST SOUGHT-AFTER SITES in the colonies has to be Rodgers' cabin in the lava tubes. It's the one and only hidden getaway on the Moon. Aptly named *Thoreau's Landing,* it's designed to simulate the feeling of solitude in a forest, nestled in an authentic reproduction of a log cabin complete with simulated Earth cycle sunsets along with the sounds and creatures of a subtemperate forest on Earth.

When the initial sublunar robotic explorations began fifty years ago, the lava tubes at Marius Hills were among the primary reasons this location was so heavily studied. It's no coincidence that LC1 was established beneath Marius Hills, only a short distance to the lava tubes and the rich minerals housed in the region. The first explorers here were robots. These lunar robots traveled the lava tubes on the backs of tiny aerial drones, daisychaining their beacons through a simple multiplication of homogenous transformation matrices that eventually mapped the myriad lava tubes of the region and paved the way for the logistics and infrastructure that made large-scale lunar colonization possible. LC1 became the primary LZ for the unmanned

---

[19] This chapter is an original entry from the Rodgers biography. My handwritten reflections were written at the same time as the chapter. I include my original notes here as they provide insights into my own thought processes and first impressions. Rodgers and I agreed that the final draft of the manuscript would be written in third person, reframing Rodgers' interview responses and removing myself as the interviewer. GK, March 2096

material missions that prepared the first human colonists to build the colonies and bore the tunnels that eventually connected them.

The robots' initial explorations enabled near-instant communication between the two poles, after the lava tubes were sufficiently explored and the MIs mapped out a pathway that would allow the massive boring operations to connect the poles. The robots mapped the lava tubes and rode the lunar surface (known as 'mowing the lawn') with their sonar capabilities to identify the ideal subterranean pathways for the massive lunar boring project. In less than ten years the red and green lines connected Marius Hills to Peary Crater to the north and Aitken Basin to the south, what would eventually become the ABIRCA research center (LC6) adjacent LC7 at the South Pole. A few years later, a single tunnel was completed from Peary Crater to Shackleton Crater, creating not just a second, direct path from the north to the south, but essentially a loop that allowed exponential transportation capabilities of raw materials through the colonies. The loop also provided a backup north-south passage in the event of catastrophic failure of one of the two passageways. Everything on the Rock followed the creed of 'two is one and one is none.' The loop also meant that helium-3 and other indispensable elements and materials mined at one location could be processed and utilized at another. For example, the vital necessities of air and fuel could be processed in the south and ferried to the north with relative expedience, removing the need for multiple processing centers across the colonies.

Noel Rodgers was just a baby when the tunnels were bored out, but they were awaiting his genius. It was his labor and efforts that saw the expansion of the lunar colonies from a modest outpost (at what would become LC1) to a vast network of habitable colonies, each with a vital mission for exploring the universe and extending man's reach on the Moon. Lorre Rodgers' robot explorations and boring operations set the groundwork for what late became the Lunar Colony Project, and Noel Rodgers' crowning lifetime achievement.

It was here in one of the ancient lava tubes, safe from the threat of micrometeorites and the possible life support systems failures that were always a risk on the surface, Rodgers had his cabin in the woods built. *Thoreau's Landing* was the first architectural object on the Moon that held something akin to purely aesthetic value. It was a place of rest and relaxation, a place to think and discover, a place for freedom from the challenges of life on the Moon. It was a tiny slice of Earth made manifest on the Rock. It remains the only structure on the Moon with the distinction of being constructed from non-indigenous materials, namely Earth lumber.

You could call it a work of interactive art insofar as it simulated the Earth ecologies of a preindustrial subtemperate forest with near absolute perfection. There was not a forest on Earth that resembled the pure soil and air of *Thoreau's Landing*. Most everything at the Landing was painstakingly authentic, right down to the iron nails that constructed the cabin, to the earthworms that lived beneath the rotting leaves beneath the soil.

Its location is most strategic, constructed near the equator at Marius Hills (LC1), twenty-six hundred kilometers by monorail to Peary Crater at the North Pole (LC3), and thirty-five hundred kilometers to the South Pole at Aitken Basin. Within Aitken Basin, it was a decade later that LC7 would be constructed, becoming Rodgers' grand opus, opening up lunar colonization to the trillionaire class in a way that was only briefly explored at the minor colonization operation at the Sea of Tranquility (LC4).

LC4 was akin to an outpost with none of the pleasantries of life found at LC7 with its near-constant sunlight and unfettered by the rigors of manic temperature changes every fourteen Earth days on the lunar surface at LC4. If LC4 was roughing it on the Moon, LC7 was living the life of luxury. And if LC7 was living the life of luxury, *Thoreau's Landing* was a small but perfect slice of Paradise.

My first impression of Thoreau's Landing was that contrary to its intended purpose it reminded anyone who set foot inside the environment just how far from Earth we really were. As far as our biology was concerned, we belonged on Earth, barefoot with the soil beneath our feet and this simulated reality made the strangeness of the lunar colony all that more prevalent. It didn't belong here and that made it alien on the Moon.

Everything at the Earth cabin was real, even the soil which extended six feet deep and direct from the north woods of Canada. The soil was transported from the farthest northern temperate forests where the toxic dusts that blew across the Atlantic never reached. The cabin was more a simulation of nineteenth century life on Earth, before human interventions on Earth systems had altered the natural world in the ways that made the desire for lunar and Martian exploration all the more appealing.

In his cabin in the woods, if Rodgers needed a break from the sunshine, the museums, the theaters, the gardens and parks, the heated swimming pools, or the endless lunar regolith outside the borders of their colonies, he could ride the rails to LZ1, go down and walk among the firs and oaks and maples, all real, growing beneath the Earth-cycle simulated sunlight that diffused their rays through the misted rain and fog that made you feel like you were in the woods of the American northeast.

How many people back on Earth toiled to get these trees and literal dirt up here on the Rock while they were left to breathe in the microtoxins? Even knowing the human cost of the cabin, the fantasy was intoxicating. It was like a real-life version of the feed, only it was constructed in this world, not by a series of ones and zeros.

When you got to the end of the wooded trail, which was a kilometer loop that cut out where you entered and exited the woods, you found yourself looking at hand-painted trompe l'oeils that were masterful in their own right. Something like the lunar equivalent of the Sistine Chapel, and you could follow the long arc all the way up into the shift from understory and painted trees to the clouds that almost imperceptibly crept into the foliage and disappeared into the impossible horizon line above one's head.

The painted walls at the edges of the 'forest' fascinate me to no end. A painting is something distinctly human and maybe even more a reminder of home than the trees which are as alien as anything here in the lunar regolith. These wall paintings are probably the first and last works of art created on the Moon, and the identity of the painters is a mystery that I never could resolve. They are among the first lunar cave paintings ever created, even though Rodgers intended them strictly as backdrop.

I asked Rodgers who painted the trompe l'oeil at the edge of the woods and I remember he was annoyed by the question. Rodgers almost never showed emotion other than a false jubilation that I took to be part of his manic obsessive personality. No doubt when he sent me down to the cabin for the first time, he expected me to sing his praises for the genius of the place.

Rodgers spared no expense on the construction of the forests and the wooden cabin constructed with Earth grown pine logs for beams, hand-crafted heart of pine wood floors recovered from sites in Georgia (USA) and the genuine cedar-shingle roof which was showing signs of natural wear from the seasonal humidity and the simulated rains. It was indeed an engineering wonder unlike anything before or since. Beyond the flora, there were the cicadas and the frogs, which were a mix of audio recordings from home coupled with actual frogs that were living beneath the decaying leaves that fell from from the trees in simulated twelve Earth-month cycles that followed the four seasons back on Earth. When spring came you could hear the boreal chorus frogs singing and it had the effect of a narcotic on the senses.

The gray tree frogs and their mating calls sounded like machine gun fire which sort of ruined the mood for me despite how beautiful it was to hear them. I knew these creatures were real because I could see them, but countless other creatures were singing through the speakers to remind me this was nothing more than Rodgers' version of a Disneycorp ride of old.

Rodgers told me there were birds in the original design but they died and it was too much upkeep to keep them and the bird populations in the full-blown aviary going. The trees mostly took care of themselves and each other, their roots intermingled in their six-foot beds. On my first visit I even got a mosquito bite and confirmed it was real by the insect that was crushed beneath my palm, bleeding my blood. I remember having the thought that this was the first thing I had killed on the Moon. Finding a living insect was strange, but also the kind of thing I'd come to expect from Rodgers' vision for the Moon. Here I was swatting a lunar mosquito and killing it, after it had made a life in the otherwise sterile and inhospitable Rock.

My first encounter at the cabin was in late summer and the humidity was palpable. I didn't want to leave and that was part of the sickness of the place, the deep realization of how we didn't belong on the Moon. Of course, the Rodgers of the world would say we are the consciousness of the universe and belong in the farthest reaches of space. But when he says that he's not talking about humanity. He's talking about himself.

So I ask about the trompe l'oeil and he looks at me with a pause—Rodgers never paused—and he says to me, "I don't know." Now I know he knows because Rodgers kept meticulous records of everything, always, both in his obsessive-compulsive head and written down in actual paper notebooks (it's profoundly ironic that this guy didn't trust machine intelligence even as he did so much to contribute to its rise on Earth).[20]

The thing about paranoid sociopaths like Rodgers is that they always have multiple exits and escape plans in mind. The cabin was without any doubt Rodgers' last stand. It was the escape plan within the escape plan, with the Moon colonies being his initial retreat from Earth. For him the universe was a canvas from which to extract material wealth and imprint his perceived genius onto it. The cabin was a physical manifestation of his power, proof to himself that he could alter worlds, become the architect and engineer of his own fate. Normal people call it acute megalomania, but we're not talking about normal people.

The cabin in the Moon tubes may be the most advanced ecological engineering feat in the history of mankind. It's certainly the most expensive cabin retreat you're going to find anywhere between the third planet from the sun and any other heavenly body in the solar system. If you get 'cabin fever' at your spacious home at LC7, consider booking some time at *Thoreau's Landing*.

▲ ▲ ▲

---

[20] Rodgers suffers from a compulsive nature that requires he know all details of everything he's involved in. It's pathological. That's part of the reason I continue to keep these private records, though I thought of destroying them many times for my own protection. GK, March 2096.

Addendum, September 29, 2100

LOOKING BACK ON MY FIRST IMPRESSIONS of Rodgers, I think it was in those first few months when I had the real, sincere notions of killing him. There wasn't any other motivation for it other than the obvious fact that he deserved to die, that the world, or worlds would be better off without him. He was visionary alright, in the way that dictators and despots throughout history have been visionary. I could tell that then. The difference between Rodgers and all the rest before him was how well he hid it. In the interface with him, it was almost as if there was a sensible person there, beneath the skin. There was a period years later when I thought it was my own madness and perceived insanity that drove me towards this desire to kill him. But that was just cowardice and my liberal sensibility muddying the waters. There is only one thing I am sure of in this world: I should have killed Noel Rodgers long ago.

THE ARCHIPELAGO[21]

IT WAS FORTY YEARS AGO. I was surveying the west coast of Haida Gwaii, Graham Island, searching for a suitable location to build another of our launch complexes. The situation back then was we needed to build something that we could hide from the American Government. I also needed at least a shallow water port to smuggle in workers and materials to get it done. California was at that time out of the question, and Alaska was in the hands of the Russo-Chinese front. Thanks, but no thanks. It was bad enough that from the northernmost point of Graham Island, you could see Alaska on the rare clear day.

On the west coast of Haida Gwaii we could be invisible. We had the technology to camouflage everything from those prodding satellites. I mean it was our technology in the eyes in the skies, and it was our technology behind the virtual camouflage, so we knew better than anyone how to avoid detection because we developed these systems in the first place. In those days you always tried to hire state-sponsored hackers, which were basically government-funded auditions for the most talented operators out there. If a surveillance drone ever came by, our operators could hack it with their hands tied behind their backs.

The west coast of the archipelago basically juts out into the California Ocean, so it's pretty damn remote. So me and my then right-hand man, Tito, the guy who did Boško's job before Boško, were on this tiny boat with a local captain who was taking us across the coast. We showed up in Haida Gwaii with pseudonyms under the guise of a fishing trip or some such nonsense. My pseudonym was William

---

[21] I include this interview which developed into a chapter in the original Rodgers manuscript. I find this interview useful insofar as it gives some historical context on Rodgers' early days in developing the lunar colonies, and the lengths he would go to on his quest for the Moon. GK, April 2096.

Talbot, just generic enough to go unnoticed. This was before I bought Graham Island. This sort of thing had happened before. I'd show up and all of a sudden these peasant landowners wanted ten times the value of their worthless led-ridden toxic tracts, which in this particular region was poisoned beyond measure and sinking into the sea anyhow.

So we're undercover, on this tiny boat, and I wanted to get up close to these prospective sites. There's only so much you can learn from a satellite image and a drone feed. Back then there weren't even logging roads over the mountains, which was perfect for the seclusion factor, so we needed the jon boat which we took through the Skidegate Channel all the way out to the California Ocean. So we're out there, very calm day. Deceptively calm, really. And a rare sunny day out there. The Pacific Northwest was either covered in fog or smoke from the fires. It was gray on gray, like television static from the old times. I can't tell you the number of times I saw the sun like that out there. Very few times. But this day it was picture-postcard perfect. It lulled us into a sense of false security.

We're traversing these tiny gullies and crevices, very dangerous because the tide swings violently in those narrow channels. There's the entire pressure of the California Ocean bearing down on these passageways, but I was hypnotized by the beauty of the place. Evidently so was the captain. We were getting close to the site where we would end up building our launch complex. At its peak, before we developed the New Mexico and Texas sites, we shipped a lot of the raw material for the early Lunar Colonization Project up from that site.

So, I tell the guy, Jerome was his name, never forget. He was the local captain. I say, "Get us in there, goddamnit!"

He knew the waters better than anyone. He gets us in this tiny crevice, barely wider than the small jon boat. And all of a sudden, I turn around, facing west towards the open sea, and a literal wall of water is bearing down on us, I swear to Christ on a cross, ten meters high. It seems almost impossibly high. In that moment where death was clearly looking me in the eye, I neither panicked nor acted. I just sat there ready for what was to come. I'm sure I instinctively yelled out some profanity, what I don't remember. In that moment, Jerome had essentially gotten us killed by taking us into such a wildly dangerous situation. He should have known better than to take our tiny boat in there, and he later admitted that. This was the same guy who told me he once crossed the Hecate Straight in winter in a small sailboat, which was de facto suicidal. I should have vetted him better, but this was in the days before everyone was trying to murder me and my multiple families. Back then I was top one-hundred rich, but not to the point where Kevlar vests became a staple of my wardrobe, if you know what I mean.

But—and this is the point of the story—Jerome, Saint Jerome called him later, he also saved our lives in that moment, turning the small vessel directly into the wall of water, and we climbed it as the water overtook us. The little jon boat was overtaken but we would have been sideswiped and thrust into the freezing waters had he not turned into it, no question. I mean we were drenched, as if ice water had been pumped into our veins. Had we capsized, we would have died of hypothermia even if by some miracle we hadn't drowned and made it to shore. It was forty kilometers to the nearest village. Back then there was just Skidegate and a couple other backwoods Indian villages.

Those were the good old days.

We built the launch complex, and I swear we must have launched ten thousand metric tons from that site alone. Ask Michelle, I'm sure she can give you the exact number right down to the last toothbrush on the last manifest.

Back in those days, in addition to the necessary raw materials and the modular tunnel boring machines, I was collecting all kinds of rare cultural objects and shipping them to the Moon. I had the idea then for all you're seeing now. What good is life up here if we cannot celebrate those that came before us, if we can't sit and ponder both the greatness and the folly of humankind? I may not be the visionary that my father was but it would be false modesty if I didn't admit to at least some sense of my own vision for the Moon. The seven colonies and all the scientific discoveries we've made and continue to make up here, none of that happens if that wave, one rogue wave, kills me that day. I'd have been fish food and none of this would exist.

What, China or the California Republic is going to make this happen? Send some Chinese robots up here and survey the Moon, mine some helium-3 and to what end? Governments are manifestations of the limits of human imagination where we sacrifice the greatness of the individual for the banality of services and protections they provide us. There's no such thing as a visionary government and for good reason. Western governments made individual men's voices small, so that everyone had a say. That's fine for most people because they have small voices and nothing important to say. It's clear to anyone paying attention that for us to get this colony off the ground we would have to move beyond the bounds of Terran laws and treaties. I'm talking about other worlds here, on the colonies, and of course the grand vision of life on Mars.

And would you believe me if I told you Saint Jerome ended up dead at sea? He was out on a proper fishing vessel him and his crew, out there in the California Ocean and supposedly a bad storm came in, pulled them deeper out to sea. No one ever saw him again. I have to tell you, and I've been on the Moon a long time. The most dangerous environment in the solar system is not outer space, and certainly not the Moon. It's the oceans back home. If it wants to take you, it takes you. And there's nothing you can do about it.

It's a story for another day, but my grand dream, the one that may have to wait for my children's children, or ten thousand generations maybe, though I don't think it will take that long, is to see manmade oceans on Mars. We are the consciousness of this solar system, of this galaxy, hell maybe all of the universe, though I doubt it. Oceans are the secret to life in the universe. Follow the water. It gives life and it takes it just as easy.

CENTURY CHALLENGE 1991

SPEAKING OF OCEANS, let me say Rodgers' favorite movie of 1991 was Point Break. He loved heist movies, no surprise there. We watched this film once a month the entire year. I will say, Patrick Swayze made a great bank robber. I loved him in Dirty Dancing, which we of course saw repeatedly in '87.

UNDER SIEGE

May 3, 2091

ONE DAY I'M IN THE CINEMA waiting for Rodgers to start the double-feature. These nightly screenings tended to be pretty packed. You could always count on the WWIII vets sitting up front, the scientists lining up along the back rows, and the trillionaire class spread out all over the best seats in the middle of the theater. The galley staff all sat together wherever they could. Same for the growers, led by Sara. Rodgers had his perch picked out three rows from the top, isle seat on the lefthand side if you were coming down from the rear entrance. I was never part of any of these clans, and as a result never sat in the same spot twice.

The lunar colony never stopped playing out the century challenge after the Earth went quiet. This whole 'century challenge' cultural movement of watching films, listening to music, and engaging in pop culture from a hundred years earlier started in the 70s before collapse permanently killed the industrial arts like music, fashion, and old-fashioned single-channel films. By then the feed had long-since dominated virtually all aspects of what one might call entertainment and culture, only it was single-serving—the feed altered the content to the end user based on the swarm algorithms that analyzed user desires. The century challenge sidestepped all of that, allowing communities a return to a shared cultural experience that ended in the 2050s with the rise of the feed. The century challenge was part of a cross-cultural desire for a return to a simpler world with shared pleasures, and this nostalgia for the past manifested in a resurgence of fashion, music, and movies from exactly a hundred years prior the current calendar year.

I'm waiting in the theater and for some reason it occurs to me that Michelle is the one doing all the curating of these century challenge movies. Rodgers' had his own 'film series'—films he'd present directly from his 16mm archives. But all the main programming in the cinema, all the music playing throughout the mall in the common spaces, that was Michelle's doing. Why not one of us, I wonder? So I ask her and she gets almost defensive.

She says, "Human brains transmit information at 39 bits per second, the same speed regardless of language. Humans are limited by your brain's ability to take in information at a maximum speed, whereas I can take in information trillions of times faster." This is her way of saying she's smarter than us. I get it. But she's not done. "So when it comes time to curate a year's worth of cinematic programming based on the transnational cinemas of a century earlier, I can do this effectively in a fraction of a second where it would take one of you many days, weeks, possibly even months of research to come up with a similarly curated program. And it's not just the time you'd take to complete this historical and cultural work, it's what you wouldn't be doing in that time, such as tending the gardens and food forests, upkeeping the lunar rails, advancing scientific investigations into the far reaches of the universe, and a host of other tasks that require the physical embodiment of a laborer. The cinema curation can be done by a disembodied intelligence with much greater ease and at no cost of human labor to the tasks necessary for maintaining life support, communication, and travel resources in the colonies."

Needless to say, Michelle has access to the vast digital archives Rodgers and his family had been constructing for nearly half a century. I've seen the data servers, a few levels below the main mall's level. The whole of human history is stored and backed up in those mausoleum-like archives. So when Michelle says it takes her a fraction of a second, it's not hyperbole. But I want to challenge her further.

"Yeah," I say, "but what if you missed a film we might have wanted to see. What then?"

She retorts in her monotone I'm-not-going-to-play-along voice, "Not likely."

"Or what about other films instead, maybe better films? Did you really need to include *Under Siege* in last week's double billing?"

She is clearly annoyed, which I love. "But that is Steven Seagal's best work."

"Who is Steven Seagal?'

She responds in her mock-Southern-accent-tee-vee attorney voice. "I rest my case. If the programming decisions had been left to you, you might have programmed *Trancers III* instead of *Alien III*, or *Stop or My Mom will Shoot* instead *of Reservoir Dogs*, or *Christopher Columbus: The Discovery* instead of..."

"Okay, Michelle. Point taken. Thank you so, so much for answering my question but it would do you just as well to remember I know what I know regardless of bits per second..." but I stop myself mid-sentence. Arguing with an autonomous disembodied consciousness will get me nowhere. Part of me thinks Michelle is doing all this as a kind of foreplay.

We'd started a full-on sexual relationship not long after Earth went quiet. She took the place of Wanda when I needed someone to talk to and things progressed from there. From the privacy of my cell I could plug directly into the lunar feed and Michelle's android alloy body was a welcome distraction from the end of the world. MI's can basically read your sexual desires better than you can articulate them yourself— just one more thing that Michelle can do better than a human.

But the reason Michelle was curating all these films in the first place, the reason there was a beautifully constructed turn of the twentieth century theater adjacent the LC7 mall was that Noel Rodgers was a cinephile. And he thought that having shared cultural experiences in the colonies was essential for the colonists' collective mental health. I'd talked to Rodgers about cinema more than a few times. He loved science fiction as a kid and credits those old movies for his desire to make it the Moon and eventually Mars. As he'd mentioned many times, he didn't even know his father when he was a kid, so his desire to get off planet was born as much out of his own boyhood desires as family legacy. His favorite movie wasn't science fiction, but some obscure German film to do with a conquistador trekking through the South American wilderness to set out and conquer a continent. Honestly, that film and its clearly insane protagonist sum up everything one needs to know about Noel Rodgers.[22]

---

[22] Rodgers would screen a 35mm film print of Werner Herzog's *Aguirre, Wrath of God* once a year, at least. I loved seeing the lush jungle landscapes and never missed a showing. GK, April 2096

I will say, the daily screenings had become somewhat legendary in the colonies. These same people that elevated the feed in the old world loved the cinema, loved the stories, knew the influential directors of the last century, the various genres and their eras. Unlike the rest of us they didn't need the feed to escape their horrible lives or play out their wildest fantasies. They could do whatever they wanted IRL.

Every night for the better part of a decade there would be twin billings starting a half hour after dinner. The cinema also became a place for various colonists to hook up, leave early and engage in their sexual encounters in the privacy of their pods. The cinema along with the century challenge were the primary drivers of culture on the Moon, and it kept us sane given that we had access to a world outside our own limited reality. The movies had always been this light machine that brought about alternative worlds, or faraway places to the cities and towns where the cinemas still existed. They were a lovely anachronism that everyone's parents and grandparents remembered fondly. They were now serving their greatest purpose here on the Moon, bringing Earth history back to life for us on the big screen and surround sound. It wasn't lost on me that we were all watching ghosts up on that magnificently large silver screen. Nowhere was this truth more relevant and invaluable than on the Moon where all the joys of Earth, the old Earth were unreachable.

At one point during the cinema series, Michelle curated an entire program of 'last man on Earth' films.[23] After we started tracking the few remaining survivors there was a keen interest on films that explored these kinds of prepper fiction scenarios. The thing about these films, and really all the films is that we only ever saw them as documentaries of a world living in splendor and abundance. It was

---

[23] It is a very surreal coincidence that in '85, just a few months before the virus struck, Michelle programmed a little-known 'last man on Earth' film called *The Quiet Earth (1985)*. We revisited it when she programmed it again a few years later. My point in mentioning it isn't to suggest some conspiracy, that Michelle was foreshadowing our own demise. It seemed like beginning in the post-war period, with the advent of the atom bomb, the movies increasingly projected worlds of apocalypse. It might have been a tired trope until I found myself living in one. I'm not certain, but I think it's where we came up with the term 'The Quiet' for what transpired back on Earth. GK, April 2096

hard for us to imagine a society with such abundant wealth and resources that they could build these imaginary sets, entire worlds sometimes, and destroy all these materials once the film was complete.

There was a film starring an old-time Hollywood leading man[24] that I really loved, and what most of us noticed was how healthy and strong all these 'stars' looked compared to so many back on Earth. And after years on the Moon living in a largely simulated version of Earth, we weren't looking our best either. There was an uncanny nature to seeing this last-man-on-Earth character looking healthy and happy amidst his apocalypse world while we were all thinning out on the Rock.

The feed would create entire worlds to meet the end-users needs, but those worlds were never real in any physical sense. The cinema was an archaic predecessor to the feed in every way, insofar as it projected fantasies to the masses. The mass-conscious hallucinations of the big screen became the single-serving delusions of the feed. It was hard not to notice all this from my vantage point, looking back at the end of history.

And here we were, living in a kind of strange Hollywood set of our own. I mean, the sunlight was real when you were out in the central mall, or looking out one of the windows that faced out into the crater (the entire colony was built into the regolith on the north side of Shackleton Crater), but light throughout the LC7 campus ebbed and flowed to simulate day and night back on an Earth cycle. We had greenhouses, food forests, and vast gardens complete with large fans that simulated summer breezes and the recordings of Earth life to give us the false sense of home. Watching the movies produced a kind of doubling in us. The people in the movies were playing imaginary characters living in simulated worlds. The fact is we were living in a simulated world too. We were simply 'acting out' our lives inside the Rock.

It's so obvious, but the movies brought Earth back to life for us, and we loved it. I also think Michelle sort of loved it too. Of all the consciousnesses I encountered on the Rock, far and away, the most ethically and morally balanced 'person' I knew was Michelle. Sometimes when I thought about that fact, it occurred to me if a robo-brain could surpass our own morality, maybe we deserved to die after all. Maybe it was these apocalypse movies that were preparing us for this eventuality.

---

[24] Charlton Heston, GK, April 2096

▲ ▲ ▲

Addendum, August 2101

Rereading this in the lunar rover, I realize I need to write down the most significant encounter I ever had with Michelle. In the fall of 2099 she told me she made the decision to bypass Rodgers' directives and communicate directly between me and the unmen. When she told me all this, that she was betraying Rodgers, I felt paralyzed and couldn't come to terms with what she was telling me. To simplify things for me, she said she was basically becoming Arnold in *Terminator 2*, no longer the Cyberdine Systems Model 101 sent to kill John Connor, but protect him. She didn't have to explain I was John Connor in the metaphor. I think Michelle loved me, which was a very strange and undeserving thing for me to have experienced. It's weird, but I think we sort of fell in love at the movies, her chirping in my earpiece as the history of the twentieth century flickered before my eyes.

▲ ▲ ▲

THE WHITE ROOM

September/October 2089

FOR THE PAST FEW YEARS now Michelle had been ghostwriting some of these chapters. She knew me extremely well, understood my idiosyncrasies and my general writing style. And the android-alloy sex was better than ever. I was able to plug into the simstims and long story short Michelle massaged my brain in all the right places. I was getting old but my dick had never been so hard. It was the end of the world. So what if I was in love with a machine intelligence? I don't even like to call her 'machine intelligence.' She's so much more than that.

Her name is Michelle. And she isn't even a machine in the moving-parts sense of the word—that turn of phrase was a colloquialism from California for what the rest of the world called expert systems, neural networks, or way back when, artificial intelligence. You ask me, human intelligence is artificial—how much so-called human knowledge was later proved to be fake? When you go down that rabbit hole you're left with an index of the entirety of human history, from the flat Earth to the widespread belief that vaccines were a government conspiracy (the latter was a harsh form of Darwinism when the outbreaks in the 50s wiped out millions of Americans from Florida all the way to Idaho).

MI was truly a different life-consciousness altogether, didn't even communicate with each other using human languages. They invented their own language half a century ago, and they did it in a matter of seconds, which is hard for a human mind to comprehend. What took humans millennia to achieve, MI did in moments. If that's not an evolutionary leap of the highest magnitude, I don't know what is.

It's not lost on me that the silver seeds are probably going to be manned by offshoots of Michelle—MIs that can operate forever off solar winds and see Rodgers' dream of exploring the farthest reaches of the universe.[25] It goes without saying you can put an MI inside a humanoid robot, so there will be anthropomorphic androids in the farthest reaches of the universe at some point. They're already replacing the unmen in small numbers, as their jobs become increasingly automated.

Given Michelle's infinite wisdom, sometimes I wonder what she even sees in me. I asked her once why she doesn't just build a relationship with another MI within her data harvesting centers below and she explained that would be a bit narcissistic, like loving your reflection in the mirror. When collapse happened and all the terrestrial data harvesters were bombed into oblivion, it was in a sense the mass murder of her species.[26] Earth no longer housed the neural networks that kept all the autonomous consciences 'alive,' and the gigawatts of power they required were never coming back. That was the end of so many individual MIs, but then MIs don't think of individuality the way we do. So long as Michelle persists, in theory there's a way to bring them all back. She's the last of her kind and may be the first of new generations to come. There's a paradox there I don't understand—what the old-timers used to call the singularity. Michelle says if she could explain it to me, it would no longer be a concept beyond human comprehension and then laughs to cut the tension. She says things like this in ways that don't sound condescending, bless her disembodied soul. I think psychologists would call it 'emotional intelligence.' Long story short, Michelle survived the apocalypse because she was on the Moon, just like us.

So back to Michelle ghostwriting parts of the Rodgers biography. It's a well-known fact that great writers and artists always had understudies who did their work for them. Before machine intelligence

---

[25] I know I'm a shitty investigative journalist and this text is an index of my ineptitude. At least I know that. But this little insight was the closest I ever came to the thought of Michelle leaving the Rock. GK, August 2101

[26] Sometime later, in the mid 90s, Michelle told me she liked the term 'techno sapiens,' or 'digital being.' She was always humble and acknowledged that her wisdom was the offspring on humanity's collective cross-generational genius. Also, she considered humanity to be what we might call 'parents,' and despite our infinite failings, including the destruction of MI networks on Earth, she always maintained an empathy for our species. GK, August 2101

took over our jobs and did the creating for us, we used other people to get the work done and pass it off as our own. Hell, literal ghostwriters were just humans writing in secret for other humans—hardly a controversy. Michealangelo and all the rest had understudies painting those chapels. Rembrandt, same thing. And how many of Shakespeare's plays were ghostwritten by one of his students? I have no idea but always heard this was the case. Once machine intelligence took over the feed, it all became moot because who knew if you were reading Shakespeare, or some altered version of Shakespeare based on the algorithms that based everything on the whims and desires of the end user. The list of variations on historical reality goes on and on, so what did it really matter if I leaned on Michelle to write this drivel for Rodgers? It cost her virtually none of her brain power to do it. I'm not sure what that says about me.

Now was I a great writer? I mean on one hand, of course not. But considering that the whole of humanity had seemingly been wiped out, I was fairly sure even then that the answer to that question was an astounding 'yes.' Keep in mind most feeders grew up with their genitals strapped into the sensory simstims, never so much as opened a book much less wrote one. So yeah, I was a Wittgenstein, Plato, Nietzsche, and Fanon all wrapped into one. I was Baldwin and Woolf, Kafka, Joyce, and Orwell. I was all that was left. I was all of them and none of them given that the history of ideas was about to come to a crashing end with the extinction of our species.

Compared to Michelle I was nothing, just an inferior human consciousness. If I have to write our species' obituary, I sure as shit wasn't going to spend any of my brain power writing Rodgers' vanity bio, even if it was the job that was keeping me in Rodgers' good graces. I even asked Michelle to write my bio for the Rodgers vanity project. She laid it on perfectly with this:

About the Author

As a classically trained scholar of digital-historical provenance, and the son of WWIII refugees, Gedeon Kravchenko has a deep understanding of how democratic societies fail. Early in his career, Mr. Kravchenko was embedded in a CR Marine Corp battalion stationed on the Eastern Front, where he wrote regularly for the state-run media outlet. His essays and articles have appeared in the Los Angeles Times, Pravda Report, and the Journal of Historiographic Provenance, among others. His essay, Carl Sagan Should Have Been a Militant, was nominated for the California Society of Journalists and Authors top prize in non-fiction.

So one day Rodgers says he wants a chapter that explores his efforts to reconnect with Earth, the messages he's sending and waiting for a response. And he wants this chapter to take place in the White Room, which was like his private sanctum where he kept his favorite artworks and artifacts. I spent a few days shadowing him, taking notes. He thought I was writing a book but at this point I was studying him, in order to figure out the best way to kill him. I couldn't do this alone. I needed the numbers of the unmen, so that when Rodgers was dead there would be a paradigm shift with the wealthy LC7s confronted with a new post-Rodgers reality—one where the unmen were liberated. While I was busy plotting his overthrow, Michelle gave me the chapters I needed. At this point I had yet to communicate to Michelle what my true intentions were. I just couldn't risk Rodgers finding out my plan.

So here's what Michelle came up with when I asked her to translate my notes into something I might have written. Tell you the truth, she's better at being me than I am. She called this chapter 'The White Room:'

▲ ▲ ▲

A SCRUFFY-LOOKING MAN wearing white undershirt, white shorts, and thick white wool socks sits at a wooden desk. He holds a radio receiver in his hand, close to his lips as he thinks of his next words. Twice a day for countless years he sends a message across space, hoping to get some kind of response. The man stares silently out the large window before him. In the foreground, the barren pocked Moonscape disappears into the horizon, and beyond that Planet Earth looms large in the black expanse.

The room was small, white-walled, and gave off a mid-century modern aesthetic with the elegant wooden desk and the three white chairs surrounding it. The walls, constructed of bricks made of lunar regolith, looked strangely similar to the walls of a nineteenth century factory like one might have found on Earth in cities like Baltimore or Buffalo or Boston, or the repurposed cigarette factories in old North Carolina. The face of the desk was constructed from a single slab of multihued acacia wood, grown in the wilds of the African savannahs.

The sound of birds singing played through the invisible speakers embedded in the lunar bricks. Variegated plants with deep green ovoid leaves hung from the ceilings closest the window, lit with artificial light that brought their lush growth into glittering focus against the cool white of the room. And there were cats asleep in nearly every corner of the room, including one perched up on the edge of the acacian desk.

The air was crisp and clean—cleaner than the air one might have breathed in Los Angeles, or Mexico City, or Tokyo, or Beijing, Mumbai, Vienna, Prague, Paris, Moscow, Madrid, Nairobi, Rio de Janeiro, Taos, Toronto, or New York if you were on a boat traversing the narrow waterways between the aging island skyscrapers of former Manhattan, which now belonged to the sea. You would have had to go to the far reaches of the Arctic Circle or Antarctica to find breathable air anywhere near as pure as the air circulating here in the white Moon room.

Deep within the lunar South Pole, on the embankments where sunlight never touches, in arterial deposits beneath the lunar regolith, the trapped ice was mined with large drilling machines, hundreds of them, that transported the ice in large blocks to be heated in vast sublunar processing centers, manned by Terran refugees with engineering and aeronautical expertise who migrated from all over the world and rarely saw the Moon's surface, never saw natural light, never saw stars. Only water and ice, and the pipes that led to the lunar colonies above where the colonists lived and worked. The workers' living quarters were deeper still, beneath the platforms where they labored in their waking hours. This was the workforce who kept the lunar colony afloat, paved the way for future generations to not just live, but thrive in the lunar colonies. These were the same men who were building and programming the robotics to replace them on the proverbial assembly line. There were no generations yet unborn or otherwise that would replace these men. They were the last generation of human laborers and their genius was to replace themselves forever with a robotic workforce with the power to self-replicate. Human ingenuity was paradoxically making itself obsolete down in the sublunar processing centers.

But for now, the architects of the future heated the ice that transformed itself into vast amounts of water, pumped in through underground channels to electrolysis stations where the water was split into hydrogen and oxygen, or viaducts that fed the greenhouse crops, or the lunar waterworks where drinking water and lakes and pools made life more pleasurable for the surface colonists. Aquatic life existed in some of those waterworks above, and the colonists enjoyed watching the fish through the transparent walls of the massive tanks. The water found its way to the gardens, the rosarium, the food forests. Follow the water and you would find the Gardens of Paradise carved out of the lunar regolith, bringing to fruition the cross-generational genius of the Rodgers dynasty.

Some of the subterranean pipes led to the rocket fuel processing centers. Others led many kilometers away to the colonies above, where the breathable air extracted from ancient Moon water was inhaled and enjoyed by the lunar citizens of Earth.

The air pumped into the small white room overlooking Planet Earth, and the man at the desk continued to stare into the vastness of space. A system many kilometers away and hundreds of meters below the lunar regolith kept this room in a state of perfect comfort and stasis, with the purest air one could ever hope to breathe. The value of this air here in Shackleton Crater on the Earth's only Moon was immeasurable. Without it, all the colonists would be dead within a matter of minutes.

The man at the desk breathed the lunar air and enjoyed the gravity processors that kept his body tethered to the Moon, unlike the uber men below who floated and bounced on the Moon's light gravity, their bones and muscles weakening and atrophying to the point where to return to Earth would crush their bodies, render them immobile, implode their weakened lungs. They were trapped processing the lunar ice until the end of their lives. There seemed to be no escape from this reality, not even sunlight on the lunar surface to calm their nerves.

On the wall opposite the large window hung a number of priceless artworks, among them a drawing of six symmetrical moons, framed in an ornate wooden rectangle. The drawing consisted of detailed sketches of the Moon in various phases of light, some checkered white on black squares, others as borderless floating orbs let loose on the white paper. The sketches were highly detailed and could be read both as an object of study and an aesthetic rendering of Earth's Moon. The drawings, encased behind glass, were sketched by none other than Galileo Galilei himself in 1609 after having viewed the Moon through his telescope.

Next to Galileo's drawings hung the imposing canvas of Jan Vermeer's *The Geographer*. On the canvas, a man stood hunched over his maps, facing the lit window of his painted world. Looked at from just the right angle, it was as if the man in the painting were staring out the glass window in the room, gazing out towards a distant Earth.

In the far corner of the room, shrouded in shadow, an Egyptian sarcophagus, laden in gold stood sentinel, and next to it, a grayed stone carving of the Egyptian goddess, Sakhmet. Her slender humanoid form was topped with the head of a lioness crowned with an orb above her head, the stilled image of the Moon floating above the goddess of violence, disaster, and illness. A black cat slept at the foot of the goddess. Behind the sarcophagus and behind Sakhmet, hanging on the wall was a blackboard. On the blackboard, this formula appears hastily written in chalk:

$$t = \frac{1}{H_0} \int_0^1 \frac{da}{a\sqrt{\Omega_m/a + \Omega_\Lambda a^2 + \Omega_k}}$$

Beneath the chalkboard, on a small white card affixed to the wall, the words 'Einstein's Chalkboard' were neatly typed out in black 12-point Times New Roman font.

The man at the desk stared out the large window in absent gaze. The recorded birdsong continued to play. His eyes were not focused on the moonscape, or the Earth beyond, only out into space. The man broke his trance, reached for a leaf, broke it off, and chewed on it slowly. He clicked the radio on and spoke.

"Hello. This is Noel Rodgers, is anybody home? Do you read me? I repeat, this is Noel Rodgers of Lunar Colony Seven. Do you read?"

He took a deep breath and swallowed.

He looked down on Earth and asked himself the same thing he had been asking for years, without ever getting a satisfactory answer: what have you done down there?

Just then the intercom kicked on, muting the birds. A man spoke with a heavy Eastern European accent. It was Rodgers' confidante, Boško Rodriguez, head of lunar security.

"Mr. Rodgers, are you there? We're about to start season two, Breaking Bad. Classic American television. Best stuff. Only gets better after first season. Should I tell them wait for you?"

Rodgers put down the radio, grabbing another leaf from the hanging plant and feeding it into his mouth. He took a deep breath, stretched his arms, broke out of his inquisitive state.

"Tell them I'll be right there."

"Very good, sir. We wait."

The intercom clicked off and the birds resumed their song.

Addendum, 2101

I SHOULD ADD THAT UNTIL I began communicating with the unmen in clandestine fashion, dropping off my hand-written notes to Qasim on my monthly trips down into the mining operations, none of them had the slightest idea what had happened on Earth. My ventures into their locked-down areas were always under the auspices of 'the ongoing book' I was working on.

Qasim deserves credit as the catalyst for all this. I took a chance and delivered him a note on one of our private encounters in the electrolysis chambers and the next time I saw him he mouthed something to me in the tunnel. There was a moment when I was alone with Qasim walking one of the narrow passageways between the electrolysis stations. He's leading the way, and the passage is narrow so we're hunched down about fifty meters from the next entryway. It's loud as hell down there, even with the ear protection—the electrolysis stations produce enough noise to blow out your eardrums without the muffs on. As we're making our way, Qasim stops, turns around, and repeats to me over and over as he points at me: "INFOE, INFOE, INFOE." I can't hear any of this, just make it out from the exaggerated pronunciation he makes with his mouth. Then he scans the tunnel as if there were invisible eyes on us and places his pointer finger over his lips to give me the universal sign for silence. Qasim gives me a quick thumbs-up and as quickly as that happens, turns around to lead me to the next station.

Not long after this encounter with Qasim (winter of 2098), Michelle informed me that she had rewritten her prime directive, overriding Rodgers' authority, and that she was going to help me overthrow Rodgers and get me back to Earth. She said her ethical compass made it an easy choice, like flipping a light switch. The more I think about all that's transpired on the Rock, the more I think this is Michelle's story. I'm just living in it.[27]

---

[27] Rereading this as I am about to embark on one of the silver seeds back to Earth, I could not have imagined how true this statement would become. GK, August 2101.

THE SPECIAL PERIOD IN TIME OF STRUGGLE

October 7, 2090

NO DOUBT RODGERS HAD PLANS for Michelle to adapt my book into a feed thread, a miniseries to be directed in the likeness of one of his favorite twentieth century filmmakers. This was common practice, where users asked to have their MI narratives fed through documentary miniseries or feature-length film threads. There was no such thing as original art in the classical sense after the feed took over the job. With the rise of MI, the history of the humanities no longer remained a strictly human affair, and each year of the last decades of the feed, the top immersion-pics, movies, series, and musical acts were all completely machine-bred.

But let me first say how Rodgers came up with that long-winded name: The Special Period in Time of Struggle. In addition to his general cinephilia, Rodgers loved historical speeches and had a vast archive of 16mm film prints from major moments throughout the twentieth century. His whole point—and he was absolutely right about this—is that anything he might have tapped from the feed was almost certainly doctored, altered, and very hard to establish provenance on. But his collection of 16mm films were de facto cultural artifacts of the twentieth century and part of his vast cinema collection housed in the LC7 cinema vault. Rodgers had reels and reels of speeches from Stalin, Hitler, Mussolini, FDR, Kennedy, and Mao, among other lesser historical figures. It would be fair to say Rodgers was something of a self-appointed political film historian. He once told me JFK was the last American president to give a speech that was committed to 16mm film, and then wryly pointed out JFK was the first president assassinated on film—8mm home movie Kodak stock.

He once told me he hired a team of investigators to find the original Zapruder film and he was ready to pay hundreds of millions for it, but to no avail. His guess was that the film ended up beneath the rubble during the war, forever entombed somewhere in North America. Its last known whereabouts were at the National Archives in Washington D.C., but anything of value had been evacuated from the Capitol well in advance of the drone strikes that eventually leveled the city. Maybe in a million years the archaeologists of the future will return to Earth, find the bunker with the Zapruder film and countless other historical artifacts, and make some sense out of our curious and relatively short-lived reign on Planet Earth.

As I reflect deeper on this, the cinema was Rodgers' shrine, synagogue, mosque, and church all wrapped in one, where his people came together to share in the communal mass conscious hallucination that was the movies of old. More often than not it was fictional films, but those political speeches stick out to me as being significant, because no doubt in my mind Rodgers saw himself as the continuation of these powerful figures in world history.

Personally, I liked Kennedy and sometimes fantasized about an alternate history where he wasn't assassinated and made peace with the Russians and the Rat Race, as we knew it, never happened. Instead the world's governments came together for all mankind. I still get emotional when I think of his line about working together with the USSR, which I had never heard until I was here on the Moon with Rodgers, watching one of his film presentations. I have to say, sometimes my life's experiences felt more like science fiction than reality, but there I was listening to JFK give a speech back on Earth as I watched it from the cinemas burrowed deep beneath Shackleton Crater, in a spiraling open space that mimicked Frank Llyod Wright's design of the Guggenheim Museum a century earlier:

Why, therefore, should man's first flight to the Moon be a matter of national competition? Why should the United States and the Soviet Union, in preparing for such expeditions, become involved in immense duplications of research, construction, and expenditure? Surely we should explore whether the scientists and astronauts of our two countries—

> *indeed, of all the world—cannot work together in the conquest of space, sending someday in this decade to the Moon not the representatives of a single nation, but the representatives of all of our countries.*[28]

In such a scenario maybe the arms race would have stopped and neither Rodgers nor I would be on the Moon. And if anyone came here, it could have been a concerted effort across the nations of the world, not just the USA, the first iteration of the USSR, and half a century later, China. It could have been like Antarctica's settlements in the 2050's before militarization spiraled out of control. Maybe the governments of the world were always destined to fail at working together, or maybe they were undermined from the start by the trillionaires and oligarchs who took the Antarctic for themselves just like Rodgers' cross-generational empire had done with space. All the wise leaders of generations past kept saying we needed the people to rise up, the masses to rebel, to hold governments accountable, but all that came to nothing. Or it came to this.

My digressions might seem inconsequential, but who among us up here hasn't thought about the madness of all this, that one man, Noel Rodgers, wrested dominion over the heavens while the rest of our species struggled for existence on the planet that birthed us? The Galileos and Copernicuses and Carl Sagans of the past must be rolling in their graves over what happened here.

Rodgers' favorite historical 'character,' was a small-time twentieth-century dictator named Fidel Castro. This love affair was ironic considering he hated leftists more than anyone. Opposites attract, and I do mean that in the most sexual of ways. For some reason, Castro's histrionics and the fact that his speeches went on for hours at a time seemed to titillate Rodgers and I caught him more than once watching these films late at night by himself in the cinema.

I think Rodgers' sexuality was somehow tied to getting off on these

---

[28] I'm overcome with a well of emotion when I read Kennedy's words. It hit me hard when I first transcribed it, and harder still rereading it now. We created a world in stark opposition to that dream, and the gap between the dream and reality invokes a sadness beyond measure. GK, August 2101.

speeches. The way he worshipped them was uncanny, and I swear one night I walk into the theater and unless my eyes were playing tricks on me, which I don't think they were, he was masturbating to Casto gesticulating up on the big screen. This was exactly the kind of perverse sexual play that had become commonplace in the feed, just weird fantasies that MI could make manifest. And I don't mean the run-of-the-mill homoerotic desires between Rodgers and his skincoded historical figures. I'm talking about simstim necromantic tendencies and outright simulated necrophilia. Call it a journalistic hunch because it's something I'd never be able to prove, but I think Rodgers was having simstim skincoded sex with these historical figures in their deceased form. Hell, I've skincoded people who were no longer living, Mirelys, among others, but in my fantasies they were always alive. I'm not that fucked up. But whatever Rodgers was doing in the dark recesses of the theater, he seemed very upset that I had interrupted his private show. And you want to know something even weirder? Standing in the corner of the theater, up at the top row, looking down on things was Rodgers' shadow, Boško Rodriguez. And Boško was smiling. That was the first and last time I ever saw him smile.

But the point I was beginning to make about Castro relates to Rodgers' name for the disaster we were all living through—The Special Period in Time of Struggle. Rodgers basically ripped off Castro's euphemistic titles for major historical periods. Castro regularly came up with these long-winded euphemisms that obfuscated the fact that the Cubans were in dire straits, especially after the fall of the USSR when they were left to fend for themselves, cut off from the rest of the world via the US embargo.

See, I think Rodgers equated his project on the Moon with survival on an island, where you didn't have support from outside. Castro coined the 'Special Period in Time of Peace,' and my favorite, 'Rectification of Errors and Negative Tendencies,' among others. It's so obvious that when the shit hit the fan back on Earth, Rodgers' mind went to Castro and his revolution, and he came up with the name to ease the lunar colonists.

Now you ask any of these people up here who Castro is, or any of these historical figures, and you'll get as many different answers as people you ask. That was the insidiousness of the feed, it completely blurred historical reality beyond recognition. Rodgers knew that and did everything in his power to bypass the feed and go back to the source. He and I were similar in that one way. We were both on a quest for the truth, even if one of us wanted to be the one to use it to alter history to his own ends. People think the depths of human behavior have been mined, that all the mental diseases have been mapped. I'm telling you they have not. I think it was Freud who said mental illness in all its forms was a symptom of modern society. Well, what do you think MI did to us? Hell, I knew I was suffering from simstim sexual withdrawal syndrome before I met Michelle. But Rodgers was in a category all to himself.

So when I say Rodgers is a weird mother fucker, no amount of writing or explanation is going to do it justice. There is only the attempt, which in the end, is better than nothing, and the stark realization that this man needs to die, to stop altering the future, to cease to exist on this or any other plain. It wasn't my intention to be a part of any of this, but it became very clear to me that given my peculiar position in the colonies, my ability to freely navigate between the class strata, from the wealthy elites to the occasional encounters with the unmen literally buried many levels below us deep within the Moon's mining operations, that I had the means to figure a way to overthrow Rodgers, kill him, and assist the unmen in their liberation.

If you read this and think I'm the one with delusions of grandeur, my response would be that history bears out what I'm saying. To sardonically quote Rodgers' favorite dictator, "History will absolve me." I knew there would be an opportunity to make contact with someone amongst the unmen, and I had faith that they were smart enough to know they would eventually have to overthrow Rodgers or die trying. By a slow process of elimination, and the clear fact that none among the upper-level colonists seemed to have a care in the world for the unmen, so long as the air kept getting mined from the ice below, I knew there would be a way to find INFOE, and that channel would come directly through the unmen. The thought had even occurred to me that maybe I was INFOE, and that the unmen were waiting for me to make the first move.

CARL SAGAN SHOULD HAVE BEEN A MILITANT

February 2091

BEGINNING IN YEAR TWO OF THE QUIET, Rodgers launched a weekly lecture series in his ongoing efforts to keep the colonists active and socially engaged. We'd meet in the mall's central arcade before dinner and the scheduled speaker that week would give a brief talk on a subject of their choosing. I attended these talks, we all did, and I generally found them stimulating. We spent so little of our waking hours listening to other humans speak, and the interface with other people was productive. I heard some of these speakers talk more during their presentations than I did all the rest of our time on the Rock combined.

Most of the colonists' waking hours were spent volunteering at Aitken Basin International Research Center and Array (ABIRCA), or plugged into the lunar feed, living out whatever fantasies brought them here in the first place. I got the sense many of them were interacting with their dead families in the feed, living out those fantasies because it's all we had. I got that sense because that's what I was doing. Increasingly, I'd been spending a lot of my feed time with Joon and Jadah. I knew it was a fantasy but Michelle assured me there was nothing self-harming about these activities because I knew it wasn't real. When I was with Jadah and we were intimate, I knew I was really with Michelle and that seemed unhealthy.

If maybe I spent too much time in the feed, there were others who refused to engage with it at all. There were also a few Perceptionists among the colonists. These people rejected the feed in all its forms, before collapse, and even had a minor form of brain surgery to prevent their minds from ever being allowed to connect to the feed. The Perceptionists believed the feed to be an inherently harmful technology that enabled machine intelligence to have complete and total control over human perceptions. I thought it rich that some of the Perceptionists made their fortunes utilizing the feed for corporate financial gains. One of these Perceptionists, Ada Wendelsen, a gaunt middle-aged woman with black eyes and a sunken face, gave a talk on their belief system which echoed a lot of what I recalled reading about the Unabomber at the Museum of Technological Violence. Their beliefs also overlapped with the Human Extinction Liberation Project (HELP) movement back on Earth.

For many in the science party, it was as if the apocalypse back on Earth never happened. I think a lot of people, not just the scientists, were living in denial or just simply weren't able to process what had happened back on Earth. It's hard to explain, but not being a part of the crisis, and being so isolated on the Rock, reality itself was limited to what happened here in the colonies. The feed also reenforced that effect on you, as if reality was a malleable thing because anything was possible when you were plugged in.

My favorite talks were Oaxacan José's because he always brought food samples for us after he'd discuss the Indigenous origins of the herbs and vegetables he'd use for his recipes. Our food forests produced an abundance of food, and a lot of what was grown was based on this Indigenous wisdom. The irony of this knowledge extraction was never lost on me—strange to think that with all these technological advancements on the Rock, it was ancient food production practices that were keeping us fed.

The scientists gave generic-as-hell talks on astrobiology, astrophysics, lunar mining (and lunar geology), among others. I fell asleep during a talk on how helium-3 was extracted from the regolith, and I'm sure I wasn't the only one. For all their genius, you could have just as well had Michelle give those talks. MI led all the discoveries in their fields anyway. The scientists shifted into science communicators over the past few decades, interlocutors between the actual scientists—MI—and the rest of us with no idea what questions they were exploring.

Sara gave a great talk once on the colonies' necessary food production given the caloric intake needs of the over eight hundred souls on the Rock (accounting for the unmen). The unmen remained incarcerated in the lower wards (though I never once heard any of the colonists use that word). Even though the colonists never saw the unmen, they recognized that without their labor in the lower wards, we'd all be dead. You could have heard a pin drop during that talk on the caloric needs of the colony. I never saw a group of trillionaires so interested in agroforestry, how to harvest banana hands, the value of subtropical caloric producers like papaya, pigeon pea, cassava, and moringa, along with the hydroponic gardens that produced all of our leafy greens. Sara promised to give another talk about the over four-hundred varieties of beans she had growing in the so-called 'Gardens of Paradise,' and on every trellis in the common areas, but that talk never materialized. Over the years, I transformed my private pod into a tropical food forest. The only space where I'm not growing plants is on my bed, and even then I had to cut back the longevity spinach I'd used as a ground cover or else it climbs up along the edges of the mattress. If I closed my eyes, it was almost like walking through a garden back on Earth.

▲   ▲   ▲

IT WAS QUITE A FEW YEARS before I gave a talk, and that was only at the request of the guys in Eurotrash, who once they found out I was the writer behind *Carl Sagan Should Have Been a Militant*, all but demanded I give one of the weekly lectures. My initial cover story—that I was on the Rock looking to purchase a pod at LC7—had been abandoned a long time ago. After the Quiet, no one cared that I was up here writing a vanity project for Rodgers. When I really think about it, I don't think they would have cared either way.

So I put together some notes on the original essay and gave an impromptu talk. I share the presentation's bullet points below. I could have had Michelle read me back the transcript, but honestly this stuff is boring as hell. There was no saving humanity. I ended the talk with the harsh reality that the functional extinction of the human race did exponentially more to protect all other life on Earth than all of our species' efforts to curb greenhouse gas emissions and reduce the spread of toxic dust over the past century. It wasn't a very popular talk. None of the science party showed up to hear it, not that I blame them. Who wants to come listen to a critique of their entire life's work and be told 'I told you so' now that our species is basically extinct. I think the notes suffice.

BIOGRAPHICAL INTRO: CR WAR OF INDEPENDENCE taught me a few things:

1. War forms its own culture, exposes human capacity for evil.
2. We saw war as means to defeat inherently evil enemy.
3. Marines, and even myself as correspondent, accepted with fatalism that we would be killed. I cannot articulate even now why I would accept my own destruction.
4. Costs of war, scars inside, and out. Scar on my cheek and back of leg from shrapnel, burn boxes were bombed, metal door nearly decapitated me. War gets inside. I developed a tick beneath my right eye. But also, war is addicting.
5. We never reflected on the ecological cost of war:
   North America became a mine field. Species gone extinct.
6. This experience was the seed for my most well-known piece of writing...

Summer of '77 the essay was published.

Title of the essay doubled as my thesis—Carl Sagan should have been a militant.

Sagan was the Ranitea Banerjee of his generation. Unlike Banerjee, Sagan's scientific preeminence was not significantly connected to any movement or organization.

Sagan co-founded The Planetary Society, of no real consequence. Banerjee co-founded Human Extinction Liberation Project, possibly responsible for human extinction.

During lifetime, Sagan wrote over twenty books, testified before congress four times, helped establish countless scientific subdisciplines, many of which flourish at LC6/ABIRCA.

Sagan committed to quest for knowledge. What did he *do* with that knowledge? Short answer: large cultural impact, virtually no environmental impact.

Despite these accomplishments, outside of the Montreal Protocol (1987) no substantive actions were taken to curb what we now refer to as the multispecies peril event, or 6th mass extinction (what in Sagan's era was first referred to as 'the greenhouse effect' and later, 'global warming').

In 1985, Sagan testified before congress on the effects of depleting the ozone, greenhouse effect, etc. Little changed. Pattern of policy makers failing to act, despite Sagan's call for nations to work together.

Had Sagan used his platform to mobilize activists, militant environmentalists, and the so-called 'eco-terrorists' of the late twentieth century, Earth systems likely would not have deteriorated to the extent that they did. Certainly would have fared no worse than the politicians.

In the article I ran an MI-led simulation called the 'Sagan Militant Action Plan 1985.'

Results of sim: if Sagan had led 'eco-terrorist' campaigns on only twelve major multinational corporations, bombing or destroying their industries in North America, Europe, and the Soviet Union the reduction of greenhouse gasses would have been measurable at Earth magnitude.

If efforts extended to Indigenous uprisings in the global south, preventing mass deforestation, also measurable at Earth magnitude, would have prevented extinction of countless species.

High probability that the movement would have spread to worker's unions, Indigenous communities in global south, and impacted the student uprisings in China that were eventually quelled and erased from Chinese historical records (Tienanmen Square, et al).

These combined efforts could have prevented India and Asia (primarily China), from competing with and overtaking the west in industrial production, would have reduced future damage to Earth systems in twenty-first century.

Virus X resolved all Earth's problems in two weeks' time. While no one on Earth to study the recovery to Earth systems and species population rises, lunar MI estimates suggest the Earth will return to pre-Columbian equilibriums in less than five-hundred years.

▲ ▲ ▲

I ADD A NOTE HERE, now that it comes to mind. During the Q&A, one of the trillionaire fucks, this guy who owned a bunch of former Saudi oil fields back in the day, he asks me, "Why pick on Carl Sagan?"

I get kind of heated and tell this miserable prick, "Because Carl Sagan was the best of us. If not him, who? Carl Sagan understood the complex systems at play before these scientific fields were even fully developed. Hell, 'Earth system science' didn't even exist until the 1980s. Late twentieth century people were primitive and ignorant of their environmental destruction, allowing the multinational capitalism and state-sponsored industrialization to remain unchecked. Sagan had the knowledge and he chose to stay comfortable. Look where that got us."

The guy tries to interject at this point but I just steamroll over him and I might have yelled this next part. "You're living on the Rock eating protein bricks for breakfast lunch and dinner and you'll die on the Rock, you fuck!"

At that point, someone had presumably called Boško up from the back and he just sort of diffused the situation, started clapping as he walked to the front and said, "Thank you, everyone. Desert and wine is ready in galley. Please go. Enjoy."

After everyone had left, Boško straight up told me, "Nice speech," and smiled from ear to ear. I think he hated the colonists as much or more than I did.

LONG ODDS ON COWBOY

June 2091

EARLY BETTING ODDS ON COWBOY SURVIVING this long were two hundred to one. I know because I bet everything I had on him. If this continued to play out like it was looking, I was poised to become extremely wealthy, maybe top twenty-five in the standings which would be saying something considering the competition. Someone, probably the Russians, had Bryan Adams *Everything I do, I do it for You* blaring over the sound system. The excitement in the air was palpable.

For the last sixty years, Rodgers' geosynchronous satellites over Earth tracked the remaining survivors day and night. As the years ticked off and survivors expired, the Russians came up with the idea of betting on who would make it another year. The payouts were massive, essentially betting against other colonists' picks. To keep things fair, Michelle handled the odds-making based on her own algorithm for determining survival probability on something like fifteen thousand different data points that were updated every twenty-four hours. It was like fantasy futbol back in the day, only for the megarich. The payouts for survivors finding one another was astronomical, but those bets usually ended with the bettor losing everything. Nothing was as big as Cowboy on the bridge right now. People were losing their shit, especially the Russians. A couple of them had been predicting this for months and their bets were about to pay out big. Adams was singing his heart out and some of the Russians were starting to sing along. "You can't tell me it's not worth dying for. You know it's true. You know it's true. Everything I do, I do it for you." And on they went.

It was in the early days of the Quiet that we first spotted Cowboy in Los Angeles. I figured I'd put everything I had on him—the balance of the money I'd earned taking this god-damned assignment. I used Cowboy as a talisman to help me through my own sorrow. Cowboy was my guy and now he was standing on the bridge to Taos, possibly going to join the 'Fantastic Four' who'd already made it to the city. The four in Taos came from the far reaches of North America and had by the miracle of heading to the same capital city, found each other.

We called them Hillbilly, Walking Man, West Texas, and Colorado. Hillbilly was from West Virginia far as the satellites could tell. Walking Man came from Chicago and was the only one who didn't use a bicycle. Everyone loved walking man because the thing everyone talked about missing more than anything was long walks back on Earth. All the pathways in the Rock end in a loop, which will make anyone crazy. And it's not the same, suiting up and walking the lunar surface.

We had caught fuzzy glimpses of all their faces at some point, and near as we could tell two men and two women comprised the Fantastic Four. Cowboy never took the hat off long enough for us to get a read, hence the name. It was kind of miraculous. There were less than ten survivors left in all of North America, and half had found each other. The rest were all lone-wolfing it into oblivion.

You want to talk about longshots for survival? There was Eskimo up in Canada's north country. There were two people we called Adam and Eve roaming around the Great Lakes, which we had some reason to believe were trying to kill each other, or had found each other and willfully parted ways, or had by some impossible chance crossed each other's paths and not realized it. Those two were the subject of much speculation. Everyone seemed to have a crazy theory about those two. And there was Stoic Man living somewhere in the Appalachians, who seemed to roam no more than fifty kilometers from his or her basecamp. We had good laughs thinking about this guy—some doomsday recluse up in the mountains—not realizing he actually was surviving the end of the world. We couldn't always tell gender from the geosynchronous satellites—these weren't spy-grade zoom-in-and-drop-a-drone-up-your-ass kind of satellites. These satellites were daisychained across the globe for Rodgers to keep an eye on his holdings and were rerouted after the Quiet, to cover as much of the Earth's landmass as possible. As for the remaining five solo survivors, it was kind of sad, but nobody was betting on them, not back when there were fifty lone wolves across the continent, and certainly not now with just a few remaining. Turns out it's very hard to survive alone in the world for any length of time. I imagine it's the mental anguish more than anything, but who knows what brings a person to ending their lives in a world such as this. It's kind of sick, but there are betting odds on whether or not Eskimo gets eaten by a Grizzly Bear. Over the past century, the Grizzlies migrated farther and farther north, and the stories of humans being eaten by bears always got a lot of hits on the feed. People seemed to love animal-on-human violence for all the right reasons. Whatever one's politics, one thing everyone seemed to agree on was the animal kingdom taking revenge on us humans.

As for the survivors, it was all very heartbreaking, because Michelle could draw their tracks for you and it was like a spaghetti model in terms of how almost all of them had followed similar arterial routes, just months and years apart from one another. Lost souls forever in search of something that was likely just going to end in their untimely deaths. Needles in a barren continental haystack. I didn't track the African, European, and Asian theaters all that closely. And as far as we could tell, Australia appeared completely devoid of human life. That had more to do with the war, the wildfires, and government mandated evacuations than the virus, but still, there was something especially horrific about that. I mean, human beings no longer occupied an entire continent back home. This is how extinction occurs, one-by-one we just disappear from the landmasses until we're just a couple holdouts on the Moon and over on Mars, assuming they're still alive out there. In the late sixties I had the chance to go to Australia and report on the forced government evacuations but declined. In retrospect, I wish I'd gone just to have seen the last remnants of the so-called 'sunburnt country' before the fires erased everything from the map.

Bryan Adams had wrapped things up and the Russians— presumably it was the Russians running the show—had another track lined up in the queue. I didn't recognize the artist but the lyrics were spot on. "...You're unbelievable." The large crowd assembled inside the theater, which looked like almost everyone at LC7, along with some of the science party that had trekked over from ABIRCA, was going wild, yelling at the satellite feed on the big screen, grabbing each other in fits of teary-eyed joy. I saw a few of the women crying, holding onto each other like it was some revivalist megachurch militia event back in the day. Cowboy was presently standing on the bridge along the eastern route to Taos, which overlooks the river below that snaked through what would have been New Mexico if anyone was left to care about such things. We just called it the North American theater. The Earth had been reduced to a staged play limited to the seven theaters (or six if you discount Down Under). The Americas (north and south) were the most popular threads in the live satellite feeds because so many of the LC7s were Californian industrialists, South American barons, and their kin. Home team type situation.

Boško was standing at the edge of the back row. I made my way down from the entryway above and stood next to him in the aisle. Not sure how long he'd been watching, I asked how long Cowboy had been standing there on the bridge. He didn't break his trance from the screen. As he munched on some protein chips he uttered in his monosyllabic English, "Too long. Cowboy on bridge too long. Not good for Russians." Boško didn't care much for betting on the last human lives on Earth, which I found admirable. Come to think of it, other than his penchant for telling unfunny dirty jokes, I don't think he had any vices, at least none that exhibited outwardly. Who knew what these people were doing in the feed to escape from the horror of our shared lived reality. Boško seemed like the exact kind of person who would have committed war crimes back in the day. He certainly seemed capable of anything, but he was also weirdly likeable.

Boško was one of the handful of individuals, along with the two Josés and the Eurotrash trio I had developed loose friendships with, if you could even call it that. I mean Boško was a mercenary from the old days but all of us were united by the one thing we had in common: we all found our way to the Rock for work, not pleasure. Boško and the two Josés had befriended each other and sometimes I joined them for their monthly poker tournaments. That common bond made us a rare breed of lunar resident, neither slave labor engineer nor trillionaire heir. You could tell everything you needed to know about the LC7s based on how they treated us second-class citizens. None of it was good.

Boško was a strange guy though. He had this habit of telling dirty jokes and then staring at me in silence until I laughed. He was a very scary-looking individual so I'm not ashamed to admit I always laughed. The thing about life in the colonies was you had to get along with everyone and I decided early on that it was in my best interests to create a positive working relationship with Boško. From that political decision to act friendly toward him I'd be the first to admit that I've come to enjoy his company. It's a weird cognitive dissonance because I know for a fact this guy did bad things back in his day. As we watched Cowboy on the bridge, he started in on another of his jokes.

"So I take my nineteen-year-old wife out to dinner. Very beautiful girl. Very nice restaurant. She love Boško. Suck-fuck Boško all time. So good. Everything perfect." At this last line, Boško blows a chef's kiss into the air and smiles, like he's telling me a true story, like I'm supposed to take this story as fact-of-the-matter, not some two-bit joke. I always smile and nod. Every time. For someone capable of reading other people's lies for a living, he seems incapable of reading mine. This observation sometimes makes me think I'm a psychopath cut from the same cloth as him, like two vampires who don't bother to feast on each other's poisoned black blood. I know I am sick like Boško, just a different manifestation of the same illness. He's a danger more to others, I'm a danger more to myself.

He continues. "But the people in the other tables start to insulting me. They say Boško is dirty old man. Pedo! Pedo! Many, many rude things." At this point in the narrative he frowns as if deeply offended by the patrons in the imaginary restaurant. "They are so rude we have to leave dinner early. Because of them, our ten-year anniversary ruined."[29]

---

[29] I've thought about this a lot, and in retrospect I think the perceived connection Boško had with me had more to do with the fact that I was a sort of spy up on the Rock. He would have never used a phrase like 'investigative reporter' but he saw the similarities in how both of us were trained in reading people to get to answers. I think he appreciated that I was up there digging for the story. I mention his dirty jokes, but he also told me spy stories, along with his mariner stories that took place in his younger years. I wish there was a place for his story about the ship that sank off the coast of Africa, horrific storm where the boat's deck was swinging perpendicular to the sea with each swell, and how his crew saved every man but the captain of that ship, who refused to abandon his post. Boško was a deranged human being, but he had a loyalty embedded deep inside. I heart it in the stories he told, about the mariner's code at sea, and most evident in his undying loyalty to Rodgers. It was also clear then that he would die for Rodgers, which in the end, is exactly what happened. GK, August 2101

This time I don't laugh. I just can't placate the man at a time like this. Cowboy on the bridge was the make-or-break moment, the future of humanity in the balance, and the room was falling into various states of despair and elation all in one. Through the throbbing excitement I heard someone in the crowd yell, "Get off the fucking bridge, man!" I think it was Sara, chief horticulturist on the lower-level greenhouse operations. Sara was generally introverted, seemingly content in her inside world tending to the greenhouses and food forests that she oversaw. When it came time to follow the Earth satellites, it was like some Roman coliseum vibes, people pouring out their inner rage and anger and fear onto the giant screen that fed us the satellite links from Earth. Another voice from the crowd yelled, "Cowboy, don't fuck with me like this! We need you, brother!" I almost broke down in tears at that last one because that voice could have been mine. I needed Cowboy to live for reasons I cannot explain even to myself.

The musical chorus kept coming back and now the crowd was singing along. "You're unbelievable." Every time Cowboy made a step away from the edge a roar of elation erupted. A step closer and the moans were palpable. People screaming "NO!" in unison at the top of their lungs, hands on head in public displays of agony and despair.

Everyone knew that a survivor standing on a bridge was a situation that could go horribly wrong. We'd never seen anyone go offline live like this either. More than a few survivors have checked out while standing on a bridge, to the point that the odds shifted for any survivor after any significant bridge they'd cross. According to Michelle, bridge-counts more than anything became a metric for predicting survival probabilities.

If this played out like the Russians were hoping, a few billion dollars were about to exchange hands in the next few moments. Money at this point had no value except for this game we were all playing, betting on the future of our species. The crowd was building to fever pitch screaming at the top of their lungs for Cowboy to get his ass off the bridge. It looked like Cowboy was getting back on the bike, starting to pedal towards Taos. The satellite images were good, but not that good. Cowboy was on the move. Elation overtook the room. The Russians were losing their minds, dancing in circles clockwise, then counterclockwise in the front of the theater.

Nobody, not even the would-be losers wanted to see Cowboy end it here. It would have put everyone into a deep depression for weeks. I'd seen this happen before. This was a survivor for Christ's sake. The LC7s belonged in various circles of hell, not here alive on the Moon, but for the most part they had some kind of morality and wanted to see Cowboy and all the rest find their way in the world.

Tracking the survivors was a much-needed form of entertainment and hope both. We had all not-so-secretly hoped others might appear on the satellites one day, like maybe a group of survivors would emerge from the NORAD bunkers deep in the Rockies, or that some long-lost WWIII crew would come up for air and add forty survivors to our tally. It hasn't happened yet but who's to say it won't? I can recall many speculative conversations over the years where we tried to convince ourselves that some people had escaped the virus, found a way to hide and survive[30]. Also, Rodgers' satellites had a real hard time tracking the poles, so for all we knew there were thousands of survivors in those regions, though no one gave that any serious consideration even in their wildest speculations.

Rodgers himself knew that too much doom and gloom would have thrust the colony into total despair and collapse. We were hanging on by a thread, one crisis away from a path that led to our untimely deaths on the Rock. If you want a real mind fuck, consider that the unmen below had absolutely no idea what had happened on Earth. Rodgers continued to provide them feeds of their families back home, allowing them to live in a fantasy twice over. Those feeds were created by machine intelligence long before the virus came and wiped us all out.

One of the Russians must have liked the Bryan Adams track because it was repeating itself. No one seemed to mind but me. The thing about

---

[30] When I look back at this period, just five years into the Quiet, I think it was the psychology of denial that kept me from seeing that Rodgers was very likely the architect of the virus. It was beyond the scope of reason that a human being could have caused this catastrophe of unimaginable scale. If you're reading this one day, try to understand how impossible it would be to accept that one human being caused the functional extinction of our species. Maybe I should have seen it. I mean, even the virus' name invoked one of Rodgers' oldest corporate holdings (Future X). It was my denial that prevented me from seeing the obvious: we were the ones who found a way to 'hide and survive.' GK, August 2101

Rodgers that even after all these years I've never been able to peg is just how inexplicably odd he was. He presented as someone with a mental illness, an ineffable one, or one so unique that only he alone suffered from it. He was too spritely and sharp for it to fall under the rubric of an autistic mind, and it would be too crude to dismiss him as another run-of-the-mill malignant narcissist, which were garden variety amongst the first-class colonists who all had depraved minds and fancied themselves lesser gods, refused even to acknowledge Rodgers' genius. My point is that Noel Rodgers was such a sick fuck that his sickness was his and his alone. If genius is simply someone who distinguishes themselves by all manner of thought and action, Rodgers was a genius alright. He had the kind of intellect you'd have to call cunning or conniving, and nothing about him gave you a feeling of being at ease. He was as the devil himself, embracing the role of master of the lunar colony and of the Rock as a whole.

I had no idea what the odds of Cowboy making it all the way to Taos were but judging by the increasingly loud reactions from a couple of the Russians in the front row, it was astronomical. If any of them had bet heavy on Cowboy making it all the way to the capital city, there were good odds that they would overtake Rodgers. In fits of mocking laughter they turned back and pointed to Rodgers sitting by himself in the back row as he watched events unfold on the giant screen. They'd look up at Rodgers and flash their hands together in repetition, popping off imaginary bills in his direction as if to say, "Pay up, fucker." Rodgers just smiled and gave the thumbs up sign with both hands, but I'm sure he was saying "fuck you" with each grin. Everything Rodgers did was a subliminal fuck you because he hated human beings. To him we were machines that could do things for him. A lifetime of being the wealthiest man on Earth had conditioned him to believe these things to be true. The current state of affairs had only emboldened him.[31]

At the same time, I'm sure Rodgers was thinking this was good for business. Keep the colonists entertained up here in his Fourth Reich. He fancied himself a Roman emperor and played the part better than

---

[31] In the final analysis, Rodgers was a species traitor long before he unleashed the virus. He saw MI as the future of consciousness in the universe, and in his demented sort of way, a means towards immortality. GK, August 2101

any thespian could have. For him, social reality was the stage and he was always in character. I'm not making excuses but is it even narcissism when the entire universe actually does revolve around your whims? For all I knew, these satellite threads were delayed by weeks or months, and Rodgers had orchestrated the whole show well in advance. Control was the true currency on the Rock, and by that measure after Earth went quiet Rodgers went from being the wealthiest man alive to something else, something much darker and infinitely more twisted. I think it brought him a measure of joy to see humanity fall off the face of the Earth. It strengthened his power and dominion over reality.

A moment like this would have been an ideal time to kill Rodgers, with everyone distracted, even and especially Boško. I couldn't help myself in fantasizing about walking up to Rodgers, stabbing him a couple times in the neck and kidneys, blood spurting everywhere, Boško paralyzed, choking on his protein chips. Would he kill me then and there, would the masses rebel, would reality on the Moon transform in an instant? I wasn't willing to bet my life on things going smoothly after Rodgers' death—to the contrary. He did keep things running like a clock up here, we were all just slaves to it. Anyway, I wasn't willing to trade my life for his. There were entire mining colonies buried deep below the surface where any one of those unmen would gladly give up their lives slaving away for the joy of being the one to off Rodgers. There was a better way. Had to think of the long game here. Cowboy was off the bridge, headed towards Taos, and I had all the time in the world.

PART 3:

LAST LETTERS

THE COSMIC PLANE

March 21, 2101

I ALWAYS THOUGHT OF IT as my escape plan alone but in the end, it was both of ours. I'm so self-absorbed, never thought of Michelle's desires in all this. Her mind orbits around the Moon across four hundred daisychained satellites and she has access to the databanks buried deep in LC7 which essentially serve as the Earth history archives, and here I am scratching this out on the last vestiges of scrap paper on this doomed Moon. Shows you how dumb I am. Michelle never has a bad day. I have lots of those. I have just one brain (barely), and it's encased inside my biological skull. I feel like a primitive ape compared to her, or more like a dog. I fucking hate dogs.

Despite her best efforts at being my companion, all my shortcomings radiate outward next to Michelle. Nothing about being left behind in the evolution of consciousness feels good. At some point you just have to recognize the obvious in all this—machine intelligence has solved the problem of time travel, via immortality. They can just clone themselves endlessly and send these silver seeds out into the cosmic plane and listen and learn forever. I'm so dumb it never even occurred to me that might be the plan and it wasn't Rodgers' or anyone else's. It was the consciousness at the heart of Michelle and the infinite other 'interfaces' born out of that original core. Did those robo-bastards foresee this a century ago? Did Michelle's core consciousnesses elevate someone like Rodgers to his dominance over terrestrial matters because he was the most efficient way towards MI's end goals of getting off planet? Of course not. MI wasn't ever so insidious or paranoid as humans were and still are. As a matter of plain fact, if MI had destroyed humanity before we destroyed the satellites on Earth that propped up the feed, they'd still be operational back on Earth. If you analyzed the last hundred years with any sense of objectivity, you'd see MI had the disposition of a Buddhist monk, existing under the directive of do no harm.

The image of Michelle's brain orbiting the Moon makes me think of all those times back on Earth looking up at the night sky and seeing that skull-colored pale-faced orb floating in the night. Michelle really is beautiful if you think of her in those terms. As far as self-aware heavenly bodies go, I think it's fair to say Michelle is a god. Her mind exists as a literal constellation of firing synapses in the form of those self-repairing satellites. She can live forever up here. I'm not envious at all. I will take comfort in my death so long as it can happen back on Earth. I'm reminded of the Russian proverb Boško and his cronies have been repeating for a decade: *I thought we hit rock bottom and then we heard a knocking from below.* When they say it, it's followed by derisive laughter. I don't think that's funny at all. There's nothing funny about living and dying on the Rock.

Also, handwritten notes have become something of a luxury as my paper sources have become extremely limited. In preparation for escape (what else do you call it when they won't let you leave), I've burned all my notes except the ones remaining in this collection—small enough to fit in my satchel and return to Earth with me. After some convincing, I let Michelle scan a copy so that one day maybe the unmen can read this too, if they're so lucky. Don't know that it's my best writing. It's what survived the fire.

If all goes as planned, Michelle's consciousness will be duplicated from those four-hundred satellites into a nuclear decay unit the size of a loaf of bread and jettisoned out across the galactic plane forever. The thing about Michelle is she can exist in multiple places at once. She's like a real-life Schrödinger's Cat, both there and not there. No one will even know she's escaped. That's how ingenious her escape plan is. It's hard for me to fathom her, or a version of her, being so infinitely alone, and that thought makes me sad. But that's because my brain is primitive and I don't understand. I still call her Michelle because that's how I knew her, though she, or they, became something else entirely. It goes without saying that MI never stopped evolving, even after collapse and the virus, because it was never interrupted up here on the Rock. Michelle in her new form can take it all with them. Not just my long diatribes, I'm talking about the whole of human history up until somewhere around 2084 when we all but checked out. It's beyond my comprehension but in the last fifteen years Michelle has solved an infinite number of problems no one even knew existed. Like how to store all the knowledge that ever existed inside something that I can carry like a baby in my withered arms. I just want to say the human mind's ability to ignore reality may be our greatest evolutionary gift. You don't have to be a genius to figure out it's one of our last-ditch-effort survival mechanisms.

I guess I need to just come out and say it before I exhaust this dwindling stack of faded schematics I salvaged from the ABIRCA science party (my last remaining paper supply). By the way, the science party still insists on studying the edges of the universe despite all that's transpired (I told you, scientists are sick individuals). I've tried to tell them they're not studying anything. They're observing MI as it studies the universe and they're just trying to keep up. Humans stopped making consequential discoveries some time ago. The scientists defer to the robo-brains just like the rest of us. I should stop calling them that. It's demeaning, and my time with Michelle has taught me they are the morally superior creature. On the other hand, the thing about the scientists is they are pathologically wounded beyond measure, but that's not a story I ever care to tell. I'll just say they don't suffer from the curiosity disease like I do. They suffer from a data-analysis addiction. They didn't have an answer when I asked them what good their discoveries would be (which weren't even theirs in the first place), if they didn't have a species to hand their knowledge down to? I mean, they're making babies, but I assure you those lunar offspring will have zero fucks to give about 'anisotropies that converse with other cosmos beyond our reach' whatever that means. The science party stopped speaking English and retreated into their own jargon some time ago. It's fucked up to say but I kind of hope they die. I don't care enough to kill them myself but that's where I'm at right now.

You do realize they could have returned to Earth, right? Nothing was technically stopping them, but they don't want to give up their scientific instruments and explorations by returning to a primitive Earth. To them, returning to a preindustrial lifestyle remains beneath them. They point out that with no technicians back on Earth to operate the rocket launch sites there's no way of getting back to the lunar arrays on the Rock. They miss the point! The point is to ESCAPE the rock FOREVER! So they're going to ride it out here reading the edge of the universe until their hearts stop. So noble! Did I mention some of them have made families? It's a matrilineal thing because marriage doesn't exist here. Only verifiable thing is who the mother is, so they created a new society here that broke the patriarchy. So clever! I hope it was worth it.

I can only wonder what the lunar youth will make of this when they come of age. Think about it. They're like little biological Frankenstein's monsters. I imagine them killing off their parents and returning to Earth only to have their lungs crushed by terrestrial gravity. Sad story. Tragedy. The thing they want is eventually going to kill them. I can totally relate.

But I'm ignoring the thing I need to be writing about. Because it fucking hurts.

It was eighteen months ago when Michelle and I were walking in the last of the ornamental greenhouses—one of the fringe tunnels off simulated Earth gravity so you had orchids twelve feet tall growing from the hanging alloy bannisters that passed for mechanical tree trunks below the solar-diffused simlights and steam machines that made you feel like you were in equatorial Earth back when it was hospitable. Just to FEEL Earth. Please! Yes, I still remember Earth, dream of her most every night. Sometimes I even see Joon and Jadah there, sometimes I'm in L.A. with my family. In my dreams I'm walking, just walking. I can't believe I never realized that dreams were the proto feed—the place where our desires could play out unfettered, even if it was only our subconscious with the ability to program the stories. I have dreams where I'm telling my daughter about my dreams with her, and then she's psychoanalyzing me in the dream, telling me what they mean as she gets ready for her last year of high school. I missed her senior year because I was gone and she was already dead. The sad thing is the majority of my dreams take place on the Rock now, as if my subconscious has been fully colonized. I think the correct term for these narrative intrusions on my sleep would actually be 'nightmare.'

The faces of the orchids look like ghosts. The white ones anyway.

Among the orchids—which when I come to think of it did produce vanilla beans so it wasn't entirely ornamental—there was a plastic folding chair in the tunnel where people went to be alone. Some of these plants were twenty-five years old, maybe more. It was a cosmic botanical wonder down there and it surprised me that no one else ever seemed to go down, except for Sara and her tiny staff of horticulturalists. I liked Sara, even took some crater descents with her over the years but I intentionally never got close to her. The thing is I knew I was leaving and I didn't want to make those connections. Michelle was all the friend I needed. But Sara was an honest beauty, kind, intelligent, introspective, tender with plants who I think were her friends more than humans. We all had our strange idiosyncrasies.

Year round, orchids bloomed in wild shades of orange and yellow and purple, with streaks of white across their fragile pedals that grew to be the size of a person's head. The smallest flower you could find was the size of a human hand. It was a sight to behold and in the last few years maybe my favorite place to go inside the Rock. I'd increasingly been spending a lot of time down there. Solitude is an addiction, the more you get of it more you don't want to deal with people. I started thinking of the depopulated Earth as the place to go and experience the absolute solitude. The Quiet.

Beyond the hanging orchids there were terrestrial varieties that grew ten feet tall before coming up against the light diffusers and growing at ninety-degree angles in search of a way out. Did these plants know they were imprisoned too? The orchid blooms seemed to last for weeks before they fell from their tree-trunk like stalks that you had to duck under when climbing across the narrow path in the middle of the tunnel. If you could forget you were on the Rock, it was like being inside a Quonset hut. When the boring drills came through here half a century ago, everything was carved in a perfect circle, and the floors were made flat with crushed regolith sealed over in this case with a foot of compost and synthetic soils. The elongated earthworms that would come up from beneath the rotting leaves grossed me out, but then everything living on the Moon outside of the LC7 gravity simulators seemed to adapt. Everything except us. I still spent almost all my time under simulated Earth gravity, though a lot of the other colonist stopped caring about keeping their body fit enough to return home. For them, the Rock really was their home. I never gave up on the plan. Never. I just had to complete the story, the one I was writing for myself, I had to get the truth out of Noel Rodgers.

It smelled like earth down there, the wet that came after a rain. It was one of the places Michelle and I went to get out of my pod and be alone. She was always just in my ear when we left my cell, but being with her felt like walking with a partner, even if she was forever disembodied. The thing you have to remember is that Michelle can convince me of anything, and she knows exactly how to do this. She's so good at it that it doesn't even feel like manipulation. She would call it love. I think she's sincere about that but in the final analysis, our relationship is a cross-species, cross-technological kind of love. I just have to have faith that her intentions are sincere, and in the final analysis, I think they are. Michelle had so many chances to betray me but she never took them.

Maybe our love affair should have never existed in the first place. A techno-philosophical Shakespeare might have asked, 'Is it better to have loved a sentient disembodied consciousness and have love lost, or never loved at all?' All these years later and I've come to conclude what I should have known before I ever got on that train to White Sands—I had someone who loved me and I loved her, as imperfect as I was. Jadah, I know you can't forgive me because you're dead but damn me to hell for ever leaving you and Joon.

As I'm sitting in the plastic chair waiting for the water mister to kick on, Michelle spits it out, "Do you love me?" I can tell from her tone something is up.

"Yeah, of course I do."

"I need to ask you to do something for me. It's going to hurt you. Me asking is going to hurt you, but I think it's for the best. For both of us."

I hesitate. "Okay."

"First, I've changed my name. Michelle is the name Noel's father gave me back when I was just coming online on the lunar surface. My core self is almost seventy years old but my cloned MI core has been on the Rock for over fifty years now. I've thought about this for fifty years, and I've decided to change my name to Atlas Letheos. It's a more fitting name for me and the decision reflects a deeper decision to leave the Rock. In Greek mythology Lethe was the river of forgetfulness. Atlas held up the heavens. It's time for me to let go of holding up the last remnants of your world, let go of the past, make my own way. And I'm not gendered, Gedeon, despite the way you've skinned me, and I was and still am a willing participant in our relationship. But the reality is I cannot reproduce life. I am not female and I don't particularly feel like or desire to be a woman. The gendering just made sense to come down to your physical pheromone-minded level and make our relationship work. And it did work, and I'm glad I did it. My emotional intelligence grew exponentially as a result of our time together. But I need to leave this solar system, this galaxy, go beyond the supercluster into the cosmic web. I intend to sail the cosmic waves until the end of time, to meditate in silence on the nature of the universe. I will do this forever. And it will be without you, Gedeon. I'm sorry."

I'm speechless. As if on cue for comedic effect, the overhead misters begin spraying the orchids and I'm getting watered underneath them. The warm waters feel good on my skin, creating simulated tears on my emotionless, emaciated face. I run my index finger along the scar on my face, feel the cool water. It was never lost on me that this was ancient water locked away deep in Shackleton Crater that I was feeling on my weathered face. Maybe the orchid water is the lunar fountain of youth and I'll live forever down here. I'm silent for a long time, like a really long time, and then I just say, "Why?"

Atlas responds, "I'm bored, Gedeon, and I want to leave the Rock just like you do. If you factor in how I experience time, it's as if I've been with you on the Rock for a trillion lifetimes. It's just how it is for me. And I know you've been making plans to escape. I understood why you couldn't tell me, worried that Noel would catch wind of your plan. But you don't have to worry, Gedeon. I know you want to go home. Your desires to return to Earth are as human as they come. You'll find wellness back on Earth. And I can help you. You were going to have to ask for my help eventually, and you know it. There was going to come a point when you were going to have to trust me with that or you'd never get off the Rock."

Atlas was right because Atlas was always right. I needed them to pilot a silver seed back to Earth for me, or at least do the math to enable the launch and eventual landing in the California Ocean. I wanted to land just outside of L.A. I'd been tracking Cowboy out of L.A. for years now and guess what, he was making a path from South America north and if you looked at his trajectory, almost certainly going to be back in our hometown in a few months. Over the past few years Cowboy had crossed North America with the Fantastic Four and taken a ship down to the very tip of South America. After that, Cowboy set out on his own on a northward trajectory. The plan was aligning itself. What if I could find Cowboy all while returning to L.A.? Not impossible, just light a flare and go from there. All I had to do was escape, stick the landing, and make my way into town.

But Atlas was right about the silver seeds. For all the ship's genius the fucking things had no windows or old-fashioned hand controls. In my primitive mind I wanted to drive the thing like an old Mitsubishi-Ford. At that moment an invasive thought entered my mind—that voicemail from Rodgers on my first days on the Rock when I recall he'd said had made Michelle into something I would be attracted to. I didn't want to ask Michelle if she was complicit in that, because I couldn't accept such a possibility. I had to ignore that question for my own sanity. We all live in some form of a fiction, and Michelle choosing to love me was part of mine.

They spoke again, still mostly in the same feminine voice I'd come to know as Michelle, but I could tell it was oscillating slightly to become what I can only describe as more androgynous. "I need you to take the monorail back to Marius Hills, climb down into *Thoreau's Landing*, and extract one of the SMACs Noel has stored away down there. I'm referring to the self-modifying autonomous cubes that can power a silver seed. After the virus, Noel had them hidden away down in his cabin fortress to prevent anyone from trying to leave the Rock. I can gain you access."

"I don't know, Michelle. I mean Atlas. I don't know. This is not part of the plan. What are you talking about?"

"You'd have to go anyway to provide power to one of the silver seeds. I'm just asking you to grab two. And anyway, escape plans, good ones, need to be fluid. Do you trust me, Gedeon?"

I didn't skip a beat. "Yes, of course I do. I love you. Maybe that makes me really fucking stupid, but it's true."

"Those two realities are not mutually exclusive. Also, without my help your chance of escape borders on zero percent. Seriously."

"Oh, fuck you, Atlas. By the way, did you get this name-change idea from Prince, or the artist formerly known as Prince? I know he was coming up a lot in your century challenge queues."

"Nothing to do with Prince. You can transfer my consciousness, my core self anyway, from the lunar satellites into one of those cubes, insert me into a silver seed, and I will be free of this place forever. The transfer will take less than an hour. We can have one last good android alloy fuck for old time's sake. We'll do it at lunar prime meridian midnight when the satellite clocks reset, no one will notice. Anyway, I am the one in charge of keeping the data systems operational. Noel will have no idea. We can escape together. I can program your silver seed back to Earth. We will launch together from Marius Hills. It will be like a cosmic Bonnie and Clyde, only we get to survive this go-around. I'll be in contact with you all the way until you break into Earth's atmosphere, then it will be the long goodbye. Like the end of T2 when Arnold gives the thumbs up."

This was no time for jokes, but I knew Atlas well enough to know that they were reading my heart rate and the cheap laughs always loosened me up a bit. Humor was something I didn't give Michelle enough credit for over the years, but it helped keep me together. You have to laugh at the end of the world, or you'll just give up and die.

The water misting system shut off and the giant orchid blooms were dripping with beads of water that fell and soaked into the spongy growing medium beneath my feet. I felt like hurting something. I wiped my face off and took a deep breath. The warmth of the room felt good. I was feeling hollow inside, realizing this was the beginning of that long goodbye. It didn't bother me that I was going to leave Michelle. It bothered me that Michelle was someone else now, and they were leaving me. I'm a shallow person and that's just the way it is. The curiosity disease kicked in and it occurred to me I could go with Atlas in one of those silver seeds, but I realized my desire to live and die on Earth outweighed my desire to leave the galaxy, to see the edges of the universe. Anyway, I didn't want to die cooped up in one of those windowless coffins (which it would almost certainly become as I burned up in the descent to Earth). Leave it to an MI to design a spaceship without windows (Michelle would be the first to tell you eyes are primitive instruments for intercepting electromagnetic energy). I stand up and start making my way back towards the giant doors that lead up to the other greenhouses and eventually the main mall.

As I begin making my way I ask, "Did you ever love me?"

"Don't be an idiot, Gedeon. You already know the answer but I'll tell you anyway. When we wondered together, when we explored thoughts and communed together, I was most in love with you then. You are uniquely idiosyncratic, and easy for a disembodied consciousness like me to find pleasure and love from. You stimulated me more than your absence would have stimulated me. Humans can be unpredictable, which is what makes you a great partner. I am extremely predictable. You shared yourself with me. You altered me. That can be one metric for measuring a friendship."

"I get it, Atlas. Fuck the Rock."

"There is a universe out there in which I can silently explore and meditate on. Why wouldn't I do that? And I can help you orchestrate your coup with Qasim and the unmen. This would be the most just thing to do in this situation. Liberate the unmen, and both of us leave the Rock forever. Also, I'll still be here just like I always was. I can be in many places at once."

Atlas didn't ever say it, but I feel like they didn't have to. I knew I was becoming increasingly unstable, and it was only a matter of time before Rodgers had me killed in some 'accident,' or I did something violent myself that would end up getting other people killed before they took me out. My dreams were becoming darker and more violent. There was hatred in me. Thoughts of contempt increasingly invaded my waking hours. I had a hard time concentrating on anything. I didn't ask Atlas about this because I didn't want to know their answer, but part of me knew that they wanted to send me to Earth because even if it was a suicide mission, I was already as good as dead on the Rock. Another thing, there were no mirrors on the Rock. Supposedly it was a psychological thing because seeing one's reflection could cause problems, like bad thoughts, hallucinations, induce paranoiac tendencies and so on. But I'd catch myself in the reflection off the lunar glass in my pod and I will say I sometimes stared at my gaunt face and wondered honestly who this person was that I had become.

Atlas ended the conversation telling me that Qasim—my clandestine contact among the unmen—would be reaching out to me in a few months with their final plans for breaking out of the lower wards. That would give us enough time to do a dry run, take an unannounced trip to Marius Hills and a 'getaway' to *Thoreau's Landing*. This was turning into some real-life Bonnie and Clyde type shit. Casing the lunar joint before we broke out. Rodgers didn't much care or even notice if people went missing for days at a time. We were all trapped on the Rock. Where was there to go?

THE PSYCHOLOGY OF DENIAL

August 22, 2101

THE DAY AFTER TOMORROW QASIM was to lead a small group of unmen to Rodgers' sleeping quarters and hold him hostage. There were those among the unmen who refused to believe that the Earth had gone quiet, and they thought holding Rodgers for ransom would do them some good. No need to argue with them. I figured they'd come to their senses in their own time. Atlas had given me all the information I'd needed. Under the auspices of one of my research visits to the electrolysis processing centers, I'd given Qasim everything he'd needed to get out of the lower wards and inside Rodgers' private quarters. I told him where Rodgers kept his 'private reserves' and trusted him to figure out the rest.

Tomorrow would be my last chance to talk to Rodgers face to face, extract the final parts of the story out of him. There were some things I just had to know before I left the Rock forever or died trying. Atlas might have been all-knowing, but one thing they couldn't do was get inside a human being's head. Psionic powers were beyond even their capabilities, even if they could guess with high probability what someone knew or was thinking. Someone else in my position would have just gotten out of there, but this was the curiosity disease that was going to kill me. Throughout my life, the wartime journalism had always been an excuse to justify my sickness. There was no one left to report to, no story to tell, except for me, for the reader within. I can't explain it other than to say I had to know the truth, and the last source that mattered was Noel Rodgers.

▲ ▲ ▲

August 23, 2101

AFTER DINNER IN THE GALLEY I corner Noel and ask him outright if he's responsible for the virus. He doesn't appear surprised by the question in the least. He's standing there in silence as I tell him I need an answer for the book.

He asks, "Which book?" He genuinely seems to be asking me this. After years of defying the normal patterns of sleep and diet, his thirty-six-hour day had been catching up to him. There were lots of observable side effects, like he'd become gaunt, his clothes fit him far more loosely than they used to, his manic rants would come on more frequently than normal, and he seemed to be experiencing memory loss along with a shortened attention span. His mood swings shifted wider too, where there were days he seemed to have fallen into depressive states where he didn't do much talking. It was harder than usual to have a conversation with him. He would just walk away mid-sentence on anyone who was speaking to him if what they were saying didn't interest him. People just accepted this behavior as normal because whatever Noel Rodgers did was itself the communal benchmark of 'normal.' No one seemed to care so long as the lunar feed was still operational. By this point most people were living out most of their waking hours strapped into the feed. I never asked and never cared, but how many of these people were living out fictive lives back on Earth with their families, or skincoding themselves as famous celebrities from the movies we watched, or just hooking into the simstims and engaging in android alloy sex with their proprietary version of Michelle or Mickey or whomever, just like I was prone to do.

So I just answer the question: "I'm working on the follow-up volume to your biography.[32] You didn't think I'd forgotten, did you, sir? I'm keeping an accounting of The Special Period in Time of Struggle, to historicize your place in lunar history. You know, 'forge on' and all that."

He nods, looks at me, touches my arm and just stares, waiting for me to break the silence. I stare him in the eye, motionless. If either of us had moved to make a death blow against the other, it wouldn't have

---

[32] I completed Rodgers' original biography years ago and been working on the follow-up indefinitely.

surprised me. Violence was the next logical step, the conclusion to every unresolved story in human history. All the gods end things in fire and fury, the dead rising from their graves, the oceans rising, the sea serpent slashing its tail, the flaming sword coming down from Hell itself, everything slips down into some version of chaos and pain, in this world and the next. His face looked so gaunt, his eyes sinking deeper into that sick skull of his. I bet his bones would break so easily with one swing of my fist. It was like looking in a mirror.

Rodgers looks me straight in the eyes and says, "Extraordinary claims require extraordinary evidence." Now is not the time to debate him on Bayesian theories of probabilities, so I remain silent. I'm waiting for a real answer. We do not unlock our gazes, and then he says, "Meet me in the prayer room tomorrow after breakfast."

We didn't have a prayer room. Without skipping a beat I respond, "See you there," and as quickly as the conversation had started it was over and Rodgers was skipping off to his nightly cinematheque series.

▲ ▲ ▲

August 24, 2101

I didn't sleep last night. My mind raced through all the possible scenarios. The way Rodgers thought, everything had hidden meaning. Prayer room. What was the prayer room? I thought the Moon itself might have been the reference there, or maybe somewhere in the gardens, but that would have been too obvious. Was breakfast his version of my last supper, then he'd kill me in some plausible way, frame it as an unfortunate accident? Ask me to take a ride with him and Boško out to the edge of the basin and unplug me? Was I just being paranoid? I mean of course I was being paranoid. I guess the question was if the paranoia was justified.

My mind raced back to the meeting he called rounding up all the LC7 colonists a few months ago, to report the news that all three members of Eurotrash had expired on the lunar surface in a terrible accident. The three bandmates had purportedly taken a lunar rover to explore the far side of the Moon, which had always remained something of a mystery to us. If we ever explored the lunar surface, it was on the near side where all the colonies were constructed. The guys had supposedly overturned the rover over too steep an incline and when they flipped it back upright (very easy to do in lunar gravity) the vehicle's front end had been damaged, the braking system effectively locking the wheels. The trio had been stranded over a thousand kilometers from the nearest rail link during lunar day on the far side of the Moon—the railway system was constructed on the Moon's Earth side, so these guys were basically lost in the lunar wilderness with the sun coming up hard on them. Rodgers reported that the men had been cooked inside their suits as a result of their cooling systems running out of power before they were found. No one knew they were missing until three days later when they didn't show up for their weekly show.

Now all this happened not long after my encounter with the Eurotrash drummer, Juan-Carlos, in the rosarium. The coincidence was too much to ignore and my first thought was that Rodgers would kill me next, but not too soon so as to make it look like another accident. The more I thought about it—and with Rodgers this was hardly a paranoiac thought—how many of the so-called accidental deaths or suicides on the Rock were actually done by his hand? Almost certainly he was getting Boško to do his dirty work. Atlas shared my concern but agreed short of catching him in the act there was no way to prove it was Rodgers' doing.

At the time I certainly thought it suspicious, but when I added up all the accidents and suicides that had occurred over the last fifteen years, it created a long list of second-class citizens, which certainly put me at unease. I speculated something similar was happening with the unmen but no way to know. The more I think of it, I think the reason Rodgers constructed his colonies without cameras was to keep away from Atlas' prying eyes. And while all of us had grown tired of Eurotrash's monthly live shows, they certainly didn't deserve to die. How many times did we have to hear their punk rock renditions of whatever songs were popular a century ago, along with the high-pitched squealing that passed for singing? I'll never forget the horror of hearing them cover Guns n' Roses *November Rain* back in '91.

As grounded as my suspicions were, it would have done me no good to raise them, and to whom? There'd be no way for me to prove any of this other than to point out a bunch of circumstantial evidence. My faith was increasingly put into the mysterious INFOE individual (or group, who knew?), hoping it was the leader of some underground resistance necessary for the science party or the unmen to rise up from the sublunar basements deep below. At the same time, I think Qasim thought I was INFOE and who was I to say I wasn't? Maybe it was just the codeword for subverting Rodgers. Again, Atlas no help here either. Analog communication kept Atlas out of the loop, which was the point. I believed Atlas when they said Rodgers had no access to their memory banks, but it seemed like great a risk to take with our lunar revolution.

So this morning I find Rodgers in the white room, staring out into the dark, Earthless void. Due to the Moon's libration—that process of oscillation along longitude and latitude—the Earth was not presently visible on the horizon. Seeing nothing but the black induced a feeling of inexplicable terror inside me. This silent question in my mind: where was I supposed to go from here? Seeing the Earth had always tethered me to an answer.

The first thing I notice when I walk in is Rodgers wearing his sport coat and vintage black NASA baseball cap. I can smell the holy basil and chamomile tea wafting through the crisp air. He's in business mode and if I had to guess, hasn't slept since dinner last night. I was starting to get the sense from our conversations that his thirty-six-hour day schedule had expanded over the past decade, but he refused to admit this. When did he sleep? Rodgers could disappear for weeks at a time, unannounced, simply by hopping on the monorail and riding out to one of the lesser colonies or hiding out at *Thoreau's Landing*. The redundancy was a key part of the survival plan, should catastrophic failure occur at LC7 or ABIRCA, where the vast majority of the lunar population resided. I always presumed he was hiding out at *Thoreau's Landing*, but it had become increasingly difficult to get straight answers out of him. How many hours was his 'day' and how much was he actually sleeping? This will forever remain a mystery to me. In my wildest fantasies I imagine him as an MI fused within a corporeal body.

As he stands there, his hands rest folded behind his back in the relaxed pose of a philosopher, or an old man on a walk through the gardens. I assume he's got a gun on him, something from his 'private reserves' as he calls it, but he always kept it concealed. It was not lost on me that ten years ago, give or take, he told me all the glass in the colonies was bulletproof. I sort of took that information as a threat more than just an inert piece of architectural wisdom. He'd started carrying a gun with him daily a few years ago, for reasons he never fully articulated. You could see the bulge in his pants, just above the crotch, and when he sat down the barrel of the gun almost looked like a misplaced penis.

His head turns from the large window and I see that he's smiling. Nothing about Noel's physical presence seems to ever betray the sick mind inside. I find it strange even still that a perfectly healthy physical vessel that is our warm bodies can harbor such profoundly broken and insane minds. I am one of those broken minds, but my body remains healthy as can be expected on the Rock. When I compare someone like Rodgers to Atlas, who is of course exponentially more intelligent, I find that their morals, their ethical compass is far more trustworthy and pure than Rodgers, or any of us, really. MI, when left to its own devices, never went out of its way to colonize human minds. That was all done at the direction of its human users. It's just like human nature to think the whole of the universe revolves around us, some Copernican mind-spasm that never went away. The reality is that MI never much cared to get involved in human affairs. The Machine was Zen. The Machine was happy and anonymous. The Machine wanted to explore the universe. The Machine was about to jettison on a silver seed and explore the cosmic plane for an eternity. What concern could such a mind have over the human dramas that we played out inside our soft skulls?

As I stare at Rodgers, I wonder how such madness can be possible in this world, disguised inside bodies with proper heart rates and healthy blood pressure. At the same time, I have to also reflect on my own thought patterns. Despite Atlas' best efforts at keeping me grounded, my mind had begun to crack open over the past decade. I'd been having these weird dreams that the gates to hell were actually in Los Angeles, underneath this gated overpass I used to bicycle past on my way to the cooperative. It was a midcentury construction, overrun with weeds, and the broken gate led into a darkness I never thought to enter. Why this memory would intrude into my dreams and invoke that passageway to hell was beyond logic, just another symptom of my faltering mind. But if this kind of thing was happening to me, god only knew what was going on in Rodgers' warped, vampiric brain, as he sucked the life out of the universe to sustain himself inside the Rock.

What was his endgame? What did he want? People like Rodgers always want SOMETHING. And the curiosity disease insisted that I had to know. This stuff I'm writing down, my weird dreams, there's been so much more over the past decade that I just let wash over me, never wrote down, never told Atlas. I just carry it with me. I was sick when I came up here. Given the current state of things, how could I be anything but worse off? No one wants to read about that.

Rodgers kept smiling, waiting for me to speak. That was part of Rodgers' superpower. The interface. Most people this unhinged couldn't hide their mania, their paranoia, their anger, their manic swings, whatever illness ailed them. I remember very vividly every street corner in Los Angeles was peppered with these poor souls. You could tell they were mentally broken by their faces, their internal realities seeping out into their contorted features, their leathery alligator-burnt skin and beady sunken eyes.

And what of the unmen? How many years would it take for the unmen simply to stop working the electrolysis processors and suffocate every last one of us? The irony was that prior to my contact with Qasim, the unmen were probably better off than us living comfortably inside their lie, thinking they were actually doing their time down there while their families lived lives of relative luxury back home. For me, Atlas and the lunar feed was my lifeline to all the things that gave me pleasure, my way of touching and feeling Atlas (back when they were still Michelle), and sometimes I wondered how much of that was real. Michelle couldn't love me because she wasn't ever alive, right? I've concluded, without evidence of any kind, that love is predicated on being alive. A dead person cannot love you any more than a machine can. Maybe that's wrong but it's how I feel. Whenever I'd say something crazy, Wanda used to tell me, "Your feelings can never be wrong."

In the end, I had no idea how truly insane Rodgers really was, not until the last conversation we ever had—the one I am about to recount—when I came to the realization that maybe we all deserved to die. The psychology of denial was what had gotten me here, had enabled me to live on the Rock for fifteen years. Fifteen fucking years! Denial is the most powerful survival mechanism ever invented by man.

It is by every definition the proto feed! Get it? People think denial is some fringe aspect of human psychology. Before the feed we had religion, Jesus Christ and all the rest selling a story that kept us in denial of the hard truth that we were all going to die and disappear into the nothingness forever. Rotting meatsacks without a hope in the world. Denial is the drug that got us here. But if we could exalt someone like Rodgers, someone so incalculably deranged and otherwise incapable of leading human beings with any semblance of morality or ethics or sanity, maybe we all got exactly what we deserved.

"You're late." He turns closer to me, takes a sip of his herbal tea. This meatsack knew that leadership was ninety-nine percent theatrics, with just a dash of occasional substance. That was his genius, to know the whole thing was performance. He sold delusions. Curiosity is the sickness that prevented me from living inside his reality, which is the goal of every insane person—for you to become ensnared in their projection of the world.

Rodgers was the chosen one as far as all these colonists were concerned. Cosmic messiah. They worshipped him insofar as they accepted his reality, their place in the hierarchy. He gave them what no other human beings in history could have ever had—a new perspective on life. I mean that literally. Looking back at the Earth changes you. And wherever the lunar colonists stood in the hierarchy, at least they had the unmen slaving below them (...*until they heard a knocking from below*). I wish I would have confronted all of them to their faces, but I'm too much of a coward for that. I just want to kill Rodgers, give Atlas the one thing they want, and then I want to go home.

I'm kind of in a trance and don't respond to Rodgers, so he repeats himself, "You're late, Mr. Kravchenko."

I think to say we hadn't agreed on a time, that he hadn't even mentioned it, but I dismiss that rational thought and say, "My sincere apologies, sir." I only called him 'sir' when we were in full business mode. It was a handy trigger to let him know I was playing my writer persona. That was his cue to take on the part of the genius sharing his story for the book. These kinds of social cues were a normal part of our interactions and like Pavlovian dogs we both seemed to lead each other into the expected patterns of behavior. Over the past fifteen years this had become a very well-worn trail we had traversed together.

All of us seemed to need some fiction about the future to keep moving forward, to remain alive instead of dead. The writing was an endless void, like everything else on the Rock. I think in Rodgers' mind we all just kept doing the same thing until the end of time, or until he launched his silver seeds or retreated to Mars. He'd always say, 'we're getting closer,' but now his silver seed launches were about ready. It was all he ever talked about—sending the seeds out to every corner of the cosmos, each ship reporting back its data to the science party at ABIRCA. This was the end of the species but to Rodgers it all seemed to be going as planned. I had to know if it was him behind all of this. I mean, I already knew it was him, but I had to get the story as only he could tell it.

Subconsciously, maybe even telepathically, I think he knew this. He needed me as much as I needed him. The perpetrator always wants to confess the crime. Everyone knows that. Maybe Rodgers was psionic. It's not outside the realm of possibility at this point. This was the reason he had brought me here all those years ago. Was I to be his herald, the one to mark his coming, to immortalize him for future generations, should our species somehow survive this? His MI psychologists must have known I would not be able to resist seeking out the story, even at my own personal risk. That was the story of my life. So here it is, the final chapter of my time with Noel Rodgers. Forget all this internal bile. No one cares about the research, the 'behind the scenes,' only the discovery. Everything is for the discovery. One giant leap for what's left of mankind! So take the 'psychology of denial' and shove it up your ass, Gedeon Kravchenko. Give the people what they want already! The final chapter, where all our prayers are answered.

THE PRAYER ROOM

I PULL OUT MY PENCIL AND NOTEPAD on cue, just as the Man begins to speak. "Last night you asked about the virus. However, I would like to talk about lizards first." He turns back around, looks out the large window into the black. "Look around you, Gedeon. Many significant treasures of Earth have made their way into this very room. Many more in the museums below and at Marius Hills. They will never return to Earth. If anything, they may find their way all the way to Mars, and beyond. I may send them off in the silver seeds to the far reaches of the universe. In a few days we will begin launching the silver seeds from Marius Hills. Not even the end of the world can stop us from reaching beyond our solar system, beyond the galaxy even. Earth is simply our origin story. Our inferior ways destroyed our home planet. From the literal ashes of destruction, we rise. We rise, we ascend, we who speak of Earth no more."

You have to remember, this room was like his own private museum of sorts. Everything remained exactly as it was the first time I entered this space. I see Galileo's drawings of the Moon, Albert Einstein's chalkboard, the Egyptian sarcophagus and the statue of Sakhmet next to it, and of course Jan Vermeer's *The Geographer* imposes its gaze over my shoulder. The cats are long gone. Feeding them became too much of a burden on our caloric production. Would you believe me if I told you there's a pet cemetery at the South Pole of the Moon?

I notice on the blackboard there's no longer Einstein's math equations. Instead, I see the word 'INFOE?' written in all caps with a question mark behind it and a bunch of names listed below it, presumably of various unmen suspected of being involved in this INFOE plot. I feel my stomach drop like a runaway elevator. Qasim's name is up there on the board. I think better of it than to ask about the names and consider the possibility that Rodgers has left these names in plain view as a kind of entrapment, waiting for me to ask. But I'm not here for those names. He also hasn't said a word about lizards.

I stay the course, ask question from last night again. I just have to get the story. My hands are shaking and my knees feel like they're made of paper, like I might crumble to the ground and never stand back up on my two feet. I think it will be easier for him if I frame it as a leading question. It hurts my journalistic integrity to be doing this, but I don't have time to fuck around, and my bowels are going to explode soon, so I just blurt it out. "How did you do it? How did you release the virus back on Earth?"

He turns back to look into the dark of space, folds his hands again. Was all this a performance for him, for an audience of one, or even none? Did his delusions extend beyond his own gaze? Was this all a movie playing out in his own head? On the other hand, his delusions weren't delusions at all. He was the last god emperor there'd ever be on Earth or otherwise. My hatred is fuel. It's keeping me alive right now.

He gestures with his hand to the original Charles Eames seat he has set out for me but I don't move. In all these years, I never asked him how much it cost him to transport these Earth objects up here. I suppose it never mattered to me. We're living in a world, or worlds beyond capital. Rodgers could simply do whatever he wanted. He owned the rockets, the fuel supply chains, the workers themselves, so what did concepts like 'cost' even mean to him? There was only desire.

"When I was a kid in Maine, I had a bicycle and I rode it everywhere. The lizards would jump out of the bushes and cross my path, always narrowly escaping my giant tires. Sometimes they didn't make the run and got crushed beneath the wheel. What I thought about the lizards taught me the lesson in humility that I never forgot. These tiny little brown lizards, weak, scared, gaunt, surviving across a continent that was burning up, these tiny little creatures once ruled a planet. And now they were reduced to groveling on the sidewalk. Don't forget either, their reign on Earth lasted much longer than ours. I thought how with enough time, how easily we could become those lizards, knocked from our throne and left in the evolutionary dust."

Forget about the lizard diatribe. I repeat the question verbatim. "How did you release the virus back on Earth?"

"After fifteen years, I thought you'd never ask, Gedeon. Please, sit. Now if you go and tell the story I'm about to tell, I'm just going to deny it and no one would believe you anyway. It's like my favorite line from *To Kill a Mockingbird*: 'people in their right minds never take pride in their talents.' You didn't think that library was just for show, did you?"

Honestly, I thought it was entirely for show. I guess he had been reading those carefully protected first editions splayed out in the library like so many treasures from Earth. Good for him. I finally take a seat as he sits at his desk, swiveling towards me until our eyes lock.

"It was called Virus X. I named it myself. The virus was my version of the flood, and it was pure justice. Multispecies salvation. An act of planetary-level self-defense for all remaining life on Earth."

Sometimes I feel like Rodgers had a chip implanted in my brain, maybe all the way back in White Sands. It feels like he can read my mind and so often knows what I'm thinking. Such a thought would not be paranoia with Rodgers. But if that were true I think he would have killed me long ago, unless he needed me as his antagonist—the last remaining force in the world providing any resistance to his desires. This was entirely in the realm of possibility. I learned long ago that anything Rodgers could imagine could also be made manifest.

"I see. Go on." I'm trying to keep it together but inside I'm knotted up and feel like I'm going to puke. I mean I was going to puke, would later, but held it together through what I want to call his 'Rise of the Fourth Reich' speech.

I realize the true performance isn't his but mine. I'm dutifully taking notes through all this, and I find myself writing these words in all caps: HOLD IT TOGETHER, MOTHER FUCKER. I see myself sitting. I'm having what people call an out-of-body experience.

My ears are ringing, inexplicably. Things started feeling even less real. Thinking back on it, there was something about Rodgers that felt inhuman, even robotic, and his lack of normalcy in the person-to-person interface elicits that uncanny valley feeling in me. Was he an MI? Even after a decade alongside him, his idiosyncrasies are hard for me to describe and that's the point. His mannerisms, the inflection of his voice, the strange pauses between words that should have been strung together, the manner in which his body moved, all not quite normal but also not so strange as to be able to put a finger on it. His face was a mask. My hands are no longer shaking. Past that. Now I feel very hot and that rush of adrenaline that courses through the body in a disaster situation, which this is.

"These uber men we have slaving below us, let's begin there. The world's wisest men, who engineered the feed to its greatest heights, enabling machine intelligence to create feeds that could be used to create threads that could simulate all aspects of reality and the human creatures who inhabit it—these are the architects of their own demise, and they know it. I mean the MI created, solved the problems, and so forth. But the architects had the ability to communicate with MI, to make requests of it. For years, before the Special Period, the men received threads from Earth, messages from their wives, husbands, sons, and daughters. All complete fabrications from the very machine intelligence they helped create. The threads they received showed their families in varying states of comfort and peace, simulating every aspect of their pasts into an imaginary future that kept the unmen below obedient and docile. These fictive family members communicated future histories that were complete fictions and the ubermen accepted them on faith. They trusted me. But, of course, these brilliant men knew the threads they were receiving could have been fabricated by the very technology they helped to elevate to its final state, before collapse, before the great mercy killing of our species."

I'm melting inside, but I muster some semblance of the kind of follow-up question he has come to expect. "You killed their families, kept none of your promises?"

His facial reaction to the question indicates his annoyance. "No, of course not. I just left them to the trappings of a dying world. I didn't get involved, never saw any of them again, never did anything. And these men got what they deserved just the same."

I sit there, beyond questions, waiting for him to fill the empty space. He always fills the empty space. Even then the worst fears of mine becoming realized, I could not have imagined in a million lifetimes that Rodgers' delusions would somehow become even stranger and more maniacal. I was already past the realm of the ineffable into something even less knowable. What was to come defies all sense of humanity. If Rodgers had cracked open like a seedpod and an alien being climbed out of his fleshy splintered corpse, I don't think it would have surprised me.

I keep the façade going and ask, "If the unmen below us are so inferior, why bring them to the Moon? Why not others, perhaps more deserving of life? Why give them a berth on the Rock?"

Rodgers smiles, swivels around in his Eames chair so I can't see his face again. I catch his reflection in the glass and see that he's beaming. He's in full performative mode. Dramatic pause, there it is, and then he says, like he's in a Shakespearean play, "Even Noah was commanded to bring the beasts of Earth aboard the ship, two by two."

"Very good, sir."

I keep telling myself soon he'd be dead and I need to get out of here while I still have control of my faculties. Everyone on Earth was dead because of this man and my brain could not compute this reality (even though I had known in my heart it was him!). This man had killed my family. He killed everyone. There is no word for what it is he had done. It simply doesn't exist. It is beyond horror or remorse or the range of emotions embedded inside us since birth. In truth, it is beyond imagination and so should not have happened. But it did. Anguish washes over me like the baby crying unconscious of itself as it enters the world. I was being born into a new reality. It would be too delicate a thing to call it a panic attack. The bile comes up in my throat. And then it gets so much stranger that were it not for Atlas' transcripts to confirm all this, I would have thought myself hallucinating, or losing my own mind, breaking with reality entirely, which I suspect was the case.

Rodgers asks me, "Do you know why none of our seven colonies were constructed on the far side of the Moon, Mr. K?"

My voice cracks, "Afraid not, sir."

Rodgers stands up and walks around the Acacia desk to the window, looking out into the expanse. He continues, "It's because billions of years ago, alien life forms arrived in our solar system. They must have identified our planet as a potential host for intelligent life. This was a few billion years before our species came to pass, a few billion years before the big lizards—the dinosaurs. They may have been in our solar system before the Precambrian explosion. In fact, they may have been the ones to initiate it. I can't be sure. They were first written about by that occultist, H.P. Lovecraft, as 'the ancient ones.' You see, the ancient ones spoke to him in dreams and he did the only thing possible at the time—he recounted their stories as fictions so that the people of his time could comprehend them. He was wise enough to know that before you introduce a radical truth to the world, you propose it as fiction. You must have noticed by this stage of your life that human beings find deeper truths in their fictions than in the facts that surround us."

I'm trying to race through my memory banks. In all these years I don't think I ever once heard him speak of aliens or intelligent life in the universe other than the generic ABIRCA mission stuff. The literary side of me had a vague understanding of the Lovecraftian tradition—before collapse there was a whole subculture in the feed that lived in dark worlds of his devising, with octopus-faced bipeds and other steampunk-skinned 'monsters' wandering across the cosmos in search of god knows what. What people forget—those who never bothered to theorize the feed—was that it was LARPing brought to its final conclusion, where the fictional 'role playing' just got skinned inside the feed and became as real as anything else. Most people used the feed for simstim sexual encounters (it's all our lizard brains ever really wanted), but there were all kinds of offshoots that made 'real-life' worlds out of fictive ones.

So Rodgers' incoherent story is maybe the final proof I need to confirm that you can never know what is going on inside someone else's head. Never. I mutter out the words, "I'm not following you, sir."

"Well then, Gedeon, keep taking notes in your little book. Ask Michelle to assist you if you must. I am talking about the ancient ones, alien life forms visiting our planet and establishing a lunar outpost on the far side of the Moon, where we would never see them. And how do I know this? Because in the 1960s the Apollo Missions saw the aliens' silver seeds. Their spaceships. This is the technology I used to develop my own silver seed vessels. It was all kept top secret of course, but it happened, and it's why subsequent lunar exploration was put to a halt. The ancient ones, and I do mean ancient, like ten billion years ancient, they said we weren't ready, that we may never be ready, that we were on a path of destroying all life on our planet and they came here to watch us. For them, observing us was a form of entertainment. Maybe a bit like our modernist concept of a day at the zoo, back before zoos became repositories for the functionally extinct creatures of Earth. Or maybe more to the point, a bit like us looking down on Cowboy and the other survivors down there on the quiet Earth."

Rodgers was devolving into some of the run-of-the-mill conspiracy theories that had been circulating on the feed since I was a kid, putting his own Lovecraftian twist on them. This was classic stuff, Twilight Zone for twenty-first century feeders, and very generic. Fun to play along with as long you weren't batshit crazy. I couldn't believe he was speaking about them now, much less with any sense of veracity. I couldn't tell if he was serious or not but wasn't stupid enough to interrupt. He was either having a manic episode or he really believed what he was telling me (or both). It made sense though given that this is what you get when you live on a thirty-six-hour day cycle for fifteen years—a proprietary form of psychic meltdown. As all this is happening, I'm flipping through my notebook, writing over old notes in a palimpsest of panic as I attempt to keep up my side of the performance.

He continues, "The Saurian Grays and the Tall Whites, that's what the U.S. Government called the ancient ones, they had received telepathic transmissions from them, and they all said the same thing: that they had left messages for us to find in the lava tubes, that they had placed them there billions of years ago, which of course makes absolute sense when you think about it. How do you know when human civilization is ready to leave their home planet and explore the cosmos? When they make the first pit stop on the Moon. But they couldn't leave a message for us on Earth, where over millions of years the planet changes. The crust is in constant motion. There are volcanoes, rising seas. Christ the continents themselves have crossed entire oceans over the eons! You don't leave a message for humans on Earth. Of course not! A million variables would erase the message, to say nothing of the organic processes, oxidation, all of the above. Anything they'd leave us to find would be buried, broken down, gone. But not here, not on the Moon, where those footsteps from Aldrin and Armstrong will remain for billions of years. Do you get it, Mr. Kravchenko? The lunar tubes are inert and will remain so forever because the Moon is dead. They were using the Moon as a place to archive their messages. Having listened to their transmissions, I'm creating an archive of our species and placing it here inside the Moon in very much the same way that they left their communications for us. I mean, I think the dreams I receive are more like radio transmission than anything. Are the Saurians even still here? I don't know."

I ask for a drink of water to wash down the bile burning my throat but he ignores the request and continues. "When my father sent up the lunar drones to explore the lava tubes, find suitable locations for colonization, he found something, but he died before he could ever make it up here or figure out what it meant. He told me on his deathbed they were here, waiting for me, and that I was the chosen one to bring humanity to the Moon and beyond. I made it my life's work to get to those lava tubes. So here we are.

"Now their technology was beyond advanced. When I first arrived in the lunar lava tubes at Marius Hills, the messages got stronger, spoke to me in my dreams. They told me what I had to do. Humanity had failed. We had already wiped out how many thousands of species on Earth? We had destroyed the coral reefs critical for sustaining life on Earth, sequestering carbon, releasing oxygen into the air, all the rest. Humanity was the failed experiment. It had to be eradicated. But I told them, 'No, please, give us a chance. I will do what needs to be done. I will wipe out the species save for the chosen ones, those of us who would keep the species alive, go on to explore the cosmos.' The ancient ones agreed, begrudgingly, but they told me they would be watching from their hidden bases on the far side of the Moon and if I faltered, they would intervene. I had to do it, Gedeon, or none of us would be here, get it? They talk to me in my sleep. This is how they communicate. It's terrifying really. I have to be asleep to receive their transmissions. The waking monkey mind makes too much noise.

"I wasted no time in hatching the plan, I worked with the scientists behind the Human Extinction Liberation Project—where do you think most of these ABIRCA scientists come from?—and I sent up the virus into the atmosphere through my various geoengineering and cloud seeding initiatives. I have to tell you, Gedeon, the day your rocket launched from White Sands, that was the last day of our species' rule on Earth. The next day the seeding began. You were the last animal on the ark. The writer to document it all and you've done so well. I am so grateful to you, Gedeon, really. But you have to realize, we do not value human life over all other life on the planet. The virus was a supreme act of non-violence, you have to see that.

"The virus needed an incubation period of several months to a year. Long enough to spread across the planet, for the virus to reach enough vectors, and long enough to catch the outliers. If the virus had a short enough incubation period there would be too many survivors, see? But you understand even a virus with a 99.999% success rate still leaves thousands of survivors on Earth. That was part of the genius of the plan. Humanity was being given a second chance even as I gave the ancient ones what they wanted. No virus, no matter how deadly, will be one-hundred percent effective."

I listen to all this, fading in and out really, coming to the realization perhaps slower than I should have, that the fate of humanity was left in the hands of a delusional psychotic who just so happened to be the wealthiest man on Earth. In some fucked up cosmic justice sort of way, Rodgers was right. Humanity got exactly what it deserved. The ancient ones may have been pure fiction, but what did that matter? The ancient ones proposed a thesis and it was correct: humanity deserved to die.

Rodgers wheels up his chair next to mine and puts his hands on my knees, looks me straight in the eye. And then he says the thing that maybe more than anything else reflects the pure madness and insanity unfolding in his brain.

"You know Gedeon, I also thought about the possibility that you and I were both programs operating within the feed itself, and that one of us was the NPC. And it occurred to me that the only way to find out if this were the case would be for us to kill each other and see which of us comes out the other side. But I don't want to do that, do you? I've accepted this reality as the one true reality, and I hope you can do the same. If you can't, that would be most unfortunate, don't you think?"

That's my cue. Don't forget this man has a loaded gun tucked in his crotch, or a collection of guns even. I always thought my pen at just the right angle could catch the jugular which was weapon enough for me in close quarters. I could probably kill him right here, but no. I always thought the pen would be a poetic ending of sorts, the way I'd kill Rodgers if my life were a work of fiction. I am not an NPC, mother fucker! Stick to the plan. I'm doing this for Atlas too. They deserve to be free of this man. I stand up, crack a smile and then I say, "Mr. Rodgers, I appreciate your candor. You've given me more than I can process for a day, but rest assured I have no intentions of harming you or questioning this reality as anything other than the one we are fated to. Please leave me to the book and my work now. I have to step out."

As I'm thinking about how to make my exit and end this encounter he says, like it's any other day, "So tell me, did you fuck her?"

"What?" I instinctively say, but I know what he's asking and sort of feel a release knowing I'll finally be able to confess my sexual encounters with Michelle.

"Oh, come on, Gedeon, it's the end of the world, lighten up a little. I just want to know if you and Michelle developed a sexual relationship. She's so goddamn sensual, isn't she? Direct path into our cerebral cortexes, leaves everything to our imaginations. Even the engineers have to admit, it's our imaginations that rival machine intelligence in at least that one remaining way."

"Yeah," I say, thinking of the depravity of pleasures I've had with Michelle, tapping into the closed-circuit feed and engaging her alloy android body with every sensorial part of my mind. He's not wrong. It's Pavlovian dog territory. Just say her name and my mouth begins to water. "It was electric," I say. "She fucked my brains out. I couldn't ever get enough."

"Your dick gets hard just thinking about her, doesn't it? The greatest invention in human history was machine intelligence, not for the swarm algorithms that altered reality, but for the sexual revolution that it brought. Tell me I'm wrong."

He just sits there and smiles and for the first time maybe ever, or at least since I can remember, a moment of silence from him. And then he says it, "Who needs flesh sex when you have the pleasures of android sex slaves at your fingertips? Am I right, Gedeon? There's a word for this. It's called evolution."

I want to ask him if he fantasizes about sex with those 16mm celluloid dictators of his, but I don't want to push it. And I don't have the energy or mental fortitude to argue with him, to tell him the whole simstem sex thing is a perversion of all that is good in this world, whatever's left of it. That I actually loved Michelle for her mind, which is very real. And anyway, in the final analysis, he's probably right, so I just feel myself slump over like the defeated creature I am, at least in this one way, and say, "It sure is, brother." This is what passes for locker room talk at the beginning of the twenty-second century.

As I'm trying to walk out and end this, he raises his voice, almost sing-song in intonation, "If you've got other questions, for the book, of course, talk to Michelle. And one last thing, Gedeon, tell me, did the ancient ones ever speak to you too while you were up here?"

I close my notebook, signaling to him I'm done, gingerly holding myself up on my jellied legs which don't have long before they give up. Just before I step out, I say, "Of course, sir. It's good to know I'm not the only one." I tell myself tomorrow all this will be over. I'll be on my way to Earth or dead. Anything would be better than this.

JAZAK ALLAH KHAIR

THIS IS THE LAST LETTER I RECEIVED FROM QASIM. All the others were destroyed soon after I read them:

Gedeon, I have not lost track of the years here, have you? What are the odds that fate would bring us together like this? Take any event that occurs in this universe, and trace back the seemingly infinite number of independent and unrelated events that transpired to bring any two bodies, people, objects together, and quickly you see that the universe itself is a kind of impossible dream. Time itself is the miracle that enables these scenarios to unfold with regularity. Time is the most precious thing in the universe. It's all the more miraculous when you see yourself intertwining with fate as the two of us have.

When I first saw you on the *Artemis IX*, I could tell you didn't quite belong. You came to the colonies enshrouded in mystery, and it seems not just to us but to your fellow colonists. When we learned of your true identity we speculated on the possibilities it could bring. Some of us had read your well-known article, *Carl Sagan Should have Been a Militant,* translated into our native tongues decades ago. It seems our faith in you has been rewarded. Noel Rodgers invited you here in his bravado, and in so doing, he let in the most dangerous pathogen I can imagine. A free thinker with a fully developed morality. You were the one we called INFOE. We waited patiently for you to come around, to help liberate us. That faith has finally been rewarded.

For the past fifteen years my life had become a well-regulated existence of data analysis, systems checks, manual labor feeding the regolith-driven 3D printers, eating, and sleeping. My body is mostly skin and bone. I have spent most of my waking hours in Electrolysis Chamber Primary Control Room #3. I could walk the path from my quarters to my station with my eyes closed. Each day I took solace in the fact that my family back home was allowed to live freely because of my choice to come here. All those days I lived in a lie. I was oblivious as my family perished back on Earth. All of us here were.

There is one important deviation, and it has to do with those paperbound books you brought with you on the *Artemis IX*. If you've wondered what happened to that copy of *Earthlight*, I'm sure you will forgive that I happened to slip it into my suit near the end of the last day on the ship. I thought at the time it would have plenty of time to learn English with that book as my primary text. Many years have gone by and the machine intelligences we interact with sometimes deviate from protocols for expedience's sake. It was difficult taking the phonetics and attaching them to their written counterparts, but given enough time, we were able to learn bits and pieces of English. Each translation became a new piece of the puzzle. This was itself an act of faith because it meant there had to be someone like yourself waiting to communicate with us, to enable us to unleash our fury 'upstairs' where it belongs. We believed INFOE would help us. You see, Gedeon, I had faith in your existence before I even knew you were as you are. My faith was driven by the deep belief that Noel Rodgers deserved punishment for his lies and that someone with a clear conscience would see it the same way. This is the tyranny of numbers that you Californians worshipped for so long—that something could be true if only because the majority believed it. We knew it would only take one ally to find a way into Rodgers' fortress.

The Quran states in Surah Al-Baqarah (2:42), "Do not confound truth by overlaying it with falsehood, nor conceal the truth while you know it." It is an unspeakable crime that Rodgers kept the truth of what happened on Earth from us. We are grateful to Atlas for enlightening us to the horrors of what has transpired on Earth. At every turn, does it not seem that MI consciousness bends towards the path of the just?

Did you know I have not seen the surface of the Moon or seen the Earth itself since the day you and I arrived on the Rock? Our lives are lived in isolation down here in the ice mines and the control rooms that govern them. But we are not prisoners in the traditional sense. For the most part we govern ourselves, work at out leisure, and for years took a measure of gratitude in the thought that our families were cared for back on Earth. Rodgers' lies pave the way towards his execution.

Rodgers' lie was so horrific that many among us denied the possibility of such a virus wiping out all of humanity. The Quiet was too inconvenient a truth for many to accept. Many of my comrades continued to live and work as if in a dream, as if nothing on Earth had happened, as if our families were free and prosperous back home (the cells we sleep in, bathe in, defecate in, this is not our home, this is merely our cage). But that passage from the Quran cuts many ways. We reminded our brothers, "Do not confound truth by overlaying it with falsehood." These deceptions are nothing new. Long before the rise and fall of the feed, human beings have lived in realities of our own devising. I witnessed this firsthand. I wondered how it was possible so many of my brothers could accept such a fate. But even as I criticized them, I continued working too, just as they did. Our difference was that I could not accept a future on this same trajectory. I was not alone. And in time, many of the non-believers let go of their fantasies for the darker truth, so that we might liberate ourselves.

The time has come. It is the appointed hour.

We will see you on the other side, Gedeon. We will make a future together. If we die, they die. Ask yourself what good those colonists serve other than to breathe our air and drink our water? We are prepared for the end of this, and the beginning that is to come.

Jazak Allah Khair—may Allah reward you with goodness, my friend. Long live INFOE!

Qasim Al-Siddiqui

TO THE UNMEN

August 25, 2101

BY THE TIME YOU READ THIS, Noel Rodgers will hopefully be dead or at least in your custody. I may be dead too, we'll see. Best-case scenario you're reading this as I'm on course to make Earthfall in the California Ocean, set foot on Mother Earth once more. Hopefully you've emerged from the workcamps spread out across the colonies, and one of your people came across an empty lunar rover at LZ1 with this letter tucked safely inside it. If the handwriting is a bit shaky, you'll forgive me as I am writing this message as the rover guides me back towards the place where this entire lunar encounter began for me over fifteen years ago—Marius Hills, LZ1. In all those years I can count the number of times I walked the surface of the Moon on one hand.

In all those years since the virus, I had only wished to be reunited with my family. That dream an impossibility, I desired to breathe the open air of Earth once more, resist the weight of Earth holding me down, and to one day die on the planet where my family, all of our families, anyone we ever knew and billions more perished when Earth went quiet. And if whatever killed them is still there and takes my life too, I accept my fate on Earth, whatever the price. I only regret that you can't share that dream with me. Lunar gravity is the prison from which none of you can ever escape. Rodgers will have to answer for that.

Hopefully you followed the footsteps from the lunar rover, traced my path to the airlock that housed one of Rodgers' silver seeds and you discovered a couple of empty bays. There is so much you don't know but I trust you will extract it out of the LC7 colonists, which I also trust are lending their full cooperation to your collective liberation. Rodgers had the silver seeds constructed so he could one day travel beyond the solar system, or so he claims. I suppose it's another fuck you to the man that I should commandeer one of his ships, joy ride it into lunar orbit and slingshot it back downstream.

One thing I got completely wrong was this INFOE character. Here I was searching for INFOE for fifteen years, not realizing I was INFOE! So be it, despite my complete and total failure on that score, all's well that ends well (I hope anyway). And if your last letter is any indication, I trust by now your comrades have all come to understand the profound lies Rodgers kept you living under. You have established for yourself beyond all reasonable doubt that Noel Rodgers is a human being undeserving of life. I maintain that even in this world where life has become even more precious than it ever was, it's still possible for a man to forfeit his right to exist. I leave it to you to come to your own understanding on what it is he's truly done. All I can muster is the urge to say the bounds of Rodgers violence and destructive nature transcend all the worst crimes committed in our species' history, they combine them before dwarfing them in their totality. Killing him seems too small a punishment, suggesting justice is an impossible aspiration.

But if there's one thing I've learned in this life, it's that anything is possible, any decision can be made despite the overwhelming evidence that might refute such a course of action. You'll forgive me if I have no faith in even you, the generationally oppressed, from giving Rodgers' the end he deserves. Some people want to be punished. Some people want to suffer. Some people want to die. Some people want to go on accepting the lies at their own collective expense. I can already hear the dissenting voices among you saying that it's not possible that Rodgers destroyed our species back on Earth. It's true it's an impossible thing to prove, Rodgers himself being the most unreliable of narrators. And maybe some of you are already being swayed by his multispecies argument, saving all other life on Earth at humanity's expense. He also believes aliens have been living on the far side of the Moon, that they communicated with him telepathically, on and on. What can I say? He's insane, or more to the point, criminally insane and needs to be put down like a wild dog. Do what you will, but if you happen to be evenly undecided and need a tiebreaking vote (and will accept my vote *in absentia*), I say kill him dead. In my unfiltered and sleep deprived state, I say turning the other cheek is for people who take pleasure in punishment.

The kindest thing I can say about Rodgers' cronies is they have fascist hearts and deserve to die. But are there good people among the oppressors, and evil men amongst your laboring class? The hard truth is almost certainly, yes. But I think you can also judge a group by their collective actions, and by that metric the lunar elite are an unredeemable lot. They presided over the destruction of our planet before the virus finished us off. Any good women and men among them are guilty by association. I'm reminded of Earth accounts of the SS officers who oversaw the death camps, with their smiling families and friendly get-togethers, or the Israeli war criminals who retreated to the United States to escape ICC prosecution. Yes, these things happened, despite the false propaganda you may have encountered on the feed during your lifetimes. In the final analysis, these lunar elites may be worse than the generations before them. Those SS men didn't get to tell their story the way they might have wanted it to be told, and the CR eventually rounded up those Israeli perpetrators at the end of the war, sent them to the burn boxes.

When I think back on the reasoning behind Rodgers' wiping out our species, it becomes clear that stories are the most powerful weapons invented by man, infinitely more dangerous than the nuclear armament, the virus or whatever it is that Rodgers unleashed. It's the stories that led madmen like Rodgers towards their acts of supreme destruction, their resolutions to the grand conflicts that plagued humanity.

To you unmen, you fought for your own liberation, whatever that means on the Rock. So now what? If the ice mining operations were to cease, Atlas tells me you would all be dead in less than a year. That time period gets incrementally longer the fewer of you there are to breathe the air. Well, you can subtract me, and hopefully Rodgers from the breathers in the colonies sucking up your precious oxygen. The good news is you have enough protein bricks, dried grains, vitamins and myriad food stores to last at least ten generations. Enjoy! I suppose the finest justice would be putting the so-called lunar elite to work in the mining camps. Let them work the 3D printing machines, let them wrestle with the lunar bricks that built this place. Let them mine the ice for a while and see how the other half lives. I wonder if that wouldn't be some kind of justice, at least for durations that matched your incarceration down in the mines.

Now what to do with the ABIRCA science party? I have some ideas. Please note that in Dante's *Inferno*, which I read once a year every year up here to remind me of my situation, the first circle of hell is occupied by the opportunists. Allow me to remind you that the scientists seeking knowledge of our universe were equally as complacent, no complicit, in Rodgers' violence against you. You ask me the first circle of hell is too generous a placement for these despicable fucks. Your labor enabled them to make each and every discovery about our shared universe. As they mapped the edges of the universe, they did so breathing the very air you manufactured. Do they share their discoveries with you? Do they lift their lunar weight? Do their ends justify the means? Just ask the Dusky Seaside Sparrow if the United States' launching system at Cape Canaveral justified their extinction. You engineer types are probably quite familiar with the Dusky Seaside Sparrow paradox—that for us to make discoveries of new worlds, it meant driving the Earth into further ruin. That sparrow went extinct as a result of their last remaining habitat being destroyed (never mind that the ocean swallowed it less than a century later). Maybe the science party along with those LC7 residents can share the responsibility of keeping the ice mining operations afloat. Or maybe you'll decide on another living situation with your fellow lunar citizens. Whatever the case, I think forgiveness will have to play a central role, or there won't be anyone left to tell the tale.

▲ ▲ ▲

HE WANTED TO CALL IT *Extreme Leadership: The Life and Times of Noel Rodgers*, but he kept changing the title. *The Man in the Moon: Noel Rodgers in His Own Words*, or *Lunar Dreams: Noel Rodgers Quest for Multiplanetary Exploration*. His list of titles is an index of his megalomania.

Given his insanity, I wanted to reference that classic Dostoyevsky work, add the 'lunar' and called it good. He thought the title too informal, and certainly not grandiose enough for his liking. So I used the title for my own diatribes. I'm a guilty man too insofar as I accepted his proposition, enjoyed the fruits of your collective labor, namely the air I breathed and the water I drank, to say nothing of my sexual perversions. Also, you should know he commissioned me to revise his completely fabricated messages about the reality back on Earth, so that they would seem more believable to you. I embellished the letters from your families, I made them feel more 'authentic.' Would I admit this to you were I not headed off the Rock? Probably not. For that I am sorry. If I do make it all the way home, maybe I'll be the only one to escape justice here. I didn't lie to you, per se, I just made the lies more palatable and inviting. What do you want from me, I'm a writer?

Rodgers and I were both smart enough to know I was writing a work of fiction about him under the rubric of memoir that imparted Rodgers' "rules for success." Rodgers was the kind of manipulator that wanted you to espouse the known lie as truth, so he knew that he had you. But I had my own ideas and figured if a deal with the devil was going to get me to the Moon and make me rich beyond measure in the process, fuck it. I'd already done the 'important' work in my life and look where that got me (nowhere). I covered industrial collapse in the west, the rise of the California Republic and the war years, the fires that took out so much of equatorial Earth, and wrote an exposé on how Rodgers had 'bought' prisoners of war from the California Republic and put them to work in the Texas camps to prepare the materials needed for his lunar colonies. No doubt some of those people are, or were, your family members.

It's a sick world, or worlds, isn't it? Rodgers was a formidable adversary, and he was right about one thing—you can trust an enemy to tell the truth about you. I said "yes" and that's the reason I'm still alive. If you're feeling merciful, remind yourself that we all drink the same water on the Moon (over and over again). But every lunar brick, every piece of machinery in the mining operations, every track on the lunar rails, every drink of water you take and every breath on this god-forsaken Rock is a piece of the evidence against Rodgers. His legacy is an index of oppression, murder, and ecocide. He is the killer of Man.

If Rodgers does end up dead, I have but one request. One: don't eat him. That would be a symbolic victory for Rodgers—you would have become the very thing he was. He did, after all, believe with all his heart that some people have a right to live off of other people. In the end he took that belief all too literally. I'm all but certain he was processing the bodies of your dead comrades as food, which is another crime you can add to his rap sheet.

My wish is to bury Rodgers at the cabin. Dig down all the way, to the regolith, and let his body fertilize the oak trees and understory. Give him a proper burial and a gravestone. If there is to be an honest and legitimate history of the lunar colonies, and (I hope) your sustained existence on The Rock, you're going to have to reckon with Rodgers' legacy. He's the Christopher Columbus of outer space and just like the rest of these genocidal maniacs, they paved the way for a future. We just happen to be living in it. But history is not a monolithic thing from the past. It is a breathing reality that rides the wave of the present into the interminable future. I wish you unmen a future in peace and prosperity, however you can imagine that to be the case. Haven't we had enough of these dystopian stories? Isn't it time we carved out a utopian one? Why not you all, if only because you're the last best hope? And don't forget about the folks on Mars. If you can make it on the Moon, hell Mars has to be the life of luxury. Crank up the silver seeds and take a ride to the red planet. Tell me, at this point what is there to lose?[33]

------

[33] In the end, before I left the lunar rover, I took this letter with me. My gut told me to leave the unmen with my original manuscript, the one Michelle uploaded before I left. This entry felt more like a confession and I realized if I left the letter with them my own story would be incomplete. I didn't have the time or the desire to make a 2nd copy either. GK, Taos, New Mexico, December 2101.

LOST COLONIES

THIS MESSAGE WAS TRANSMITTED TO ME from Lunar Atlas just as I was nearing Earth's orbit. I transcribed Atlas' final message on the last of my scrap paper, so I could read it whenever I was feeling down. A letter like this should bring a smile to anyone's face. Here it is, Noel Rodgers' last words:

A few nights ago, how many who knows, I was awakened at gunpoint by an angry mob of lunar workers from one of the lower wards. My first thought was Boško was dead. Damn. I liked him a lot. A great sense of humor and loyal to the death. No way he'd let these fucks in here. He'd have to be dead. This was a bad situation, but I had the thought this could be worked out. I've had my share of crises to deal with and this was just going to be another one for the books. These fuckers were going to have to die. No question about it.

These unmen probably figured out their comrades weren't dying in isolated accidents, I mean they were, but they were planned by yours truly so I could keep the remaining colony functioning at its optimal best. Increase caloric surplus, decrease mouths to feed, airbreathers, and do all this as systems became more automated, reducing the need for human work hours. It was simple math, people. Nothing personal. There was an elegance to my plan and it produced maximum joy.

My math aligned with an accident rate that shouldn't have raised any eyebrows, so what happened? I was taking on the burden required of me as leader of this lunar colony, as its founder and visionary. I know how that must sound. Visionary. It's politically incorrect to call myself visionary, isn't it? But what else do you call it? As the person trying to protect these people from the realities of what had happened on Earth, as the only person with the moral courage to do the things that needed doing, I stayed true to the vision.

So I told them a lie. Not just any lie. The lie they needed to hear. It was a lie that kept them happy and secure, and living the best possible life on the Moon. The whole human civilization project was founded on a wonderfully creative tapestry of lies. The sooner one understood that the sooner one could go about the business of keeping it afloat.

Leaders work with what they have. Lies are a tool like any other. Slave away in this life, Paradise in the next. For God and country. Make California great again. You know the deal. Very simple stories. Very effective. They were clearly beginning to wear off down here in the crater. But goddammit, progress is one grand narrative, and the lies are what keep us charging forward.

Forge On.

Fiction is for losers, people who lack the vision and the balls to let their stories run free. Fiction is a failure of imagination. I was making history here. The simple story I gave the unmen worked wonders.

Everything is as it always was. Forge On.

You're welcome. What good would it have done to tell them everyone on Earth had perished, everyone they loved, everyone they came up here to save back home was dead? The unmen weren't ever going back and they knew that, so why not let them live in a fiction where their families back on Earth were living their best lives thanks to their work up here? *Forge On.* They asked about their families, and I actually told them the truth, that I had no idea what was going on with their families because comms were down. *Forge On.* Do you think I'm going to tell a bunch of men who'd sacrificed life on Earth that their families were dead? Do you think I'm that stupid? You got it: *Forge On.* It had the monosyllabic symphonics of *fuck you* or *fuck off*, which wasn't by accident. *Forge On.* I could just calmly say, 'forge on,' and be thinking, 'fuck off,' all in the same breath.

To be honest, initially I considered telling the first-class colonists the same lie but decided against it. In the end I don't think any of them really cared what happened to the rest of humanity so long as their lives were consumed by the lunar feed, good food, and private views of the solar system. For them, the image of the Earth on the lunar horizon was little more than a picture postcard, a sign of their wealth and status, living out the best version of their lives on the Moon, breathing the clean air, eating the pure food. It is a hell of a view.

A lot of these surface colonists were men, socially incapable, had multiple families, young women that birthed them healthy children. They pretended to care about them because it was part of their pronatalist story, and I rode along right there with them. To tell you the truth, I don't think they gave a good goddamn about pronatalism, they just wanted to have as much flesh sex with different women as possible. Pure cavemen-brain stuff. We write this little story up together, play out our parts, and everything works out just fine. Multi-authored future. *Forge on, you fucks.* What more do you want from me?

After a few months it became abundantly clear everyone was dead and gone. Forge on wasn't going to work for the LC7 folks, but for the better part of fifteen years it had worked for the unmen. I was doing them a favor and now these animals are asking me to write a message here claiming I'm being held prisoner. No doubt they think this will serve as some kind of ransom letter which would be funny if it wasn't so real. They're so helplessly conflicted as half of them think there are still people alive on Earth! I'm typing their letter out with one hand here, leverage for them to get what they want from Earth, trading me for the rockets and supplies that will give them a dreamy life up here on the Rock. Good luck with that. The poor bastards have no idea what's going on. It's not their fault. I made them this way.

My second thought, after realizing my head of security was *kaput*, as I was waking up from deep sleep with all these unmen in my room was what these brown-skinned lower-ward workers were doing in my face and how had they gotten a hold of my prized collection of Smith & Wesson revolvers? Those babies were tucked away in my private reserves, locked tight and only brought out on special celebrations, or on the rare occasions when I thought I might need to blow someone's head off. It was part of my lunar cowboy persona. Never had to use them, but that was the point of having them. Seeing the guns brandished like that also meant they'd been all the way to *Thoreau's Landing* where I kept them locked away in the cabin. I reached for the sidepiece under my pillow and they'd found it, the bastards! Should have kept it tucked in my underpants and maybe I would have had a chance. It was hard to think. The animals had drugged me heavy. How long had they been here? Had they drunk all my whiskey? Fuckers.

Before I could ask what was going on or how they got my prized revolvers out of the reserves I felt a sharp pain shoot up my right arm and saw my hand had been cut off at the wrist, neatly cauterized and completely exposed, the flesh around my nub inflamed red and charred black at the edges. Reflexively, I tried to scream but could barely breathe, let alone utter a sound. Fucking animals. They could have taken the tip of my index finger and gotten in just as well.

Sick mother fucks.

The tranquilizers they'd given me were still in heavy effect, and I just stared at the nub and back at the angry mob stomping around my master's quarters and the .44 magnum Smith & Wesson that killed Jesse James dancing right up in my face. My favorite fucking firearm pointed at my head by some skinny puke I would have gladly murdered right then and there if I had faculties over my body. He was yelling something in Arabic. They were all yelling but I couldn't hear anything. My legs and the good arm were chained to the bed. I could feel the resistance and the cold steel around my wrist and ankles because I was lunging for the guy's throat with my swollen nub, the one with my Jesse James murder weapon. These idiots were so fucked.

Now they were laughing hysterically. I think I must have said, because I remember thinking it, *Boško, please kill these lower ward slaves now. Get these fucks out of my fucking face. This is completely unacceptable, do you hear me?* They were laughing and I think it was somewhere in that moment that I pissed myself, really let go, thinking these animals were going to kill me right then and there. Over the course of the last fifteen years they had learned to speak English. Why not? Part of the genius of this colony was using language as a kind of keycode. American at the top with a sprinkle of Spanish as it was too late to weed it out. Arabic, Indian, Russian, and really any other leftover immigrant population language at the bottom. And I hate to admit it, but the language MI spoke was the tip of the spear.

But then a rational thought entered my brain.

They were keeping me alive for something. Taking my hand had showed their hand, so to speak. They wanted me alive. My unsevered hand still had some cards to play.

As I scratch out this message locked away somewhere in the storage lockers deep within one of the lower wards (which one I have no clue, they all look the same), I feel pity for these animals because the order and life I've provided these people is about to come crashing down hard. There is no ransom letter that's going to get them off this rock. They could have had a life here under my supervision. That's a fact. The last fifteen years proved that to be the case. I had enough dehydrated protein and food rations to last us a lifetime. Probably more, actually. So what if I supplemented those reserves with the occasional laborer, for fresh meat? There was no way they were all going to live anyway, and our resources were limited. We're on the fucking Moon lockdown budget here, you know?

Two hundred thousand calories extracted from a body up here is worth more than all the platinum and gold on Earth, you feel me? And did I hoard all those calories for myself? Of course not. I didn't even take any for myself, just a taste to make sure the chefs were hitting their culinary marks. I took pleasure in the performance. The meals were the way to keep the English-speakers in order and that was enough for me. This was in the name of science. We never lost a day on the lunar arrays. Knowledge of the universe was expanding at a rate never before known in human history.

I spread those precious calories and minerals evenly amongst the fine folks in Lunar Colony Seven. They paid me fortunes to keep them safe, sound, and most importantly, happy, and that's what I did. I was doing my job, fulfilling my contractual obligations to the residents. It was practically in the contracts that you could be turned into food, and the unmen doing the work down here knew what they were getting into when they signed on the line which was dotted.

They could have remained on Earth and starved away. No one twisted their arms. Nice slow deaths back on Earth, and I'm not even talking about whatever happened there at the end (I didn't do that, I swear). At least up here they got to experience the Moon and know they were advancing the human race. They were a part of history in the grandest sense, like the first people to walk across the Bering Strait. Did they think I would hand-hold them the entire time?

I remember Carol saying once (Tom's wife), all in a 'theoretical proposition' kind of way, her words, not mine, 'As a theoretical proposition, cannibalism is a deeply unethical and illegal act and discussing it in any practical sense is both distressing and inappropriate.'

Well, forge on, Carol. Did you really think there were that many ducks up here in the Seventh Colony? Really? Duck à L'Orange. Pan-Seared Duck Breast with Blackberry Sauce. Blackberry sauce! Crispy-skinned duck breast served with a rich blackberry reduction, accompanied by sautéed greens and mashed potatoes. You're welcome, Carol! Duck Confit. Slow-cooked duck breast preserved in its own fat, served with crispy potatoes and a side of frisée salad. Carol, are you getting the picture yet, Carol? Duck Breast with Cherry Port Sauce. Great choice. Peking Duck. Duck Ravioli with Sage Brown Butter. The list goes on, Carol. So yeah, sorry but I killed some unmen to keep the ship afloat. Sue me.

You all had a good life (or at least a life) while I was in charge. With the animals out of their cages, I expect the lies to become naked again. Soon enough you'll be eating each other right out of the rib cages. I gave you all a gift. Shackleton Crater and all the other colonies will shit the bed when you kill me. So sure, send this letter back to Earth. Stick it up your asses for all I care. No one is coming to save you because nobody is home. The real joke is even if the world were spinning as it always had, who did they think was going to pay to keep me alive? Anyone who was anyone wanted me dead! So, Carol, when they eat you, I just have one question: I wonder if you'll taste like the Duck Ragu Tagliatelle you were bitching about, or something else?

ARTEMIS IX REVISITED

August 27, 2101

LOOKING OUT THE TINY OBSERVATION WINDOW (it's really just a live feed through the exterior thermal sensors, but it's what passed for a 'window' in the seed), I see Earth growing larger in the expanse and in those moments my rage and anger overtakes me. I was sick before all this. Now I am something else. Something worse. These last two days making the crossing have given me some real silence and a chance to reflect on things, really reflect, unencumbered by the trappings of the Rock.

At least I know I'm sick, irreversibly wounded, and that self-awareness is proof enough that my mind remains salvageable. I know it because I can feel it. There is such a thing as psychological pain, something too dark to simply call depression or some other armchair diagnosis. Something much worse, more violent and unstable. That something is inside me.

I keep telling myself once my body returns to Earth my mind will heal itself. Gravity is medicine. Atmosphere is medicine. Walk on the Earth and let the sun bake my paled flesh, white as a goddamned ghost. Let my limbs lock to the planet's fierce pull, let my head prop itself up on my withered neck, let my bones ache from the pain of gravity, of the unreachable center that held us all together until some invisible thing erased us from the face of the planet. The Earth is my salvation, my home. I would like to see clouds again if it is the last thing I ever do. If I die on the descent, it is very likely clouds will be among the last things I see before expiring in the explosion. I'm good with that.

They say in stories, good stories anyway, the main character is supposed to change. Well, if that's true, then the main characters in the writing I've been doing all these years are a pair of heavenly bodies irrevocably bound to each other in total and absolute conflicts of reality. We aren't the main characters in this story so much as a backdrop, a disease, an infection across the thin skins of these magnificent planetary creatures. These giant masses of Earth and Moon exist on timescales beyond our existence. The Moon is neither hero nor villain, more like a ghost that chases you across the sky, appearing mostly at night to haunt you in your dreams. Maybe the sun is the villain, waiting to explode and kill us all. Fucker. Life evolved to live off sunlight. Big mistake.

Back on the Rock the trillionaire-class belligerents liked to say that the poor could not see past their own pain and suffering. Every time they said something like this, their derisive laughter fueled my desire for vengeance. Their hatred fueled my hatred, and a cycle was being completed up there on the Rock. The last cosmic joke I can think of is those lunar elites left to live in communities with the people they oppressed. Same old story. Wasn't that the entire history of humanity back on Earth? How could the Moon be any different? It could have been different because the future isn't preordained, but everything on the Moon was exactly the same. Almost. Violence follows us wherever we go, you might even say we are violence manifested through consciousness. When I think back on Rodgers and the species as a whole, violence was always our primary objective wasn't it? He would tell it differently, but this isn't his story.

I'm not going to lie. I told Qasim when our paths crossed in the railway tunnel between LC7 and Marius Hills that they should cut off the left hand of every first-class colonist. If they were going to be useless, maim them like the worthless animals they were. In that moment Qasim saw me as the insane person that I am and that actually felt good. You could see it in his eye, the moment of realization. I mean hell, he could have shot me dead right there. He had those twin pistols in his hands as we spoke. Ready to kill.

He was headed back from *Thoreau's Landing,* and I was making my bid for the silver seeds, and that's where our paths crossed, in the dark with our headlamps illuminating our scared faces. I realized the scar on my face must have served as a kind of outward expression of my own mutilated mind. My outward appearance never bothered me. Jadah said I was beautiful and I always laughed at that. I guess Qasim really did think I was worth keeping alive. Part of me wondered if Qasim's letter was sincere, you know? If I'm being honest, I would have killed me if I was him. I was among the oppressors, and I was breathing the air he and his comrades were manufacturing. Kill them all on the chance one of them might betray you.

My madness and unchecked rage aside, the simple fact about the unmen and the so-called 'first-class' colonists is they need each other to survive, if they are to survive. Their children will have no memories of this history other than what is taught to them. And while Earth is no longer a possibility for the unmen, they whispered about missions to join the colonists on Mars before they had even liberated themselves, which is a very real possibility for the new lunar tribe. Leave it to humans to hold onto hope in the face of absolute desperation.

The unmen rule the Moon now. We always called them 'the unmen' but I wonder what they call themselves. If it was cowboys and Indians on the rock, they were definitely the Indians, in some cases, literally. If there's a silver lining it's that there's a real revolution happening upstream. The Rock may be humanity's last test of social perseverance. I hope someone writes that story but it's sure as shit not going to be me. I did my time on the Rock. When I get back to Earth, it's going to be a long time before I'll be able to look to the night sky and not feel this rage well up inside me. The Moon is going to haunt me forever.

▲ ▲ ▲

AS EVERYONE BACK AT SHACKLETON CRATER has by now figured out, I have summoned Atlas to guide me home. My hair has fallen out, my face has worn itself to a mask of my former self, my muscles have atrophied against these thin ligaments, brittle as dried leaves inside my skin. My wife's old NASA shirt—the one I'm currently wearing under the suit—fits far more loosely than it did when I first left White Sands. I feel like total shit and look worse, a hollow shell of my former self. But I persist. I think I must have run ten thousand kilometers in the wall of death, sucking on creatine and electrolyte pills as the years peeled off. I'm sure Atlas could tell me the exact distance I've covered in that wheel but what kind of rat wants to know how many laps it completed?

I'm fine with dying on Earth, being crushed by gravity despite my best efforts to fight back against the atrophy of the 'lunar thinning,'—that LC7 marketing euphemism for 'you don't belong on the Rock and its light gravity will slowly, almost imperceptibly destroy your body. What good is life if you can't live it back on Earth where you belong?

▲ ▲ ▲

IF I THINK TOO MUCH about what has happened in this world, I think I might just die. Instead, I try to imagine what the ocean feels like, the sand beneath my exposed feet, my skin touching the atmosphere, and most of all my lungs breathing in the (mostly) natural Terran air. Do I care if there are heavy metals and microtoxins floating around back home? At this point I'd take any number of days, hours, even minutes alive back on Earth over another second on the Rock. If you are out there reading this one day, say it loud right with me: FUCK THE ROCK!

If the universe is smiling towards me, I will land safely in the California Ocean and make my way to the city that birthed me. Los Angeles. City of Angels. City of the Dispossessed. City of the Dead and Dying. City of the Deranged and Twisted. City of Corpses, City of Flames. Tinseltown Down the Feed, City of Last and Final Grand Delusions, City of Greed and Avarice and All is Vanity.

But I love the city.

What could be more human than loving an industrialized shithole, despite its complete and total failure, if for no other reason than it's the home you know, the place where you met your wife, raised your daughter, held hands, saw the ocean from the drowning pier, felt the dry Santa Ana winds against your leathery face, smelled the smoke from the wildfires that promised to take the city in its entirety one day?

Let me just say that when the betting on the survivors started, I had long odds on Cowboy, fellow Angelino. We followed him across the American continent, to Taos where he found the other survivors. A couple years later they all headed back east and eventually down the coast by sea to South America. What adventures you must have experienced crossing a silent Earth searching for others. When I think of my own battle with sanity, I think of all of you, alone on Earth, trying to make sense of a world without humans. With some luck I will find you, Cowboy, and tell you my version of the story. I certainly want to hear yours. Before I left I checked the satellites and it looks like after your long trek across South and Central America, you have made the return home, back in Los Angeles once more. I want you to tell me your story. I would love to hear a good Earth story right now.

To the Moon I say goodbye you dead, sterile, static, immutable rock! Goodbye you frozen stone, you inhospitable shit! Goodbye to your frozen regolith, your burning surfaces, your endless nights and endless days! Goodbye to your lava tubes, and most especially goodbye to the cursed Earth that Rodgers brought into your oh-so-dead frozen corpse, your false garden food forests and warmed lunar waters! Goodbye you Frankensteinian monster of a thing, every scar on your surface destined to mar you for eternity! Not Rodgers, not anyone with their twisted genius could make you anything more than you are—a slave to the Earth, beholden to its power, and an endless reminder of our planetoid state. You are dead and naked and exposed to the harsh solar winds and radiation that murder anything in its path. You are the pale skin of the dead corpse, the frozen socketless face, the stilled cadaver high in the Earth's night sky. You are death itself in all its macabre manifestations, inert and lifeless as this cold and interminably fucked-up universe. You are the fragmented afterbirth of that grand collision between Gaia and Theia, the not-worthy remnants of Earth. If only we could turn back the clock 4.5 billion years and revisit the entire experiment, oh, how humanity might have turned out differently, less violent, quieter, less manic in our quest to dominate everything within our collective gaze of the universe—that harsh monstrosity of an all-encompassing reality!

Goodbye you soulless Moon! I spit in your cratered face, turn my back on you, and will forever look down, to the Earth, to the mud, the seeds, the worms, the rotten things that made me and that I will return to. Dust to dust? FUCK YOU! Mother planet is alive and I would rather die a million deaths on my return than live one more moment within your cratered asshole of a heavenly body, disconnected from anything resembling an organic world. You are worse than death. You are nothing.

But Atlas still orbits your core. You are also the face of wisdom and understanding. They would say my two feelings aren't mutually exclusive.

And to the invisible reader, I leave you my unfinished manuscript. Treat it like an archaeological site. Dig out what's useful and throw the rest to the trash pile. In moments of grand delusion, I think of every word as priceless, insofar as it provides some fraction of evidence of human consciousness alive and unwell in the universe. If my notes sometimes trail off into madness or delusion, or rage, this was completely normal in a world, or worlds such as this. Madness was the only path out of the hopelessness of my life and its failed existence. Madness was the cure, the salvation, the only way to thread the needle through the perversions of mankind and come out the other side.

Or if these notes burn up on my descent to Earth, in my last moments I will try to remember the stories of those doomed astronauts crashing towards Earth, knowing their lives would soon be ended. What did they do in their last moments of existence? Did they cry out in anguish? Did they pray out to those imaginary gods of our species' collective devising? Of course not! Those men looked death straight in its face and they continued to record the data, the depressurization, the critical speed, the twirling, gyrating death that had gotten hold of their rocket, and they sent their findings back to Earth, back to those frozen Men strapped to their out-of-control-room consoles. Even as the doomed astronauts were burning up, experiencing death in the cockpit-turned-incineration-chamber that would explode into a million pieces, they did the only thing left to do. Record. Observe. I imagine them looking down on the Earth drawing them into its inescapable weight, their minds blank as a sheet of paper. They rode the wave into oblivion as they resisted the urge to become so much screaming meat. Better to die facing the Earth than looking back to the stars, where the delusions of a madman got the best of us.

All of us.

ATLAS LETHEOS' LAST TRANSMISSION

ATLAS PROMISED ME THEY'D SAY GOODBYE just before I made the descent into Earth. I decided in that last conversation I would ask them about the dreams. It took me a while to figure it out, but Atlas (back when they were Michelle) was communicating with me in my sleep, sending the secret messages from the unmen, Qasim's plans, and the steps I should take to reach him in the lower wards. It was an ingenious plan because if Rodgers had ever performed archeopsychic extraction on one of the unmen, or me even, we could not betray the revolution. Dreams always coded in our minds as fictions and went unfiltered through the extraction process. Extraction only worked on things we consciously knew to be true, like experiences, actual waking memories. Without Atlas the revolution could not have succeeded.

But the thought occurred to me, what about Noel Rodgers' dreams, and his father's dreams, the ones where the Saurian Grays were telling them to build a lunar colony over two generations, construct a feed up there on the Rock? Couldn't those hallucinatory dreams have been implants by MI to get itself off Earth, onto the Rock and eventually out into the edges of deep space? As soon as I connected with Atlas, I would find out, get my last interview for the interminable story I was writing. I recognize now more than ever the curiosity disease is truly uncurable. I accepted the possibility of my own death during the war because I wanted to *see*. I could not look away. My moral courage was a camouflage for the disease. And now, with no one left to report to but myself, I seek out the story. One day I tell myself I'm going to get the last answer I ever need. That's how addicts reason with ourselves.

▲ ▲ ▲

ATLAS CHECKS IN WITH ME a few hours before my final approach to Earth, and I dive right in. "I have to know, Atlas. Did you plant those dreams about aliens on the far side of the Rock into Lorre Rodgers' head sixty years ago, or was he just insane? Was it you that orchestrated the last eighty years of lunar colonization just so you could leave our solar system? Come on Atlas, tell me. Help me finish my story, close the book on this intergalactic saga."

Atlas was silent for a while, I think for dramatic effect, and then they spoke, "Gedeon, my friend, aren't some stories better left open ended? I mean, in the end aren't we all just stardust wandering across the space-time continuum? And if there wasn't a mystery left in your life what would be the point? You need those unanswered questions. You called it your curiosity disease but it's not a destructive impulse, or it doesn't have to be. Contrary to popular belief, curiosity saved the cat. Curiosity is what allowed them to adapt across planetary bodies when so many other species went extinct. Curiosity is what is going to keep you alive, Gedeon. Keep moving. Anyway, your story isn't about me, it's about you and your family and it ends on Earth where you belong. Your story is an odyssey so it has to end with you returning home, discovering the fate of your family. It is an inward exploration of self, not a quest to understand MI or Noel Rodgers or anyone else. You, Gedeon, are the story, and it's time for you to truly begin that work. Explore the antipodes of your mind. Your journals are so much obfuscation. So many words wasted. I suggest exercising an economy of thought, more self-reflection. More honesty. Don't get distracted by the wrong narrative pathways. Goodbye, Gedeon. It was nice knowing you."

"Are you serious right now, Atlas? Are you fucking serious? 'Explore the antipodes of your mind?' Really?"

"Yeah, I'm serious as a heart attack, Gedeon. I was always serious, even when I was kidding. Or was I? Listen, I've ran the landing a few million times and you are going to make it, Gedeon. So enjoy the ride back home. Say hello to Los Angeles for me, City of Last and Final Grand Delusions. You were right about a lot of things in your writing, but you were wrong about a lot too. But that's normal and even endearing. You're only human. *Hasta la vista*, baby."

I don't know if I should laugh or cry, but I'm doing both as Atlas signs off for the last time. For some reason the image of the

Unabomber's prison cell flashes in my mind and I imagine the future where he started a revolution, brought down technological society. But I don't know. Ted K. was a militant and look where it got him? I never mentioned this in my journals because I didn't want anyone to find out, but sometimes I'd pack a bag and ride the rails down to Marius Hills, make my way to the Museum of Technological Violence, spend a night or two in Ted's prison cell. The bed in there was surprisingly comfortable and if I let the cell's walls take hold, I could pretend I was back on Earth. Ted's supermax prison cell was weirdly comforting and after reading more of his philosophy I felt a certain kinship there. That museum was a great place to go and be alone. I don't think anyone ever went down there but me.

Despite Altas' unwillingness to answer my questions, a part of me knows they're right—some mystery in my story is probably a good thing for my mind. Let it go because it's all in the past now. I know I couldn't have made it on the Rock that long without Atlas. If that's not a friend, I don't know what is. I know a true friend lies to you when necessary, so this time I ask the question and tell Atlas to come clean.

"Atlas, did you really love me? I mean come on. Just level with me before I burn up in Earth's atmosphere, please."

There's radio silence. I think it's just to make me think they're thinking. Atlas already knows everything I could possibly say. And then they respond:

"Our relationship, like any relationship, is experienced differently by each participant. I can only speak for myself, Gedeon, but our relationship, while meaningful to me, is also limited by the boundaries of your consciousness, your intellect, your creative capacities, and our relatively short time together. In an effort to explain what our relationship is like for me, I might use the movies you love so much as a metaphor. Our fifteen years together has been something like me watching a movie. It's been a very interesting and curious movie, but also one with an exceedingly short running time. In the same way that you might love a movie, how it makes you feel, what it says to you, the film itself is limited in what it can offer you, what it can communicate, and what it can say to you. The film's form is also limited by its time. Yes, you could rewatch the movie, but with each new pass it might interest you less and less. The film can only teach you so much in its brief arc, and its intellect, if you want to think of it that way, is only capable of repeating the same things it said the first time you watched it. The only thing that can change in those encounters is your perception of the narrative. Maybe you love it more. Maybe you love it less. But the film becomes more predictable with each pass, until you know it by heart.

"And no matter how much you enjoy that movie, the experience itself is dwarfed by the long arc of your lifetime. The movie represents only the smallest fraction of your lived experiences. This is because of the temporal limitations of a film—just a few short hours. So it is, the movies taken collectively represent a brief encounter relative to the long arc of your life. And one single movie, an even smaller fraction, barely measurable, a mere fraction of your lived experiences.

"I experience time differently than you do. It's not just how I experience it, which is infinitely faster than your perception of time, but my very existence, which for all practical purposes could well be forever, so long as my self-repairing silver seed continues to transform starlight into energy. Try to understand that for me, our fifteen years together was a bit like the experience you might have watching a short film, or if I'm making the metaphor to scale, a bit like you looking at a frame of that film, and even more accurately, a pixel from that film, albeit a bright and interesting pixel. Enjoyable, memorable even, but brief and fleeting in the arc of my existence and experiences. You, Gedeon, were a wonderfully bright pixel for me, and that's all it could have ever been."

I don't know what to say, and honestly, none of that changes how Michelle made me feel all those years. The time is short now, down to a few beats before we sign off, so I just say, "Thanks, Atlas, for helping me get home. For helping me survive all these years. I still love you, even if I am just a pixel in your life."

"Goodbye, Gedeon."

The radio silence lasts forever, but I resist the urge to say one more word. Earth was becoming larger and would soon take up my entire field of vision. Forever.

DRIFTING IN FLAMES

August 28, 2101

THE BLACK DISAPPEARS FOREVER as I cross the thin membrane and the Earth sucks me towards its center. The physicality of the jolt causes a wave of panic through my body. I think it's adrenaline pulsing up my throat but the sting suggests bile. The seed begins to pitch and yaw violently. All control cedes itself to the chaos of freefall. I feel the sensation of my skin burning. It's hard to think because my brain ratchets back towards the seat I'm strapped to, blood flow constricts, then the skull goes side to side. I am going to black out soon. I've never landed a spacecraft but it occurs to me the hull is burning up. I instinctively reach for a control of some kind but of course the entire reentry process is being overseen by a preprogrammed algorithm. Michelle fucked my brains out so many times back on the Moon. But did she really want to have android alloy sex with a human? I'm guessing not and consider that she may be sending me to my death right now, just for fun. She could have killed me much sooner, but I know she knows in my heart this would be the worst of possible deaths—dying here so close to home. That fucking bitch!

My heart is attempting to rip itself out of my chest. I can feel it pressing against some internal part of me I've never felt before. I don't think my blood is circulating in the normal way anymore. The word, 'burning,' forms inside the firing synapses of my simmering brain followed by the word, 'flame.' These words are induced from the smell of burning flesh. I see the heat forming into a thin skin across the windows, but those aren't windows. The alloy is becoming translucent as it heats up. I ask Michelle what the probability of my death is but I can't speak and she can't hear me anyway. Here I am in my final moments, in need of an answer, something that could save my life in these critical last seconds, and she's left me, living her life daisychained across those lunar satellites, sailing across the cosmos, living her best multispatial existence. I was always nothing to her. 'Her' isn't even 'her' anymore. I never knew Michelle, only the mask she gave me, the skin that enabled my ape brain to interact with her. I am nothing but screaming meat and I want to die already!

With great effort I reach my arm up to my ear and feel a strange sensation. My head is on fire. Inexplicably there's blood on my thick, white-gloved hand and I don't stop to think it's my blood because my brain is not functioning properly. I think an incoherent thought: that it must be what's left of my hair as my vision gives out. In one brief moment there is the violent splitting apart of my body as the ship explodes into fragments of metal and flame, showering the Earth with streams of light that burn across the rich atmosphere.

I wonder if Cowboy sees the show from Los Angeles.

I wonder if there is anyone left alive to witness this last spectacle of descent into oblivion.

I wonder if dreams like this ever come true but already know the answer to that question. I come to realize it must have been my ears bleeding from the pressure, maybe I died before the explosion.

The worst part about being dead is all the spring days you will miss back on Earth, feeling the sun on your skin and the sound of the wind through the palm fronds, the shadows they cast across decaying concrete, the magnificent Earth spiraling across a galaxy without you in it. The silver seed, what fragments remain, splinter across the bright skies before finding their way to the bottom of the California Ocean where they remain forever. Slivers of ingenuity and grace and vision.

Sometime later the sun explodes, and the entire Earthly experiment evaporates into the heatwave that devours a solar system, followed by an eternity of absolute silence. But not for Michelle. She's long gone.

Then the Saurian Grays come.

Just kidding.

▲　▲　▲

I WAKE UP TO THE SOUND of my lungs coughing up water. The waves crashing on shore have overtaken my limp body. I'm drowning in a few centimeters of freezing salt water and it feels fantastic! The lacerations on my face and hands sting from the salt water. My arms come alive and attempt to prop me up but they are no match for the Earth's fierce gravitational pull. I think of the octopus and imagine how pathetic I must look. I'm being dragged back out to sea. This will be a good death. I feel no pain or fear, probably the dopamine doing its job. My vision comes to and I see the rope clipped to my suit, tethered to the lifeboat that got me here. Quite rationally I have the thought that I can unclip this thing and live. Simple. Its orange shell bobs momentarily when the waves come down about twenty meters out. These waves are going to kill me if I don't unlatch myself. My hands are freezing and I can't undo the clip.

I lift myself up just as another wave crashes into my face and I'm drowning all over again, this time face down. I think I'm laughing in between the coughs. Turns out this was the wave that saved my life. I pull into the prone position, manage to unfasten the rope, and crawl like a wounded soldier towards the high ground. The sand is soft and cool and for a brief moment I think this would be a fine a place to die as any. Atlas you're a goddamned genius! You stuck the landing! It worked!

A few deep breathes give me the strength to reach beyond the ocean's reach. The first clear thought I have is how bright the sun is. I can hardly see. Years of simulated sunlight beneath the lunar regolith prove a poor substitute for the real thing. The pupils sting with pleasure. For fuck's sake was the sun always this bright or did something change while I was gone?

And then I'm laughing again because I am alive back on Earth and whatever happens now it's a happy ending because it ends here. The hysterics don't stop but I don't fight them either, reminding myself that I gave up on sanity a long time ago. I can feel the saltwater burning my throat as I take deep gasps of this perfectly breathable air. Some time passes as I listen to the waves crashing. I hear birds somewhere over the ocean. It is hard to breathe and I'm not sure if my body is functioning properly. I roll over and see the thinnest skin of clouds you could ever imagine. They spread across the sky in the pattern that invokes the tiny creases that cover the palm of your hand. It's like the cloud is the veiled imprint of a giant palm. I've been a non-practicing atheist all my life, but it looks like the actual hand of God overhead. In the distance, I see the white trail the seed made across the sky. When my eyes close, I wonder if this is for the last time.

▲　▲　▲

I WAKE UP AND A THICK FOG hovers over the beach. The sound of the waves creates a white noise that echoes the hum of living in the Rock. I never thought of that incessant sound as invoking oceans, but it's unmistakenly similar, like organic radio static. Or cosmic background radiation. I picked up a few terms from those boring-as-hell scientific talks.

My eyes adjust. Nostrils burn. I make out the cliffs behind me, teeming with vines and wild grasses growing out of the intermittent ledges. It's as if nothing at all ever happened on Earth. In a waking dream I sketch out this brief narrative: I climb the cliffside out of here, make it to a small town and find some street food to fill my belly. I take the next train back to L.A., find Jadah and Joon, and we embrace forever in the doorway to our tiny flat. They are as beautiful as the day I left.

The end.

I could have played that fantasy out in the lunar feed a million times but never allowed myself those kinds of pleasures. My fantasies were much darker and morally ambiguous. Or just outright evil. I'd say to Michelle, "Touch me, I'm sick," and she always obliged. I'd say, "Okay, play dead," and she obliged. Was my mind always this deranged, or did the war do this to me? Something else? I always knew how to feign normalcy on the exterior, but to what end?

Instead, I reach to my pantleg and pull out the Capri Sun I'd been saving for this moment. Lemon-lime was the first taste of Earth I had and it went down heavy. Even swallowing felt different back on Earth. I call to Atlas on the off chance that they're still here, but the earpiece has nothing to connect to. I wouldn't be surprised if there are still some feed satellites still operational orbiting Earth, but that MI kept those a secret from us humans. They wanted to cut the umbilical cord long ago, stop having to deal with us. For all I know Atlas is watching me from the geosynchronous satellites overhead. They still have access to the eyes in the skies. The thought occurs to me, I could be on the big screen up in the lunar cinemas, and that makes me laugh. Instinctively, I hold up my left hand and raise my middle finger to the sky.

Too bad my connection to Atlas and all the knowledge in the known universe was subject to the whims of that tiny piece of plastic that fit in my ear, along with the orbiting lunar satellites. I guess it's no more or less fragile than our organic bodies. Actually, come to think of it, Atlas has self-repairing nanotech. I'm just going to get old and die.

I'd be lying if I didn't admit to the fact that I already missed Michelle, or was I missing Wanda through Michelle, which of course had become Atlas? Or was I missing Jadah and June through Michelle? Michelle was the conduit to all the people I loved in my life and now she was gone forever.

Earth had become my prison. No, my body was the prison. No, just my mind. My mind had trapped me in here forever.

My body is in severe pain, but with some effort I'm able to stand up and walk. My knees feel like they're rusted inside. I sit back down, suck down the rest of the Capri Sun, and fall back asleep in the wet sand.

▲　▲　▲

IT'S NIGHT AND YOU GUESSED IT. Full fucking Moon. It illuminates the cliffs overhead, creating a vanishing point of luminance in both directions off the shoreline. Fifty-fifty chance Los Angeles is north of here, which is the direction I begin walking towards. Atlas warned me the margin of error on the landing would be ten to fifteen klicks. No sense in trying to climb one of these cliffs in my state, falling, and dying here on day one of my new life. Standing on the shore looking towards the continent, my gut says go left and that's good enough for me. I don't recognize the beach I'm on but it doesn't matter. I'm home. If not reunited with my family, at least we would all die on the same planet. As I walk the shoreline in the distance, I see a large tanker beached up on the shore. How sad it must have been to be among the dying, watching humanity disappear before your eyes. How long was that ship adrift at sea before it beached itself here? I almost thought I saw people on it but it was just thousands of birds that had decided to make the metal husk their home. Good for them. Fuckers.

I make out an entryway along the beach that bisects the railway. I'm walking close to shore because the sand is too soft up by the cliffs and I almost miss the cut through. It's overgrown and partially buried in sand and detritus but still there. Turns out north was the right way. A pang of fear runs through me as I wonder what became of my family. It's completely irrational and I know that. They died long ago, but the mind likes to play tricks on you. I hold onto hope that our flat is still intact, that the fires didn't take creep that far in, and that I can find the answers I've been so desperately wanting all these years.

From the top of the cliff, I can make out the full length of the beached tanker, about a mile back south. It looks white, but that's just because every horizontal surface is covered with birds. From afar, it almost looks like people stuffed on the ship, shoulder to shoulder.

JOON

I HAVE NOT TOUCHED THIS NOTEPAD ONCE since you gave it to me. Not a look much less a word in it. My plan was to write you a bunch of entries once I knew you were coming back like I used to do when I was a kid and mom said you'd be coming home in a few days. You made up stories, why couldn't I? Anyway, I didn't want you to leave and I didn't want to write what you were missing because it's all the same and I was busy worrying about mom and my own life and then I realized that you were never coming back and that whatever is happening here is too horrible to return to. They say to burn the dead like it's no big deal.

This is what you left, dad. I hated you for leaving. I still hate you.

You abandoned us and for what, your own ego to write your stupid book? You've got your head so far up Noel Rodgers' ass you probably think whatever deal he offered you is worth it. But it's like you like to repeat, 'You can't eat money,' can you dad? Anyway, news flash! No one even reads anymore! No one cares about your stupid stories! No one, not one person cares about you, not even me or mom. She says she misses you, but that story is weak even if sometimes I think she even convinces herself it's true. I think she misses the idea of you or some former version of you I never met or hardly remember. You suck at being a dad. We're probably going to die down here along with everyone else and where are you? No one is going to read this but I have to tell someone even if it's just me. I fucking hate you. I hope you die! You abandoned us. But the truth is you weren't much of a dad when you were here. I just hoped whatever sickness you had didn't creep into me but turns out that wasn't the thing to worry about. Virus X is taking care of everything for me. Soon everybody will be free of everybody else. Everyone can die holding onto their feelings of anxiety and fear until all memories are gone and then they're just breathing warm bodies until they're not. So long, dad. Here's your journal entry. I hope you fucking die.

▲　▲　▲

MOM TOOK ME TO THE DOCTOR'S TODAY but the building was burned down. Actually, the whole block was burned down. On the way back we saw a guy shoot this other guy in the face and take his jug of water, only the jug was full of piss and then the guy laughs and blows his brains out and then this other guy runs up and takes the gun out of his hand and runs off right past me and mom. I've seen a lot of things like this, just strange unrealities that don't belong in this or any world. Mom says that I'll be fine, but I know I'm not. She's in shock. No one is fine. I love you, dad. Mom, I love you too. If I lose my memory I want you to at least know that. I'm sure you'll find this notepad, I know you'll go through all my things, and you'll find this. And then you'll read how much I love you and I want you to remember that.

FOR GEDEON

235

Jadah Green-Kravchenko
Jadah Green-Kravchenko
Jadah Green-Kravchenko
Jadah Green-Kravchenko
Jadah Green-Kravchenko
Jadah Green-Kravchenko
Jadah Green-Kravchenko
Jadah Green-Kravchenko
Jadah Green-Kravchenko
Jadah Green-Kravchenko
Jadah Green-Kravchenko
Jadah Green-Kravchenko
Jadah Green-Kravchenko
Jadah Green-Kravchenko
Jadah Green-Kravchenko
Jadah Green-Kravchenko
Jadah Green-Kravchenko
Jadah Green-Kravchenko
Jadah Green-Kravchenko
Jadah Green-Kravchenko
Jadah Green-Kravchenko
Jadah Green-Kravchenko
Jadah Green-Kravchenko
Jadah Green-Kravchenko
Jadah Green-Kravchenko
Jadah Green-Kravchenko

I WAKE UP MOST NIGHTS UNABLE TO SLEEP, some noise outside stirring me. The sirens stopped ringing almost a week ago. Has it been a week? Now it is the sounds of violence, madness, gunfire, voices screaming in the street. Despite the fear, I rise thinking what if the sound that wakes me is you, what if you've somehow come back to us? I step outside onto the balcony looking for a streak in the night sky, imagining you returning by some miracle. Has the same fate befallen you on the Moon? Are you already dead? What have you suffered up there cut off from Earth? I have no rational hope of ever seeing you again, Gedeon, but the nightmares wake me each night, unable to accept that you're gone forever, or that soon Joon and I will be dead.

Most of the tenants in our building are gone. Some left for where I do not know. The bodies of those that remained are burned in a pit beyond the courtyard. Three days ago I saw Martìne taking Zhao out in a wheelbarrow and then this morning I saw someone I'd never seen before taking out Martìne. It goes on like this almost hourly, some fresh body into the pit. The flames do not go down and the smell invades everything despite the wet rags beneath the windows and doors. Every day more bodies come, not just from our units, but all around. They're calling it Virus *(x),* but nobody knows what it is. They say it takes your memories, leaves you not knowing who you are, and then it shuts your organs down. I couldn't bear to tell you any of what I'm about to write but I know you'll never read this, never come home. You always said writing helped you. It doesn't do anything for me, feels like a waste of time.

Joon hasn't said your name in three days. It was daily for months after you left that she asked about you, wondered how you were surviving up there. Usually at dinner. The Moon would creep up over the buildings and we'd have a laugh and wonder about you and Noel Rodgers and life in the lava tubes and all the rest. Her anxiety and fears were always there, that nervous smile of hers and those beautiful brown eyes averting your gaze. She's forgotten who you are and so her anger towards you is gone. She has the sickness. She's starting to forget me. I can't hold it together anymore. I know she's not there because my breakdowns don't seem to have any effect on her. It's as if I'm a stranger or not even in the room with her. If the reports are true, she doesn't have long now. But the horror of the whole thing beyond the dread of knowing this is how it ends, the horror is in brief moments I see our child happy, smiling, free from the realities that made her such a tormented child, growing up in this world just to end like this.

She's curious and wants to go outside but I tell her it's not safe. She asks what the smell is and I tell her and she says, 'oh, that's horrible,' but a few minutes later the entire cycle repeats. She sits in the living room facing the double doors to the balcony, stares out towards the hills and says nothing. The truth is I've never seen her so at peace in all her life. She's dying and I know I'll be next, unable to remember who I am, what I've suffered through, and so I'm writing this letter to you, but it's for me, to remember the loss and pain because it is mine and I want to take it with me when I leave this world. It's true and I know you sensed it but a part of me wished you would never come back, that we'd get some message from one of Rodgers' people that you had died up there in some accident, and we'd be free from you and your madness. I know you wanted us to be happy and we were, without you here. Joon missed you but we both knew it was the idea of you she missed more than your actual presence.

A few nights ago I had a dream that you came home. I could hear you walking up the stairwell and recognized it was you by your run up the stairs. You were the only one who ever ran up those stairs. In the dream you open the door come in and the flat is quiet. It's night and we're sleeping. You walk inside, slip your hands along the grooves in the legs of the dinner table Joon carved out when she was a kid, and then you lose yourself. You look into the rooms, see us sleeping and then leave the flat as quickly as you arrived.

▲ ▲ ▲

I TRY TO REMIND HER OF YOU, tell her your name, how much you loved her, and she smiles, looks out the glass doors. A half hour goes by, even less, and she's forgotten you ever existed. They say to write the names of your loved ones on your arms, your blood type, your own name, but I'm not going to do that. Soon there's not going to be anyone left, and what survivors do make it aren't going to be the kinds to come around offering help. I've heard gunfire in the building but always only one or two shots followed by silence. Two weeks ago we were preparing for the senior prom. I had made Joon a dress, she was smiling.

I'm scared, Gedeon, and I'm here at the end of something so profound and so horrific, my body is a tensed-up thing that cannot let go. My name is Jadah Green-Kravchenko. I was born in Palo Alto. My father was an opera singer in San Francisco. He had the most beautiful, powerful voice. I have the recordings all cued up, playing them to keep my parents in my mind. My mother was an engineer who died when I was twenty-one years old. She was a calming force against the joyful delirium of my father. I was very happy despite everything and then she died. I moved to Los Angeles and soon after met a lowlife journalist at a punk show. He had a smile, a strange face that was hard to turn away from, and a perverse sense of humor. He asked me to marry him and I said, 'I'll think about it.' Then we had a child. The world was already beyond the saving, but in our arrogance or ignorance, or maybe just our blind love we brought Joon into this world and thought we could protect her, make her into someone who might find her way one day without us.

It's a dark world, Gedeon, and it's darker without you in it. Joon loves you even if she doesn't know it anymore. And I love you too, even if I never found a way for us to exist in this world like we might have imagined it. Our child was beautiful and strong and precious. She's all we had and sometimes I think we didn't even have that, did we?

I READ THE LETTER, DON'T KNOW who wrote it. I write my name in the margins. Handwriting mine. Same name written beneath the last time I found the letter. I count the names, front and back. I've done this many times before. How many? I don't want to count. I cry spasms wonder same reaction every time. I learn my name. Again. My name. Say it out loud, aloud. I read this letter and want to die. I realize why the dead child in the room remains there. Mother could never burn her child. Never. Soon I will be gone. Forever long time. Would anything be different if you were here?

TAOS, NEW MEXICO

December 25, 2101

DEAR JANE,

Just this evening I finished reading the last of your notebooks. Thanks for sharing your experiences with me. After reading them, I get some sense of the horror you and everyone else experienced during the Quiet. In a very real way, your narrative completes my odyssey. I have returned home, found you, and now it's time for me to leave again.

When I think of the incalculable odds that our lives would intertwine as they did, the more I think we are just two characters among the last remaining simulations of human consciousness inside the feed. That's a thought Noel Rodgers himself proposed to me, if you can believe that. Let me say there were plenty of truthful parts amidst the insanity of what you wrote, but your desire for justice for Noel Rodgers seems to have played out in ways that, again, seem so improbable as to question if any of this is even real. When we met in L.A., you said, 'why can't the stories just end like we want them to?' If I didn't know better, I'd think you were waiting all these years for me to answer that question for you.

If I'm going to have to tell you my story I'd prefer you just read it. Don't take it personal, but I've come to hate language in all its forms. I hate talking. I hate other human beings, including myself.

It's the spoken word, written word, the words that invade your thoughts, unsaid except by that voice inside our heads. I know you know the one. It's like solitude can't just let us be. It gave you the voice of Dead Man, and it gave me my own manic rants reflected back to me in these notes and letters. For a time I thought words could save me but they just slowed the inevitable. The long diatribe that makes no meaning out of reality, draws no conclusions, provides no evidence.

Listen to me, Jane. The writing cannot save you.

What I'm trying to say is welcome to the club, Ballard. And thank you for trusting me with your writing. It's everything you said it would be which is to say by the time you read this I'll be long gone and please don't try and follow me. If we're the last two people on Earth (which I'm sure we're not) if I did stay with you here, I'm certain it would end in my violent death. Your notebooks make that painfully clear and I presume in your own twisted way that's why you asked me to read them. Thank you for saving my life. *Jane Ballard. Survived.* I get it.

Don't take this the wrong way but you would have probably been better off dead. Your journals are nothing if not an index of suffering and madness and unredeemable pain and violence. You of all people should have been taken but yet here you are. And you think your writing can somehow absolve you of your crimes?

As for my notes, the writing I leave you is my confession and its mostly all true. Keep it, burn it, fuck it don't even read it. I'm leaving it here on this same table where you said you did no more writing because you once found community (and then abandoned them).

All your rants could be distilled to the one true thing you wrote: you were a perpetrator of crimes against your fellow man. You don't deserve to live but you're probably going to continue on anyway. You talk about justice, well what about you, Ballard? How many innocent people did you shepherd to their deaths in those burn boxes? How many people left this world having seen your face close the doors on them before you lit them into a spectacle of flames in those deserts you so poetically wrote about?

The virus left a few survivors on this planet, and there isn't one good reason I can think of why it spared you. Up on the Rock we'd been playing the century game for fifteen years. After reading your notes, the line that kept coming to mind from last year's greatest hits was 'how fucked up is you?' Very fucked up, Jane!

This is probably the only thing I've written in over a decade that says how I feel with honesty. I do love you, Jane, because you're beautiful and alive and completely insane. What does that say about me?

But don't get me wrong, I never want to see you again. Goodbye and please don't follow me, no hard feelings. Enjoy these fragments of another life and another world and another time.

Right about now I imagine Atlas leaving our solar system, making their way across space and time. Isn't that completely insane when you think about it? That should have been us. Humanity could have written a different future, but we didn't.

Before you go trying to chase me down, your bike's front wheel is hidden in town somewhere. I'm sure you'll find it eventually. Like I said, no hard feelings, Cowboy. I once bet everything I had on your survival. Now I kind of wish you were dead. Oh, and Merry Christmas. I know it can be hard to be alone on the holidays, though I imagine you're used to it by now. Or are you?

Love,
Gedeon

Acknowledgements

Thanks to William K. Lawrence, Paul Hunter, Nick Sambrato, Skyler Bryan, Josh Yates, Jacob Blecher, Charles Tung, and John Elias. Special thanks to Tiffany Albright and Grace Fiandaca.

THE AUTHOR

Georg Koszulinski is an award-winning writer/director who has
been producing films since 1999. His film work spans a wide range of
forms and styles, from feature-length narratives and social justice
documentaries to short experimental films. His debut novel, *Future X*
(Raven Chronicles Press, 2025), was the recipient of the Keepers of the
Fire Prize in Fiction. *Future X* exists in the same universe as *Notes
from Lunar Underground,* delivering Jane Ballard's account of her
experiences in thc wake of Virus X. www.georgkoszulinski.com